D.M. MARLOWE

OBSIDIAN'S EYE

This is a work of fiction. Characters and events portrayed in this book are fictitious and not to be construed as real. Any similarity to actual events or persons, living or dead is entirely coincidental and not intended by the author.

For more information:
www.dmmarlowe.com

To nerds everywhere--my costume loving, t-shirt wearing, fandom-embracing brothers and sisters. Long may our geek flags fly

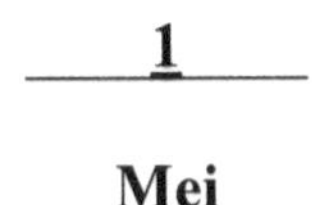

1

Mei

We crept through the darkened streets of the village.

Ryu was in an uproar. People huddled together, talking in whispers. Others ran by, faces in the torchlight showing grim with purpose. Everyone was on high alert. No one could be sure what creatures might be sent against us, now that the wards were down.

My companions and I kept to the shadows, creeping close to the buildings and avoiding contact. We quickly passed beyond the village proper, heading slightly northwest on a path that I had not been on before. Gradually, it narrowed into little more than a slight trail through the woods. A tiny portion of my tension eased as the forest closed in around us. I always felt better surrounded by green and growing things, especially here in these familiar mountains. The why of that was one of the many things I needed to explore.

We all relaxed a little as we moved deeper into the woods, spreading out along the trail. "Boru insisted on being taken to her own home," Hitomi said from just ahead of me.

Feeling grateful to have them, I let my gaze touch upon everyone in our little party. Hitomi, the girl who had become my first friend. Sho, a fierce fighter, wickedly skilled with a sword, but also shockingly talented and clever.

And Ken Sato, who was . . . more than a friend. Maybe. It seemed incredible that we'd only known each other for a few weeks. Sneaking around in the dark, avoiding monsters with him somehow felt like old times.

"Are you all right, Mei?" he asked me.

I'd stumbled a bit, catching on an up thrust of exposed root. Ken knew me well enough to know how unusual that was.

"Fine. I'll be fine." I still felt shaky, not completely recovered from the battle I'd fought—when? An hour earlier? More? I shook my head to clear the lingering fog. Mere hours since I accomplished the driving goal of my last four years—I'd defeated the creature that had killed my father. At last I had destroyed the wind demon that had hunted me every day since then. The relief was enormous, but the cost had been high.

My mission now was clear—I must lessen that toll. "How much further is it?"

I was anxious to get to Boru, to see for myself that she had survived. In the dark, I shook my head against how far I'd come. Two months ago, I'd been alone, disconnected—and entirely unaware that the string of natural disasters that had befallen and changed the world might have supernatural causes—and that a war was being fought to prevent more. Now I had friends, allies of sorts—and I was poised to enter the battle.

But I was going to do it on my own terms.

"It isn't far," Ken answered, his tone low. "It was a smart move. She'll do better in her in her own place."

I knew what he meant. Boru was a loner—perhaps because she was also a witch. A powerful one, too. Another thing I hadn't known existed just a short time ago. But I'd felt her power. And I knew she'd been the one to save the temple and the village of Ryu, transporting it here to the mountains in North Carolina even as Japan had been destroyed around them.

Boru had been the one who created and maintained the wards—the magical barriers that had protected this place for so long. But she had been tricked and betrayed. We all had. The wards were gone. The first of the malignant Inaba's minions had been deflected or destroyed, but who knew how long it would be before more showed up?

"There it is," Hitomi said quietly.

It took me a moment to see what she meant. The small cottage had been crafted of woven trunks and branches, daubed with mud-colored mortar and partially hidden behind a profusion of creeping vines and blossoms. It looked like it had sprung straight from the mountainous soil. It had to be difficult to spot during the day. If I'd been alone out here in the dark tonight, I might have walked right past it.

"All of you wait here and keep hidden. I'll get rid of the guard." Ken took a hold of my wrist and squeezed. "We'll only have a short time."

Hitomi, Sho and I crouched down behind a tangled mass of rhododendron as Ken approached the cabin. He eased the door open and went inside.

We waited. I saw that Sho had his favorite blade buckled at his waist. He gripped it tight and kept his gaze locked on the door. We all breathed a sigh of relief when a middle-aged woman emerged and hurried past, never pausing as she headed down the path.

"Guys," I whispered. "I need to see her alone for a minute, okay?"

There was a moment's silence, then Hitomi spoke, a warning in her voice. "Be quick."

Sho nodded. "Rin and the rest of the council will be looking for you. Soon, if not already."

I murmured agreement as we stepped out. Ken stopped me on the threshold. "I'll wait out here. Try not to tire her. She's been . . . weakened."

I nodded and crossed into the cottage—only to stop in wonder.

Here was magic indeed. Another concept I'd run smack into at Ryu. Magic was real, and many of the ninja living here were born with nature-based abilities to manipulate it.

Minding, they called it. Hitomi could change her appearance. Sho could tap into the natural force of the energy that surrounds us and use it to read deeply into a person's character. And Ken—Ken could manipulate the wind in a myriad of ways.

Boru could do more than most, because she was not only a ninja, but also a witch. And here lay the proof. The room stretched out, cozy and welcoming and impossibly bigger than the outside had made it look. A large hearth took up much of one wall. A nook beyond it had been set up with a battered wooden table and shelves covered with mortars, pestles, and glass bottles of every size, shape and color. Another corner held a similar set up, but was nearly buried under stones. From small, faceted gems to large, rough chunks, they were sorted into piles, stacked and in some cases, displayed in assorted cases and frames.

Plants popped up throughout the space, both living and in drying bundles of herbs. And books—books were scattered everywhere.

I wanted to sink into the nearest comfy chair and stay forever.

"I don't care if your grand-nephew is marrying a gold-digger." The familiar voice emerged so weak and thready it barely carried across the room. I turned toward it to find a small bed perched on a dais. "Leave me be."

I knew my time was short, but still my feet began to drag as I drew nearer. Boru had been thin and ethereal looking before. Now she was nearly translucent. My knees shook as I stepped up to the bed, and knelt beside it.

"Boru," I whispered.

"No, I cannot tell your daughter where you hid the jewelry," she answered irritably. Her fingers, lying near her face, twitched in a shooing motion.

I took her hand. "Are you all right?" My throat tightened. "I'd thought she'd killed you."

Yuki-Onna, the Snow Woman, the first *yokai*, or supernatural creature, I'd fought with tonight, had hinted that she'd killed Boru in order to bring down the wards. Now I could see just how close she'd come to telling the truth. The witch's cheek twitched and she pulled away, but she didn't open her eyes.

"Boru?" Tears spilled out. "It's me, Mei. Please. I need to talk to you."

I startled as her eyes flashed open, vibrant green against the unnatural paleness of her skin. "Mei!" she gasped, alarm in her face and in her sudden grip. "You're not dead, are you?"

"Dead?" And then I understood. Boru had told me that much of her knowledge and skills came from her ability to communicate with spirits—and that her first wards had been the ones she'd built to protect herself from their ever-insistent importuning. That's who she'd been talking to—the spirits of the dead, or perhaps nature spirits or *yokai*.

I glanced about, a bit uneasy. "No, Boru. I'm not dead. I'm here, in your home, with you. Still breathing."

She closed her eyes again in relief.

"I need to talk to you," I said again.

"No," she looked up again and protested feebly. "You must run. The Yuki-Onna is here for you. Inaba has done something to her, altered her. She was the one who drained that boy outside of the village—of both blood and chi. She attacked me, too, so the wards would come down and she could get to you. They know about you, Mei. They know about your eyes. About the prophecy. You have to get out of here."

"She's gone." I lowered my head. "The Yuki-Onna has come and gone. She took Akemi."

"Oh, no." Her eyes closed again and she lay, so very still.

They know about your eyes. They were the words that haunted my nightmares. I was *kawad*. A freak. A mutant, born affected by the toxins, poisons and radiation that had leaked into the atmosphere after the round of disastrous quakes and tsunamis that destroyed so much, years ago. My eyes, with irises too large and too blue, and pupils like a ragged silver starburst, had made me the focus of scorn and hate.

Never let them see. That had been my mantra—until I came to Ryu and found that the villagers saw my deformed eyes as a sign of hope and promise, not as something to be despised and feared.

I hadn't been the only one with different eyes, either. Another girl, Akemi, had been born with a mutation too, similar but not quite the same. Growing up in Ryu, she'd never been the focus of hate—and she hadn't been happy to share the attention her role as Girl With the Stars in Her Eyes had garnered her.

I sighed, and waited for Boru to continue. And waited. After a moment I looked frantically to see if her chest moved, fearing—

"Oh, will you *hush*!" she said suddenly. Her eyes popped open and she stared over my shoulder even as she reached for my hand.

"Run, Mei," she breathed, focusing on me. "They'll realize their mistake soon enough. Something else will come. Something worse, perhaps."

Nodding, I squeezed her hand. "It was worse. It was the wind demon—*my* wind demon." I bent, moving closer. "We did it, Boru. Somehow, with help that I don't even understand, we did it. We destroyed him."

Her eyes blazed, feverishly bright. "Good girl. Tell me everything."

I did, starting with the moment we'd realized the wards had fallen.

"It was Reik, wasn't it?" she asked sadly. "I knew what he was after, but I'd hoped that our friendship would prevent him from going through with it. I don't know how he—"

"He didn't," I interrupted. "I know he hasn't been completely honest, but you can rest easier knowing that he didn't ultimately betray you. The Yuki-Onna—she's his mother, did you know?"

Her face fell. "I'd only just begun to suspect something like that, but she confirmed it when she . . ." She waved a hand and her words trailed away.

"He didn't do as she wished. The Snow Woman brought something herself to help her break the seals. An object of power. She said as much to Reik."

Her relief was obvious. "Thank you for sharing that. It does help, a little, knowing he didn't abuse my trust."

I told her the rest, describing every bit of the battle that Ken and Reik and I had fought. She listened avidly, but by the time I'd finished, she was visibly tiring further.

"Tell me again about the last bit—those eyes that opened in the mountain, and the creatures who came to help."

I told the tale again, hoping she'd know something about what I'd seen. "It was the strangest thing. I could see them better when my eyes were closed. I think I was the only one who knew they were there. Not even the wind demon seemed to realize. Until the end, when Ken caught a flash of them, right before they disappeared."

She was frowning. "I can scarcely believe . . . Could it really be. . ?" Her tone faded away, as if she couldn't gather the strength to speak further. Irritably, she swatted around her ear.

Abruptly, I stood. "Boru, you are whiter than your sheets." I looked around. "Isn't there something here that can help you, heal you? Make you stronger?"

"I'll be fine." She grimaced. "I just need time. But we

must talk now. There are things . . ." Her gaze unfocused. "Yes, I hear you. I will look into it, but I must recover first."

I frowned. The uninterrupted access of her spirits looked to drain her further every time. I straightened as an idea struck me. "Listen, Boru . . . Do you have such a thing as a summoning or transport spell? Something I could use or trigger?"

She frowned and I continued. "Ken and I met a couple of Kappa on the way to Ryu. They have a ring, and it allows for the transfer of chi energy. If we could get them here, I know they'd allow us to use it—and I could give you some of my energy. Enough to at least raise your personal barriers."

Tired yearning crossed her face. "I wish I did have something like that. But I'd have to be at full strength to cast a summoning spell."

"You are turning into a wisp right in front of me," I insisted. "Surely there is something I can do to help."

She stared beyond me again, blinking. "Energy," she whispered. "Energy." She rolled over onto her side and stared across the room. "Yes. It might work."

"What? What do I need to do?"

"Over there. On the table with the stones. Do you see the pierced tin box?"

I left her to cross over and look. After a few seconds I found it. "Yes?"

"Look behind it. There should be a hook—and a necklace."

I moved the box—and gasped.

"The pendant—is it still there?"

"Yes." Reverently, I reached for it—a gorgeous pendant on a silver chain. It was fashioned of a sparkling metal setting made of elegantly curved wires carefully positioned to hold an oblong stone. I'd never seen a stone like it—light blue, with scattered whitish spots. Light glowed from the depths.

"What is it?" Carefully, I brought it to her.

She smiled. "A moonstone—but a very special one. Long ago, it was spelled by a very skilled witch. It might help us with a transfer of energy."

"Okay, good. What do we do?"

"You must wear the necklace."

For a second, I hesitated. I was still in the training clothes I'd put on this morning—it seemed a lifetime ago. Surely it was a sacrilege to put something so beautiful next to the sweaty tank I'd fought in. But I draped it over my neck. I'd won that battle. At last. The fight I'd been waiting for—for years. And now I had more work to do.

"Center the stone over your heart," Boru instructed.

I did. The pendant gleamed against the black fabric.

"Now what?"

"We wait. The moonstone will decide."

The *stone* will decide? I frowned, then jumped as a bright light suddenly emanated from the pendant. It lit up the dark corner of the room.

Boru breathed deeply, gathering strength. "Good. It's accepted you. Now, I'll generate a ward. It's like a barrier, an invisible shield. I'll do my best to make it tangible. You lay your hands on it. If this works, then the moonstone should help you with the transfer."

Tension rose in her face. "Stretch out your hands," she gasped. "Can you feel it?"

I reached about between us. "No. I don't think so."

She closed her eyes, concentrating harder and for a moment, I feared what the attempt might do to her. But suddenly the heel of my hand struck something. "There it is."

She nodded, her eyes still closed. "Now, you know how to *see* your energy, right?"

"Yes." I'd practiced meditation and chi techniques as a girl with my father, and more recently with both Hitomi and Sho.

"Imagine the transfer. A *slow* process, drawing only from the top layer of your aura—the one that interfaces with the world. The stone will take care of the rest."

The pendant grew warm against my chest and soon I could feel the slight drain, even as the unseen barrier beneath my hands grew more solid.

Boru sighed in relief. "Not too much," she ordered. "You have trouble ahead of you. You are going to need your strength."

I let the energy flow. I needed Boru's wisdom and advice, but we also shared a special bond, a connection because we were both linked to Rialka, the spirit guide to the village of Ryu and the founder of the fight against the wicked Inaba and the destruction he wrought. I needed to know that Boru was going to be well. And all of Ryu needed her to recover quickly.

"That's enough." The barrier popped like a bubble beneath my fingers. The warmth and the light quickly faded from the stone.

"What happened?"

"I dropped the physical manifestation of the ward." Boru sat up. She quickly leaned back against the pillows, but she already looked much stronger. "I cut you off." She smiled at me. "Thank you so much, Mei. It's been so long since I went without the protection of a shield, I'd forgotten how noisy and exhausting it is. I'll heal faster now that I have a measure of peace and quiet."

"You looked more drained every time you spoke to . . . someone else."

"It takes a great deal of energy for a spirit to communicate. And for me to hear them. It is draining."

"You sound better already. And your color has already begun to return." Relief welled inside me.

"So much is happening, so fast." Boru frowned. "Will you help me with the pillows so that I can sit straighter?" She sighed in frustration when she was settled. "I'd meant to help in your training. Now . . ." She sighed again.

I shook my head. "I'm not staying, in any case."

She merely looked at me.

"I'm going after Akemi."

"Ah." And then her eyes widened. "Going where? To Inaba?"

"I have to go. Akemi would not let herself be my friend, but neither am I her enemy. She went to fight that Snow Woman because she was afraid—afraid that I was going to steal everything she wanted for herself."

"It was never her role," Boru said gently.

"I know that now. But I can't help but see everything that's happened from her perspective. I showed up and everything she believed about herself, everything she wanted, started to disappear."

"And from your perspective?"

I sighed. "I've accepted my fate. You and Rin and Ken and everyone else have convinced me. I am the Girl with the Stars in Her Eyes—and it means more than just an excuse for people in the outside world to throw stones at me."

"It means so much more," the witch answered. "You know that."

"I do." Everything was moving so fast. I'd only just learned about the prophecy earlier today—it seemed like so long ago! I'd acknowledged my own part in it, for several reasons.

My eyes couldn't be denied. Neither could my connection with Rialka, the spirit of Ryu and the guide the ninja followed in the fight against Inaba's evil. The other predictions had all fallen quickly into place and I'd been forced to acknowledge my role—and fight.

Now questions and other considerations began to rush in. Had Inaba known it was me all along? What would he do with Akemi, in that case? And then it hit me—sudden, terrible confirmation of my worst fear. If Inaba had known, then I'd been right all along.

It was my fault. All of it. My mother's death. Our need to live isolated and apart. My father's murder at the hands of Inaba's wicked henchman.

The weight of it pressed down on me. I sucked in a breath, fighting to keep from breaking.

"Mei?" Boru struggled to sit straight. "Are you all right?"

Another jagged breath. The blame was mine. Fine.

Vengeance would be mine, too.

"Mei?"

I nodded. When I spoke, my emotion roughened my tone. "I know my part. And if it means that I'll have to be the one to face Inaba, eventually, then I might as well do it on my terms, for a good reason, and to save Akemi."

"You have to save us all, Mei. I know it's a heavy load, but like all of us who've been born into this fight, Rialka has given you gifts to balance it. Your burden is the biggest, but so is your potential. Your skills—"

I laughed bitterly. "Skills? I hope you don't mean *minding* or magic. I can do parlor tricks, at best. The only real skills I have so far are the knowledge of fighting and hiding that I came to Ryu already knowing. But I'm willing to use them."

"You are right about Akemi's situation not being her fault, but neither is it yours."

I shrugged that off. "But I'm the one who can do something about it."

"Rin won't like this."

"That's another reason I have to go. I wasn't raised here. I cannot be Rin's good little soldier. I've been on my own too long. I have to do this my way."

Boru nodded. "I can understand that. In fact, I think it's a good idea that you go. You already know how to fight, but you need knowledge and different skills if you are to win this battle with Inaba. Rialka has given us hints of what will come in that battle. And based on that, you aren't ready. To defeat Inaba, it is said that you must be adept at both Zai and at Zen." She spoke of two of the traits that lent the ninja their powers of spiritual and mental strength.

"Zai—harmony with and control of nature. Zen— enlightenment and understanding." She scowled. "Today's battle is a good example. You fought well, but if you'd had more training, you might have been able to control those streams of ice and air."

"It's a long way to JanFran. I'll practice all I can."

"There are people who can help you along the way. I can get you in contact with them." She gave me a sardonic look. "I assume you don't go alone?"

I shook my head.

"Well, Hitomi knows how to scry. You can keep in contact with me and I'll find you all the help I can." She frowned. "But before you leave, tell me once more about the creatures who helped you tonight."

I conjured up every detail I could remember. "What was it you said earlier?" I asked eventually. "Do you have an idea of what those creatures might have been?"

"Perhaps. I can't be sure." A troubled look passed over her face. "Mei, they might have been Elementals."

I made a face. "That doesn't help me, I'm afraid. I'm not

knowledgeable about the creatures of folklore like all of you at Ryu."

"No one knows much of Elementals. I've been in contact with nearly every sort of human or *yokai* spirit, but I've never tasted even a hint of an Elemental presence. It's very rare. And possibly not a good sign." Her gaze fell to the moonstone.

Her gaze reminded me and I reached for the chain. "Oh! I forgot."

She stopped me when I would have taken it off. "No. Keep it. Listen, Mei, I do think I know someone who can help you. She might be able to explain what happened tonight. She's familiar with Elementals, and she might be able to help you with your training too."

"Who is she?"

"A friend. To all of us. She's a witch, like me, and she's not that far away." She nodded toward the necklace. "Wear that pendant, show it to her and she'll help you all she can."

She sank a little further back into her pile of pillows. "But before you go, we must talk about that Yuki-Onna." She raised her arm and I flinched at that sight of two inflamed-looking puncture wounds.

"How she's changed, you mean?"

"Exactly."

"Has she grown more powerful?"

"She's powerful in a different way—and that might be incredibly significant. The Snow Woman has existed for hundreds of years, and the basic fundamentals of how she operates, whom she chooses as victims, and how she preys on them—never changed. Until now."

"It's Inaba, it must be. He has her preying on the people of Ryu, coming to fetch me . . ."

"But is he also behind her sudden habit of draining her prey of blood as well as chi? And what of the fact that she birthed a half human child?" Her frustration shone clear. "There's never been a child like Reik, born of human and *yokai*, not that I know of. And what about that Tengu that you and Ken fought weeks back? Ken reported changes in that one's behavior as well." Her fingers clenched. "These are creatures that we have been familiar with for generations—and now they are changing, evolving . . . I can't get rid of the feeling that all of this is vitally important."

"Rin told me that you suspect that Inaba is responsible for the disasters—the quakes and the tsunamis and even the Rift that destroyed Japan. Do you think it's all related?"

"I feel that it must be. But how? Why? It's another thing you must figure out before you meet Inaba, I'm afraid." She reached out and ran a hand along my arm, circling my wrist with her delicate fingers. "I will do all I can to help you from here."

"Without risking your recovery," I insisted.

"Agreed. Now listen and I'll tell you how to reach Effie."

I must have made a face.

"Don't let the name fool you. Effie Couts is a woman in command of a great deal of power and she could help you begin to answer these questions."

I nodded. "Okay. Where do I find her?"

"Not too far. A couple of days hike, on foot, in a little grove just off of the Appalachian Trail." She narrowed her eyes on me. "Yes, you can all act the part of a group of teens hiking the trail. Now, here's where you should go . . ."

2

Mei

Ken was approaching when I emerged from the cottage. "We've got to go. The nurse is coming back—and she's not alone."

"I'm ready." I felt a twinge of conscience. Ken had likely ruined his good name, going along with us in this unsanctioned escape. He was one of Ryu's most respected scouts, universally loved in the village. General Rin, the village leader, was going to be furious with him—and all of us. Guilt struck harder then, but my friends had all wanted to come—insisted on it—and I was so tired of being alone.

Ken turned his head and tucked his chin. "Thank you for your help," he said.

He wasn't talking to me. In the dim light coming from the house, I caught the quick movement close to his face. A sleepy chirp answered him.

"Oh," I breathed. "That's the first time I've actually seen you do that."

Birds talked to him, I'd heard. It had been an early hint of his *minding* gift—the ability to manipulate and control the air.

His shoulders hunched slightly. A defensive posture.

"I think it's adorable."

He relaxed and another peep sounded from his shoulder.

"He likes you," Ken told me.

A more complicated series of chirps came from the little bird then. "No," Ken answered it. He set off, obviously expecting me to follow. I could see the flutter of wings as the little creature kept its balance. "Thank you for your help," he told it again. "We have to get going now."

It rose from his shoulder and hovered a moment before landing in his hair, right at his crown. It gave a quick peck to the top of his head, then swooped away into the night.

"Was that a love peck?" I asked.

"Something like that."

"Yep. Adorable."

"You might not think so, if you knew what he was saying."

"Well, now you have to tell me."

His shoulders hunched again. "You don't want to know."

"Uh, yeah. I do." Ahead, the rhododendron loomed and I strained to see a sign of the others.

"He wanted to know if I was going to build you a nest and make eggs with you."

Involuntarily, I laughed. "Ah. Well, you're right. Maybe adorable is too strong a word."

Sho popped out from behind the shrubbery, with Hitomi right behind him.

"Did you find out what you needed?" she asked.

"Not everything, but I know where we're going," I told her.

"Then let's head out." Sho turned to go back the way we'd come.

"Wait." Boru's words were still skittering around in my head. "Can we leave through the second gate?"

"Are you sure, Mei?" Ken sounded concerned at the idea of returning to the scene of the battle we'd fought tonight. "Is that such a good idea?"

"I'm sure. We have to." I grew more certain as I thought about it. "There's something that we need to check out."

It took nearly thirty minutes of quick travel through the woods to reach the spot. I stumbled or slowed several times— not my usual mode of operation. I could feel Ken's concern growing.

We reached the clearing and the three of them stopped, ranging out along the edge. I stepped past them and continued into the space alone. Reaching into my pack, I pulled out a flashlight and cast it about.

The place showed signs of the recent fight. The snow had melted away, leaving the ground wet and mushy. The flagstones were covered with leaves, branches and bits of long, dark hair.

I looked up, but I could only see the outline of the elaborate toori gate against the night sky. There was no sign of the creatures who had invaded or of the others who had helped us.

I cast back, trying to remember those last moments before I'd passed out from exhaustion and strain. Ken, Reik and I had been *here* . . . and the demon had been . . . there.

"Ken," I called. "When the wind demon . . . imploded . . ." I didn't know how else to describe what I'd seen. "Did you see something drop?"

"I saw . . . something . . . towards the end of the battle. I don't know what it was. But at that moment after Fuma Jinae popped . . . I was too busy catching you as you fell."

I was glad they couldn't see the color rising in my face. I'd never fainted before in my life. "Do you remember the Tengu we fought?" I asked him. "When it disappeared, it left something behind."

"Oh, yes. The little eagle."

It had been a small, resin figure. "I swear I remember something of a similar size dropping to the ground when the demon popped away."

"That's what we're looking for?" Ken pulled out a light too, and the others followed suit.

"You don't know what we're supposed to be looking for?" Hitomi asked.

"Something small," Ken answered.

"Something that doesn't belong," I added. I aimed my light toward her foot. She was standing just where—

"Like this?" Just beyond Hitomi, Sho swopped down and came up with something in his hand.

Hesitantly, I drew close. He held it up, and all of our lights focused on it.

It shone, translucent. A square of clear plastic.

"There's something etched in it," Hitomi whispered.

It was an icon, representing a funnel cloud. Like you might see on a tornado warning sign.

"That's it." I was reluctant to touch it.

"Just toss it," Ken said in disgust. "That's what we did with the last one."

"No!" I spoke out even as Sho drew his hand back. "We need to keep it. It could be important."

Ken snorted.

"Boru says we must find out why these *yokai* have

changed."

"We have a thousand other things to worry about," Ken began.

I interrupted him. "She says the answers will help me to defeat Inaba."

"Oh." They all exchanged solemn glances.

"I'll take it." I reached for it, determined to touch it only with my fingertips, but Hitomi stopped me.

"Here." She untied a scarf from the outside of her pack. "Wrap it in this. Don't touch it."

I took the fabric with relief and wrapped the thing tight before stuffing it in an outside, zipped pocket of my own pack.

"Okay, now that that's finished, let's go!"

The excitement in Hitomi's voice only emphasized my own weariness. It was more than just exhaustion—and the sheer number of monumental events I'd survived today. I knew my friend had rarely been outside of remote Ryu, and never without supervision. This was an adventure for her, a chance to experience everything she'd longed to see, hear and do. An opportunity to put a lifetime of preparation to the test.

It wasn't the same for me. I'd been on the road, on the run, for years. The last few weeks at Ryu had been unsettling, as I'd discovered so much that I didn't know, but they'd also been a respite. The village had become a refuge, a place to make connections.

Now I was leaving many of them behind. I'd thought that once I defeated the wind demon that had hunted me for so long, that I'd be done with running away. Instead I was now running toward a bigger monster—and feeling even less prepared than I had for four long years.

The thought weighed on me. My pack grew heavier as we moved on. We headed generally downhill as we left the highlands. The forest grew thicker as we came down the mountain, and our progress slowed. The others debated our route toward civilization and kept watch for both natural predators and otherworldly foes. Numb, tired, and daunted at the size of the burden I was taking on, I left them to it. I merely plodded along, head down, misery in a million aching muscles and mind disconnected from it all.

I was working so hard to focus only on the balance of my pack and the effort to put one foot in front of the other, I didn't even realize that the others had stopped until Ken came running to take my arm and lead me back.

"Come on," he said in his quiet, comforting way. "You can rest now. We're making camp."

I nodded as if I'd known it all along.

"She's so exhausted, she's nearly catatonic," he said to the others.

"Yes. Tired," I whispered.

"I'll hang your hammock," Ken said. He reached around to unhook the small nylon roll from my pack.

"Don't bother," I managed to say. Sho was hanging a tarp to make a rough shelter, but I couldn't wait. I set down my pack, laid down with my head on it like a pillow and was asleep before anyone spoke another word.

3

Mei

I woke in the morning, scratching at my wrist as a dream vision of a smiling Rialka faded. Somehow I'd grown tangled in a weedy vine while I slept. I sat up, shaking and pulling my arm. I had to work at it before I could get free.

But I forgot the itch as I looked around. Sunlight streamed through the trees. The birds were singing so loudly I could hardly believe I'd been sleeping through the chorus. Nearby, a couple of squirrels rooted through last year's leaves. It had to be at least a couple of hours past sunrise.

Hitomi sat not far away, on the other side of a small fire. She had a rock in her hand and as I watched, her fingers began to morph, fusing and changing to match the tones and striations of the rock she held. I was awed once again at her *minding* ability. And I understood how happy she was to have a chance to put it to good use at last.

Seeing me move, she grinned across at me. "Good morning, sleepyhead!"

"Morning." I wondered if I would ever stop viewing her easy manner and complete disregard for my eyes as the gift they were.

She nodded toward a leaf-wrapped bundle near the flames. "Rice balls for breakfast. Pickled salmon in them. I saved you two because I thought you could use the extra calories after everything that went on yesterday."

"Thank you," I said grateful and thinking that she was probably right. "I've never been so tired—"

I stopped. I was a bit hungry, but taking stock, I was surprised to find that I felt . . . amazing. I rotated my shoulders, but they were fine, not sore from sleeping on the ground. Experimentally, I hopped to my feet and stretched toward the sky. All of my aches were gone. No lingering exhaustion or discomfort. My head was clear, my joints felt springy. I eyed the sky again. "How long was I asleep?"

"I don't know . . ." Hitomi pulled her micro-tab from her pocket and checked the time. "Six hours, maybe?" She brandished the small computer. "I hope we find ourselves in civilization tonight. I'll want to charge this again. It will work now that I'm finally out from under the wards."

I took one of the rice balls and waved away the other one she offered. "One is good, thanks." I eyed her gadget as she bent avidly over it. "What are you doing?"

"Well, I've been keeping track of our position—and checking out the towns we might possibly pass through."

"Why?"

She lifted a shoulder. "I'm just looking for news of unusual activity, any trouble we might need to steer clear of. I've checked out some places we might like to eat or stay." She glanced up at me. "I'm going to show you guys that I can be an asset—and a good Scout for Ryu."

"I've never doubted it," I said around a mouthful of rice.

She grinned her thanks. "I just can hardly believe I'm out here!" She lifted the micro-tab. "I should make a list. There's so much I want to see, do and try!"

"What will you put at the top?"

Her smile faded as she gave the question serious thought, but she still seemed to glow with happy anticipation. "Tacos!" she exclaimed suddenly. "I've always wondered how they taste. And gyros."

Absently, I corrected her pronunciation.

"Really? That's how you say it?"

"Really." My mouth puckered a bit as I hit the pickled salmon.

"See—I don't even know what I don't know! But I can't wait to find it out—all of it." She was quiet for a moment, then suddenly burst out with, "A sweatshirt! Do you know I've never owned one?"

"Well, that's easy enough to fix."

She went back to tapping on her monitor. I watched her for a moment, thinking. "What about boys, Hitomi? Do you have something in mind . . . in that direction?"

Her mouth quirked. "Now that you mention it, it might be

nice to meet a guy that I haven't known since the cradle."

I blinked at her. I couldn't even imagine such a thing.

She gestured behind her. "How can you get interested in a guy when you've seen him get swatted for pulling pigtails and picking his nose?"

I laughed, and yet my mind's eye was suddenly busy conjuring an image of a young Ken, a big, mischievous grin on his cute little face. "Where have they gone to?" I asked, only partly to distract myself.

"Filtering water for our bottles." She tucked the extra food away.

I stared at the little screen, where it sat next to her. It showed a map, with our current position marked. "Can I see that?" I asked, struck by a sudden thought.

"Sure."

I struggled a bit, but finally figured out how to enlarge the map. "You know, I think we may be near one of the caches that my dad and I set up." I studied the screen. "Can you find our coordinates on this thing?"

"Yep." She tapped the thing a couple of times and the numbers popped up in the corner.

"Yes," I said, excited. "I never went near this one after . . . I lost my dad. It should be just a slight detour, but it's probably worth it to get the weapons and rations."

But now that I held the micro-tab in my hands—I was struck by something. "You know, Hitomi, I can't recall Ken carrying one of these when we met. And you know I never got jacked up," I pointed toward my temple, indicating the spot where so many kids had had chips installed. "Or carried a portable, either."

"Yes, I did read that implants are way down. It makes sense when you think of it. Kids older than us were trapped inside so much when the air was still so bad. They wanted the connectivity and instant access. But micro-tabs are coming back. We have other interests and activities, now that the filters are working and we can go outside again without the masks and all the gear, but we still want to be able to hook in."

"It does make sense." I began.

"How did you connect?" she asked. Since we'd first met,

she'd been interested in how I lived alone for so long. She liked to pump me for info. And though I was woefully ignorant of many of the fashions and fads of popular culture—a major disappointment to her—she'd accepted me as a friend anyway.

"Public libraries. Schools. Community centers."

"It must have been frustrating, not being able to do and see what everyone else does." She frowned a little. "I know it's been driving me crazy."

I shrugged. "I was a little busy trying to stay alive."

"Oh, I'm sorry. I know that. I didn't mean—"

I waved it off. "I did manage to get the broad strokes of popular culture, if not the intricate details." Even if I had never had an implant or a phone or computer. "I couldn't carry technology with me, because I was afraid it would be too easily tracked via satellite feed." Speaking of which . . . "Hitomi, I hate to harsh out on your fun, but maybe you'd better turn that off until we know it can't be used to find us."

She started and her hand, still rough and bumpy like stone, abruptly switched back to normal. "Oh!" She turned the micro-tab off and set it down, staring at it like it was a kitten that had suddenly sunk its teeth into her. "I didn't even think of that."

"That's because you are not used to being on the run," I said gently. "And I'm not used to having people along. But we'll get the hang of it eventually."

We both turned as Ken and Sho tramped back into camp, each carrying several bottles of water.

"Sleeping Beauty awakes," Sho called, laughing.

"I'm awake." And alert. And . . . ready. I couldn't remember the last time I felt so good.

"Awake enough to tell us where we're going? Last night we just wanted to get away from Ryu, but now we should take stock and pick a heading." Ken tilted his head at me. "And we all want to know what Boru told you."

I gave them all a quick summary, including the location of the nearby cache. "Boru says we are to find this witch. Effie Couts is her name. She lives in Hot Springs, which should only be—a day and a half or so?" I looked to Ken for confirmation.

But Hitomi sat up and broke in, all smiles. "Hot Springs? You mean Hot New Hollywood Hills?"

I stared at her, blankly. Neither of the two boys looked any more enlightened than I felt.

"Guys!" she crowed. "Don't you know what this means? We're going to see all the vid celebs!"

"Wait—what?" I asked, confused. "Boru said we'd find her just off the Appalachian Trail."

"I think I did see that the trail goes through there—but didn't you know that several of the vid studios have set up shop in these mountains?"

"Oh, yeah!" Sho perked up. He came from a family steeped in the tradition of Japanese theater, and his interests naturally extended to today's vids and shows. "Before the Rift, they were already using spots here for location shoots, so when parts of Los Angeles buckled and so many evacuated, Hot Springs became one of the new vid hubs."

I just nodded. I knew Hitomi was also a huge fan of some of the popular vids, but except for a few free showings in parks and libraries, they just had never been much on my radar.

She laughed at me now. "Oh, I know . . . you wouldn't know a vid celeb if one walked up and smacked you with a kiss."

Ken handed her a couple of bottles and then passed me two as well. "If they did that, they'd likely get smacked back," he said with a grin. "And not on the lips."

Hitomi simpered at him. "Yes, but who would do the smacking? Mei—or you?"

He ignored her and squatted down in front of the fire. He glanced around at all of us and his look was solemn.

"All kidding aside, I was wondering if perhaps we should make Asheville our first stop on the way out of here? Maybe we should go to the Dragon's Eye and talk to Neil?"

I frowned. "Personally, I'd love to go the Dragon's Eye again, but that's the opposite direction from Hot Springs."

"Bad idea, anyway," Sho commented. "That's the first place Rin will look. She'd likely be standing in there waiting on us when we walked in."

I watched Ken closely. He was experienced and smart— and troubled.

"Why make the suggestion, Ken?" I asked. "Is there a

reason we should head there?"

His gaze flicked from Sho to Hitomi as he answered. "It was something the Yuki-Onna said. She broke the wards using an object of power. A dragon's scale."

Hitomi paled.

"Carp crap on a cracker!" Sho exclaimed.

"What? Why is that significant?" I stared from one to the other of them. "Does Neil sell dragon scales at the shop?"

"Something like that," Ken answered. He shot Sho a look. "She said something about battling a mother dragon protecting her young."

Sho paled. He stood and looked up at the sky. "Then it's not likely Neil is even at the Dragon's Eye right now, is it? He's out looking for that Snow Woman."

"If Neil wants us, he can find us," Hitomi said softly.

"That's true enough." Ken stood too, and began to kick dirt over the fire. "And in that case, we might as well get moving and get some answers." He glanced askance at me. "I'd like to meet this friend of Boru's."

Together, we broke camp and soon we were on our way.

I scarfed the rest of my rice ball as we set out, heading north. The normal racket of the forest carried on around us, as if the birds and animals took no objection to our presence. I puzzled over my own ramped up energy level—but then a thought hit me. This was it. The first day of freedom. The first day in four years that I did not have to carry the knowledge that the wind demon was hunting me.

It made no sense. Soon enough another of Inaba's minions would likely be after me—but knowing Fuma Jinnae was gone—defeated—made my steps feel lighter.

I glanced around at our little band. So did knowing that I wouldn't have to face the next monster alone.

My thoughts ranged then, while we walked. After a bit of travel, I brought up the question I'd been wanting to ask.

"So what do you guys know of these Elementals? Were they mentioned in your training?" It seemed that everyone in Ryu grew up preparing for battles in a war that the rest of the world was unaware of.

"I don't know anything about them—and that makes me

nervous," Ken answered. "I hope this witch can help us."

Hitomi frowned back at me from the trail ahead. "You were with me when I told my siblings the old story of the Bamboo Princess, right? I've seen her mentioned along with the concept of Elementals somewhere . . ." She frowned. "Something to do with her emergence as the Moon Princess . . . but I don't remember any details."

"There is mention of them in a couple of the older plays," Sho broke in. "They show up as a form of judgment or justice, I think." He made a face. "The protagonists rarely come out whole, after an encounter with them. Coming to their attention rarely seems to be a good thing."

"Great," I groaned. But then I paused. "Well, they were a real help to us yesterday. There's no denying that."

Ahead, Ken paused and turned to face us. "It may be that we should count ourselves lucky, then," he said, speaking slowly. "Maybe we should try and avoid their notice for now—at least until we know more about them."

Sho shrugged. "I don't think it's up to us. They'll do as they wish."

"Well, we can at least try," Ken cautioned. He turned to me. "Do you know how it happened? Did you, maybe, *call* them?"

I swallowed. "That's just it. I think they were called, but it wasn't me who summoned them."

Hitomi's eyes grew wide. "What is powerful enough to summon an Elemental?"

"I don't know what it was. It was big. Powerful." I remembered the pressure, the feeling of something huge and awe-inspiring that had arrived on the scene. And the mingled fear and joy I'd felt.

"The eyes," Ken said. "You said you saw eyes open in the hillside. You think—whatever that was—it called the Elementals?"

"Yes." A shiver ran through me at the remembered sensation. "It sent up a signal. A flare of light. Even the wind demon sensed it, though the light winked in and out."

"But how did the . . . bigger thing get there? It wasn't Rialka, was it? So far from her tree?"

"No, it wasn't her." I shook my head. "I don't know how to explain it. I just . . . asked for help. Sent out a plea. And it answered."

Silence reigned for a few moments between us—while the forest noise continued. Then Ken heaved a huge sigh. "Well, let's hope we don't get into a situation in which we need that sort of help, before we know what we are asking for."

My shoulders slumped. "Boru contradicts you. She says I need a lot of help before I'll be ready to face Inaba."

They all exchanged worried glances. "We'll help you," Hitomi pledged. "All we can."

My heart warmed despite my misgivings. "Thank you. I know you will."

I only wished it would be enough.

We hiked on in silence after that. The day had grown into one of those beautiful late spring/early summer days of high blue sky and low humidity—always a treat in North Carolina. I pushed aside my worries and let myself enjoy it. Insects and birds kept up a happy racket as we traveled. I breathed in sweet, clean air and the memories crept in.

I'd grown up in these mountains. Not nearby, but tucked away from the world with only my father for company. I'd trained here. Learned how to fight, to hide, and to adapt. I'd learned to bond with nature too, which was how I recognized the wild strawberries growing on the edge of a little clearing. I knew most of the flora and fauna hereabouts. I paused. It was just late enough in the season—there might be a handful or two of berries . . .

I was bent over, searching beneath the broad leaves, when the clearing darkened suddenly. It lit up again, as if a dark cloud had passed over, but very quickly.

I rose slowly, reaching for the knife in my boot as the forest fell abruptly silent around us. Even the bees buzzing in the clover took shelter.

I eased into the shadow of a tree. I could see no sign of Sho or Hitomi, but Ken stood a few feet away, staring up through the trees.

The light faded again. My mouth fell open as something filled the sky above the meadow. Something massive.

Something dark, with a lighter underbelly and four legs ending in dagger-clawed feet.

I backed against the thick trunk behind me and struggled to breath past shock and disbelief as the creature settled awkwardly into the too-small clearing.

Scales. Claws. Giant, swiveling ears. A sinewy neck rippled as the great head turned and a *dragon* looked me in the eye.

I crouched, ready, as its mouth opened. Heart pounding, I ignored the fact that its gleaming teeth were nearly as long as my arm.

"You kids are in a mess of trouble," it said.

4

Mei

I blinked, but held my position. Nearby, Hitomi stepped away from an oak, her skin transforming from rough, textured bark to smooth again. Beyond her, Sho dropped from a high branch. Ken stepped into the clearing to face the monster.

I hissed at him to stop. "What are you—"

My words faded as the beast sat back, then used a clawed talon to lift a bulging messenger bag from where it had been looped over an armored neck spike. "Rin is about to bust a gut," it said, throwing the bag at Ken's feet.

I crouched again as the dragon stretched its neck out, shook like a dog, then abruptly . . . shrunk. Faster than my eye could register, it changed, morphing into . . .

"Neil?" I nearly dropped my knife. Neil, the kind, soft-spoken storekeeper from the Dragon's Eye, was an actual *dragon*?

"What did you bring?" Ken eyed the sack.

"Well, while Rin is railing about making all of you come back to Ryu, Tak and Noff have figured that you are all going after Akemi. They sent travel rations and a selection of *seihoukei*.

Sho made an appreciative sound and joined the two in the meadow. He opened the sack and began to rummage through it. "Yes! Food and weapons!"

I gripped my blade tighter and stepped out as well. "Seriously? A dragon? Someone might have told me, don't you think? I was this close to launching a knife at your eye!"

Ken raised his hands. "Sorry! We all thought you should know—but it wasn't our secret to tell."

Neil stepped forward. "Not many know the truth, but I would have told you, Mei, had we met again under more normal circumstances." He raised his hands. "I liked you when we first met, and I like what I've heard of you since, but you can appreciate that we must be careful, if only for my family's sake."

"Your family?" Suddenly I put the Snow Woman's and Ken's words together. "You mean Tomoe and Tai?" I breathed. I'd met his wife and son a few weeks ago, when Ken and Reik had taken me to the Dragon's Eye. "That's who the Yoki Onna meant—when she spoke of battling a mother dragon to steal a scale? Are they all right?"

"They're fine," he growled. "Unsettled, but fine." His eyes flashed an unearthly green. "And I'll be a sight better when I get my claws around that snow creature's neck."

"There aren't that many dragons left," Ken said quietly. "Young ones are rare and precious."

"Hundreds of years ago, my great-grandfather traded the men of Ryu that first scale, when it was Inaba's wards that they needed to breach, so that they could rescue Rialka. We've allied ourselves with your people since then, but Inaba and his creature have made a grave mistake, invading my home and threatening my family."

"But Tomoe and Tai are okay, aren't they, Neil?" Hitomi sounded anxious, and I wondered if she might be worried about more than Neil's family.

It appeared that he had the same thought. Some of the fury faded from his expression. "They'll be fine, Hitomi, thank you. And I'll be sure to tell them that you all asked after them." A twitch of sympathy showed in his face. "Your family is fine, too, for all that your father is in a rage. I think you quite shocked him."

I was surprised to see my friend's fists tighten. "Good," she said between clenched teeth.

Everyone stared.

"What?" Her chin lifted. "He wouldn't be shocked now if he'd been listening *at all*, for a long time."

Sho touched her shoulder, but she flinched away. "You know what he's been like. He belittles my abilities. Every time I mention the scout trials, he brushes it off or talks of marrying me off. He wouldn't listen. So now I'm doing it my way." I'd never seen mild-mannered Hitomi vibrate with such intensity. "He'll see that my *parlor tricks* can be a valuable tool for a scout."

"Your mother, at least, is in sympathy with you." Neil nodded toward the bag. "She sent your extra set of *nekote*. And your make-up kit and props as well."

Hitomi's anger suddenly drained away. "Did she?" She fell to her knees next to Sho and grabbed the bag and came up with one of the finger talons so long associated with female ninja. "Thank you, Neil." She looked up. "And if you speak to my mother before I do . . ." She swallowed. "Tell her that her faith means everything to me."

Neil sighed. He looked around, from one to the other, until he'd met each of our gazes. "Listen, all of you. I know you set out to find Akemi. It's damned gracious of you, considering her attitude all of this time." His gaze hardened. "But I'm going to JanFran." He spoke of the ruined city of San Francisco, where many Japanese refugees had settled to try to rebuild after the Rift. "Inaba is there—and his cronies likely are too. I'm going to find that Yuki Onna." He sighed. "And that's where that snow woman likely took Akemi. If there is anything to be found of the girl, anything to be done to help her, I'll do it." He frowned around at us. "You don't have to go. You can all turn back."

I shook my head.

Neil held my gaze. "It will take you weeks to get there. I'll be there tomorrow."

My lips pressed together. I was not going back. My path was not yet clear, but I knew it led away from Ryu, at least temporarily. But my friends might not feel the same.

"I'm going to JanFran too." Sho stood straight now. "I'm going to find out the truth of what happened to my parents there—and I'm going to fight Inaba in any way I can."

"I'm going with Mei." Hitomi met my gaze. "And I'll prove myself on the way."

Ken merely took a step closer to me.

"I'll keep going until I hear Akemi is safe," I said stubbornly. "But even if you rescue her before I get out of North Carolina, I still can't stay in Ryu."

Neil sighed. "That's what I thought." His attention returned to me. He looked me over for a moment, then frowned. "What is it that you've got there, Mei?"

I looked down to find the knife still in my hand. "Oh, sorry." I tucked it back in my boot.

"Not that." He nodded toward my chest and gave me a toothy grin. "Did you think you could hide a jewel from a dragon?"

"Jewel?" Suddenly, I remembered. "Oh, yes!" I pulled the pendant out from inside my tank. "I forgot. Boru gave it to me."

"A moonstone?" Neil's eyes lit in appreciation, then narrowed. "Quite a special specimen, too—is it not? I can smell the spells wrapped around it." His expression took on a knowing cast. "Rin said that Boru suddenly seemed quite remarkably recovered."

I shifted, but didn't reply.

He cocked his head. "I've heard of moonstones that could facilitate an energy transfer, but this is the first time I've actually encountered one."

"Energy transfer?" Ken spoke up. He frowned at me. "Energy transfer? Is that why you were in such a state of exhaustion last night? On top of everything else you went through yesterday, you gave some of your chi energy to Boru?"

I bristled. "Yes. It was frightening how weak she was. I could almost see the bed sheets right through her. And every time a spirit nagged at her, she grew weaker." I shrugged. "I gave her just enough to protect herself."

Ken still scowled, but Neil merely raised a brow. "Now, Ken, don't berate her for something we all know you might have done as well."

"Exactly!" Ken folded his arms. "You should have called me in, let me donate the energy. You're too important to risk."

"Why?" I was growing angrier by the second. "Because I'm the Girl With the Stars in Her Eyes?" I raised my head and scoffed. "I don't even know who she is. None of us do, really." I glared around at all of them. "But I know who *I* am. And that's someone who helps a friend when they need it."

"But . . ."

I glared at Ken and he smartened up enough not to continue.

"But nothing. You are the one with the formidable *minding*

ability." I looked pointedly at Sho, and then Hitomi. "I'm the weakling in the bunch when it comes to that."

"None of you are weak," Neil broke in. "And you're out here trying to help Akemi, who I highly doubt can be counted a friend. It all only confirms my first impression of you, Mei. But I'm offering to take that burden from you—and you are not going back." He raised a brow at me. "I assume then, that Boru has also given you a mission?"

I swallowed, then nodded.

Neil stared at me for a long moment. His gaze dropped to the moonstone. "It's not my place, but still, I'll ask you to be cautious. That's no ordinary gemstone." He shook his head. "I don't know what the witch has you mixed up with, but Elemental magic is an ancient and powerful thing. Elementals are older even, than dragons. They are strong, unpredictable and often dangerous."

"But if they've chosen to help us—"

"Don't count on it," Neil interrupted. "An Elemental's loyalties lie far beyond our understanding." He frowned at Ken. "And don't even think that your minding ability gives you anything in common with such a creature. Even if you could summon and control a hurricane, an Elemental could put it out and crush you with the same second's thought."

He backed up a few steps. "I have to go. I cannot let that snow creature's trail get cold. Be careful." He looked up and I could see that his attention was turning toward the sky—and his mission.

I jumped a little when he suddenly thrust a finger at us. "One of you can scry, yes?"

Hitomi and Ken nodded.

"Keep in touch with Boru. I'll send her any news of Akemi."

We all nodded—and suddenly the clearing was full of dragon again.

I marveled at how absurd—and awesome—it was, and then I jumped back as he crouched low and launched himself skyward.

We all stood watching, our hands over our eyes, until he disappeared beyond the trees. And then we stood some more.

Several minutes later, Sho sighed. "Let's go."

We set off again, all of us gone thoughtful and quiet. My mind was fixed on what Neil, and Boru too, had said about Akemi.

They had both been right. She wasn't a friend—but that had been her choice, not mine. I knew I didn't owe her anything, but that didn't mean I didn't want to help her.

Hitomi moved up next to me. "Are you thinking of Akemi?"

"How did you know?"

"You've got a wrinkle in your forehead and a slightly sour look on your face. I'm sure I look the same way when I think of her."

I just sighed. We walked in silence for a few moments then I said, "I know what it feels like to have your world upended."

"Yep." It was a simple acknowledgement of something huge—another reason why I enjoyed Hitomi's company so much. She made so much of the insane stuff that happened to me somehow seem like just another thing. "The difference is all in how you handled it."

"I don't know . . ." I thought about it. "I did some pretty stupid stuff right after my dad died."

"Listen to your own words. Your dad was murdered. You were to be next. Akemi's losses are disappointments, not tragedies."

She had a point, but there were other factors. My own trauma had come surgically quick. One moment all was well, the next my father was gone and I was on the run, fighting for survival.

Akemi, on the other hand, had been forced to watch as everything important to her drained away—at least from her perspective. Her status as the girl from the village prophecy—The Girl With the Stars in her Eyes—had started to erode as soon as I showed up. I'd been welcomed to Ryu and made much of. General Rin and Boru and the Elder Council had given me the sort of attention that she thought was her due.

Even Reik—I suffered a pang at the thought of him—had circled around me. And she'd had feelings for him. I knew it had cut her deeply.

"She went to fight the Snow Woman—it was brave, if boneheaded."

"It was brave—and desperate. Akemi has never liked to give up anything she considered hers. She doesn't like to share. She doesn't like much, except feeling superior to everyone else. Even if you save her, Mei, she won't be your friend."

"It doesn't matter how awful she is, if Inaba is as bad as you all have told me, she doesn't deserve to be left in his clutches."

"That's true. And it's one of the reasons we are all here with you. But it's not the most important one to any of us."

"It's only one of the reasons I'm out here too, Hitomi, but I think that you all know that." My fists clenched. "I just keep thinking—that wind demon was so evil, so relentless. Imagine how much worse Inaba must be."

She paled.

"I'm glad Neil is going to look for her. He stands a better—and quicker—chance than we do, of getting her out."

"But we are not going back," Hitomi said with certainty. "Even if we hear tomorrow that Neil has rescued her, we not going back."

I felt a pang, but I also thought of what going back would mean. The wards were down. I'd be training in Ryu—and watching and waiting while Inaba's creatures came after us in waves. I remembered the people I'd befriended there—and all of the men, women and children who lived there, but I still hadn't met. At least while we were out here, we stood a chance of hiding—and of drawing them away from the village.

I thought of Boru's certainty that we had to learn what was changing the *yokai* we'd encountered. And I realized how very many questions I had, questions that Rin and her Council had been unable to answer.

"No." I shook my head. "I'm not going back. Not until this is over."

5

Akemi

$\mathbf{A}$kemi pushed through the fog, fighting to come slowly awake. With great effort she opened her eyes, then quickly shut them again, against the stark, bright light.

What had happened? Where was she? With caution, she looked again.

She struggled to remember. That awful Snow Woman. So powerful. Akemi had trained all of her life at Ryu. She'd listened to the stories the Scouts spun about their battles with *yokai.* Still, she hadn't been prepared for how strong the Yuki-Onna had been.

She clutched her head. Well, the creature was gone now. As were the familiar mountains of home. She was in a small room, windowless and relentlessly white. Not the infirmary at Ryu. A hospital in Asheville?

She let herself believe that for a while, but when no one came, when she called and yelled and no one answered . . . she knew. She didn't like it, either. She was *not* used to being so relentlessly ignored.

A large mirror on one wall reflected the light everywhere. She reclined in a bed, the hospital kind that raised and lowered you with a push of a button—and she was too tired to do much more than adjust her position. A soft beeping sounded somewhere behind her and when she raised her hand, plastic tubing came with it and she realized she was hooked up to an IV.

Tired. She was so tired her hand shook just from raising it to touch her brow.

Rest. The voice sounded close. *Rest now. There is work to be done, but first you must heal.*

Straining, she looked everywhere, even pulling herself to a sitting position so that she could look behind her.

She was alone.

Rest.

It was an order, and she couldn't fight it. Perhaps there was something in her IV. She sank down, surrendering to the foggy ether.

Just as she drifted away, something snagged her attention. Movement. From a figure in the mirror.

But she slipped into the darkness, and was gone.

6

Mei

Hours later, the sun was on the descent and the air had grown warm. Hitomi paused to remove a layer of clothes and the rest of us took the chance to get off of our feet.

Sho leaned back against a tree and looked over at me, eyebrows high. "I've been watching you all afternoon," he said, marveling. "You move like the mist. You never set a foot wrong or make a sound."

"That's not true." I could feel the heat rising in my cheeks. "And I was thinking the same thing about all of you this morning." I paused. "It makes me wonder how similar our training must have been."

"Well, you've seen the training grounds at Ryu, but we did also do a lot of training in the forest," Ken said.

"And our teacher was relentless," Hitomi groaned.

"Harsh, that's what she was," Sho corrected. "And particularly inventive. Make one mistake and old Chou could come up with a punishment that would make your life a misery."

"Chou—that nice old lady?" I'd had breakfast with her several times during my stay in Ryu.

"Yeah—you should see that nice old lady in the woods," scoffed Hitomi.

"That's just it, you can't see her," Ken broke in. "Not unless she wants you to. She's like a ghost out here." He cast a glance back the way we'd came. "She could be right here, right now and we'd never know it."

"Reik was one of her best students," Hitomi recalled. "As long as he covered those blue runes and white hair."

"Yes. Hiding. Something Reik was always good at," Ken sniped.

"Your bitterness is showing, dude," laughter tinted Sho's tone.

"You can't stay mad at him forever," Hitomi chided.

"Watch me." Ken bent over, picked up a rock and tossed it high, knocking a swinging pinecone from a tree.

"Remember when Chou made Reik stand in the cafeteria, making slushie drinks for everyone who asked? He hated it." Sho chortled at the memory.

"Maybe she taught my dad, too, back in the day," I mused. "He always made me suffer if I messed up, too."

"I fell out of a tree once, right into a stream. Not exactly invisible," Ken said.

I laughed.

"Yeah, it wasn't funny when she enlisted my parents to get in on my punishment. I had to clean the toilets for a month." He shuddered.

"That's nothing," Hitomi scoffed. "I got stuck on diaper duty."

"For *one* baby," Ken said. "Do you know how many brothers I have? And what they can do to a bathroom?"

"Toilets? Diapers? *Slushies?*" I stared at them, indignant. "That's it?"

They all stared.

"Why?" Sho asked. "What did your dad come up with?"

"I had to make my way through bear territory without attracting their notice. If he caught me making a *sound*, he'd send me back to start over—with a dead fish in my pack."

Three pairs of eyes widened.

"What if you messed up again?" Hitomi whispered.

"Then I got another fish."

"Did you get chased by bears?"

I stood. "Of *course*, I got chased by bears!" I let my exasperation show. "I had rotten fish on me!"

"Wow," Sho breathed. "You win."

I frowned at him. "Don't look at me like that. I had to get myself out of the situation, but my father would never have let me come to any real harm."

"No, he wouldn't, I am sure," Ken agreed. "And the next time, you worked extra hard to be quiet, right? He was deadly serious about your training."

"With good reason, it turns out," Sho agreed.

"So it would seem," I said grimly.

We moved on, with that sober thought weighing on us all. The afternoon was wearing on when Ken called a halt and consulted a map. "There's a nice wide curve in a creek ahead. Why don't we—"

"Yes!" I interrupted. "I need a bath!"

Everyone chuckled.

"How far to the cache?" I asked. We'd let Ken keep track of the navigation.

"A couple of hours, I think. We could camp here tonight and head there first in the morning."

"We should probably do an inventory of the weapons we have and come up with a basic plan of attack or defense," I mused. "Just so we have an idea what to do, if we should run into something."

Ken nodded, but he had an odd look on his face.

"We should reach Hot Springs tomorrow, right, though, Ken?" asked Hitomi. She hadn't been thrilled to have to leave her tab back at the first camp, and had asked a lot of pointed questions as we moved, to show it.

"Yes. By early afternoon, if we set out at first light."

Her friend gave a little jump of joy. "Yes. A bath, then. We want to be fresh in case we meet a vid celebrity, right Mei?"

"Sure." I went along with her, but she'd been right before, about me not recognizing celebrities. I just desperately wanted to get two days worth of stink off of me.

I was not alone in my eagerness, in the end. We found a spot and made camp in record time, then split up. The girls headed upstream, the boys down. I sighed in relief and pleasure as I soaped my hair twice over. After we were scrubbed clean, we swam back toward the camp. Ken and Sho were waiting for us, however, and ambushed us in a frenzy of splashing.

Shocked at first, I froze—then told myself to relax. I breathed deep and smiled at the sight of Hitomi's sputtering indignation—and then jumped into the fray.

I was a whirlwind. But Ken, with his wind *minding* ability, kept sending little waterspouts against us. I laid out a steady stream of counter splashes, laughing madly and giving everything I had to drench those boys mercilessly. They fought back and the battle raged fiercely for a few minutes. We were laughing and breathless—and then Ken dove for me and dragged me under.

I stopped fighting and just enjoyed the feel of his arms around me.

It was only a brief, blind flash of time, but we both felt it. The awareness, the potential that crackled between us was growing into something that felt like a real connection. It warmed me in all the spots where we touched, a marked contrast with the cold water. We floated, our hair mingling in a lazy swirl, just enjoying the moment. When we came sputtering to the surface, the mood had changed.

Sho floated on his back now, staring at the sky. Hitomi stopped squeezing water from her hair and headed for shore. "I'm starving," she announced. "And I want something hot. I'll start a fire."

I struck out for the curve in the creek, where a couple of long, flat rocks stretched into the water.

"What are you doing?" Ken asked.

"Making like a lizard and soaking up the sun's heat," I said, boosting myself up.

"Good idea." He hesitated though, and called after Hitomi. "Are you okay on your own?"

She waved him on. After a moment, he climbed up and stretched out on the other rock.

The stone was warm. I lay full out and pressed my cheek into it. It felt wonderful after the chill of the mountain water. I let my eyes float closed. I was clean and content, warm and at peace. My mind drifted and my soul soaked in the solid strength of the place.

I think I dozed. I was half dreaming, imagining that Rialka was here, that she was introducing me to the spirits of this place, the water spirit, those from the trees and the rocks.

It was a pleasant, happy daydream. Long minutes passed, maybe half an hour, before I felt a tingle of awareness. I opened my eyes.

Ken was staring at me.

"What are you thinking?" he asked.

"About the absurdity of my life," I hedged.

He chuckled, low. "Which part?"

"Oh, you know—a nice, friendly man I met turned out to be a dragon today. And his wife and kid, too, it seems. And somehow I've reached a point where I just nod at the idea, shrug and move on."

"Just be thankful that the dragon is on our side." Ken grinned.

"Oh, I am." I smiled lazily. "And really, after everything that's happened the last few weeks, a dragon is par for the course."

"Sounds about right," Ken said on a yawn.

I smiled again, and my mind wandered. Briefly, I wondered what would happen if I stretched my hand out and touched my fingers to Ken's. I was contemplating it when that buzz started up my spine again.

Languid, I opened my eyes—and instantly stiffened.

"Ken."

"Hmmm?"

"Ken. Open your eyes."

"I don't want to," he yawned.

"Ken. We are not alone."

His eyes snapped open and we both stared.

A creature knelt between us. I'd set my soap and washcloth out to dry and now something—a *yokai*—held the soap in his hand, delicately smelling it.

He was small, about the size of a ten-year-old, with impossibly long legs and a short torso. He had long brown hair and a light layer of hair over the rest of him, too. But most disconcerting—he only had one eye in the middle of his forehead.

I shrank back as it lifted the soap toward me, almost in question. Was it asking permission to keep it?

Suddenly, it spoke.

"Ken," it said. "We are not alone."

In my voice. It said it in my voice.

I sat up and scrambled back. It straightened too, but Ken held out a hand to both of us.

"Easy," he breathed. "It's fine. Harmless. It's a Yamawaro."

"A what?" I croaked.

But it was nodding. "A Yamawaro," it said.

In Ken's voice.

That was seriously freaking me out.

"It's okay, Mei. They are simple mountain spirits. They won't hurt us."

"They? As in, more than one?"

The Yamawaro held up the soap again. Ken nodded and it grinned.

I backed up again as it stood straight. It gave us both a nod then scampered off into the woods.

I stared after it.

"Really?" Ken asked. "You look seriously horrified." There was laughter in his voice. "After the Tengu, the Kappa, shape-shifting Kitsune, the Snow Woman, the Wind Demon . . ."

"Don't forget the dragon," I reminded him.

"Yes, and after all that—this is what gives you the skeeves?"

"It talked in my voice," I said defensively, and shuddered. "And it snuck up on me. It got so close and I didn't know it was there."

"Well, get a grip, because it will be back."

"What? Why?"

"It will want to make a trade for the soap. Yamawaro are notorious for insisting on a fair trade. It will offer something it thinks of equal value—and we'll take it. Or it will get mad."

"No," I shuddered. "We don't want to make it mad."

He laughed and picked up his own packet of sundries. "Come on, let's go help Hitomi."

***

The Yamawaro did come back, bearing a stack of kindling and a bundle of wild carrots, spring Onions and a bit of edible tree fungus. Hitomi took it with thanks and managed a credible rice stir-fry. The little creature accepted his portion—and a bit of the fish that Sho brought in and roasted over the fire.

I watched it as it ate delicately. It was growing on me, although I still shivered when it mimicked one of us so perfectly. Ken nudged me with his foot as we ate and pointed . .

. and I saw another Yamawaro peering at us from high in a hickory tree.

"There are probably more," he whispered.

I was struck by a sudden thought. "Why are they here?" I asked. "The Yamawaro and the Kappa too—they aren't like the others—not like the Tengu and the Snow Woman—they are not *yokai* sent against us by Inaba. They *live* here. So far from Japan. How did that come about?"

"It's Rialka's doing," Ken answered. "She saved Ryu when the Rift hit the islands, and she's worked hard since then, to relocate people, creatures and *yokai* that were displaced . . . or that were being slowly starved or poisoned in the aftermath."

"There is a band of raccoon dogs running wild outside of Boone," Hitomi said. "They are so cute! My father said that Rialka rescued them from their home, and placed them there."

"Partly because these mountains are similar to some of the ranges in Japan," Sho explained. "My parents said that many of the people felt at home here, once the shock of the tragedy wore off."

"But Rialka places her creatures wherever suits them best," Ken interjected. "Like the Baku—scouts have seen them out in the west."

"Baku, that sounds familiar." My knowledge was not as extensive as theirs, but I had done some research on supernatural creatures, while I was on the run from the Wind Demon, trying to discover what it was and how I could defeat it. "They are good luck, aren't they? And odd looking?"

"Odd, yes. They have the head of an elephant, legs of a tiger and tail of an ox," said Ken. "They eat bad dreams, too, the legends say. The scouts say that she placed them out west near the refugee camps and orphanages, after the worst of the disasters. They took away the bad dreams of the children and helped them to adjust."

"What sort of talents do these ones have?" Hitomi asked. She'd been fascinated with the Yamawaro and it had returned her interest, especially after she showed him her *minding*. It was now sitting next to her, holding her hand. It took turns placing rocks, sticks, leaves and branches in her hand, and looking delighted when she shifted her palm to match.

"They are friendly, if you treat them with respect," Ken answered. "And that is enough." He stood and went to rummage in his pack. "But I do think we should douse the fire for the night."

I had been wondering whether to suggest the same thing. Clearly the Yamaworu *lived* here. We had wandered into its territory, not the other way around. But I couldn't help wondering if there might be something else out there, looking for us.

We all exchanged glances.

"We have water," Sho said. "Which means we can scry. Why don't we check in with home?"

"Because we don't want to hear the lectures?" Hitomi cringed a little as she said it.

"There won't be any from Boru," I assured her. "And we need to know what is happening."

"Okay." She sighed and flicked her fingers at Sho. "Fill that collapsible pot with water? You will all want to see, I imagine, and it's bigger than my pocket mirror."

The water was fetched, and I watched, curious, as Hitomi prepared herself. I'd only ever seen General Rin scry, and that had been different, as she had been showing me the history of Ryu, not making direct communication.

Hitomi sat quietly. The Yamaworu had taken the chance to slip away, but the rest of us ranged behind her. I saw her go still, her breathing slowing, becoming even and regular. Her hands were crossed and I wondered if she was touching the scar on the inside of her wrist, the one that was associated with her *minding*. Suddenly she sat forward and blew a long breath across the surface of the water.

"Boru," she whispered. "Boru."

 We waited.

"Boru."

The water rippled. I leaned forward—and my eyes widened as the witch's face appeared on the surface. "Hitomi?" she asked. "I hear you."

I leaned in. "Oh, you look much better already!" I breathed.

"Mei? Are you all there? All safe?"

A chorus of greetings answered her.

Some of the anxiety faded from her expression. "Oh, good. Everyone will be relieved. And thank you—I feel better—they are stuffing me like a fatted calf. All I do is eat and sleep." A pained expression crossed her face. "Nearly."

"Is everyone there all right?" Hitomi asked.

"Everyone is fine."

"But there's been an attack?" I could hear it in what she wasn't saying. "What's happened?"

She sighed. "That swarm of Kitsune—the ones that chased you into Ryu? They've returned."

I shuddered at the memory of the horde of fox-spirits. They could all shift into a crude, clumsy human form and back again. I exchanged a glance with Ken. We'd barely escaped them.

"We're fine. A few injuries, but no losses," Boru assured us. "I've managed to create a ward around the Temple and the main part of the village. We're all gathered here. They've done a bit of damage to some of the outlying farms—"

"My family?" Ken interrupted.

"All fine. Your dad was key to helping us repel them. He and Noff came up with several explosive concoctions. A more experienced shifter led them this time, but Rin set all four of his tails ablaze. And Tak sent several wolves to chase off the rest."

"Be careful," I pleaded. "Inaba won't give up so easily, now that he's made his move. Something else will come." And I feared it would be bigger and more dangerous.

"We are watching, but Mei—and all of you—you should know. My spirits tell me that the word is out that you are gone from Ryu. Inaba knows. You *must* be watchful. He'll have his creatures out there hunting you, now."

I drew a deep breath and nodded. "Okay. We'll be ready."

"We will," Ken echoed.

"Know that we are all thinking of you, and worrying for you. We will do all that we can to help."

"You're starting to fade," I said. "We'll go now."

"Check back in. Keep in contact so that we can share information."

We agreed . . . and Boru disappeared as Hitomi slumped back, tired from her exertions. We fed her a protein bar and hard candy from the provisions that Neil had left us, and made her rest while we straightened up the camp site in preparation for a quick departure in the morning.

My nerves were frazzled. I wandered about the camp, unable to settle to a task. Finally, I rifled again through Neil's bag. "Ten *seihoukei*," I marveled. The weapons were difficult to produce, blending technology, spells and plant magic, as they did—but they also sent *yokai* speeding back to the spirit world when they were used correctly. Ten of them was literally a treasure.

Slowly, I continued to catalogue our weapons. Somehow it helped me to restore my equilibrium. "Sho has his blade," I recounted out loud. "My knife. Hitomi's *nekote.*" I tossed her the set of claws historically worn by female ninja. "And Ken's winds, of course," I said, shooting him a grin.

Just looking at him calmed me further. His hair was down. I liked to watch the swing of his just-a-tad-too-long tresses, the curve of his muscled arm. I remembered the peace that had surrounded us this afternoon at the rocks and reached for a bit of that again.

He didn't return my smile. I didn't let it bother me. I breathed in the cooling mountain air, rich with scent of growing things and the small rustlings of the forest around us. Sometimes, I felt like the wood around us was awake and watching. Not in the same way that I felt the presence of Rialka in Ryu. Different, more scattered and diffuse, but still there. Surprisingly, it didn't spook me. I listened and felt better, calmer.

But Ken looked unusually serious as he took a seat nearby. "Mei, come over here? I have something to show you."

I raised my brows in question, not wanting to let go of my hard-won tranquility.

He straightened and I could see a long, thin, fabric wrapped bundle in his hand.

The air grew thicker around us. My heart began to pound.

He unwrapped the object he held with reverence, but I already knew, somehow, what was inside.

I moved then, and felt other eyes on us as I crouched beside him. From a plain leather scabbard he pulled a blade. A gorgeous, small sword.

I recognized the workmanship and my heart contracted. My father had forged this blade. Set the contrasting blued-steel guard with care. Crafted the rosewood handle himself. I sighed when I saw the design carved into the wood—the vine, the scarlet trumpet flower vine that he planted near his forges, because they reminded him of my mother.

"It's beautiful," I whispered. "Where did you get it?"

"Your father gave it to me."

I waited, breathless.

He shifted uneasily and spoke with an air of confession. "I was just a boy. We all loved to gather and watch him work, on his short visits to Ryu. He was so strong and talented and we'd heard the stories of his exploits as a scout. We all worshipped him."

I smiled. "I know what you mean."

He swallowed. "I don't know why he singled me out, but one day he called me closer. He knelt down and asked my name—and he gave a knife—that short, sharp throwing knife you've seen me use before."

I nodded, my throat too thick for words.

"I was thrilled. The other boys were envious, of course, but he'd done the same for a few others, so no one thought too much of it. But later that night . . ."

"What?" I asked. "What happened?"

"He came to my home. He sat with my parents and talked for a long while. And then he called me over. He presented this blade to me in formal fashion. I . . . I didn't know what to do but accept it. He bade me to keep it safe. And he made me promise to use it for the good of Ryu."

Tears welled. I could see it so clearly in my mind. My dad's soot streaked face and startling blue eyes. The solemnity with which he could imbue a promise or a lesson.

"I've carried it with me, ever since."

"It's part of a set," I said.

His eyes widened. "A *daisho*?"

"Yes." He spoke of a pairing of a long and short sword that ancient samurais used to wear.

"Then this is the short *wakizashi*. Where is the *katana*?" he asked.

"I don't know. I wish I did." The long sword had looked very like the one he held, but with a slender, curved, double-edged blade. "It was the best sword he ever made," I said longingly. "I trained with it for several years." It had been light and balanced and fit me perfectly. I still missed it, every time I drew a blade. Maybe that's why I preferred a bo staff, these days.

"Did you leave it behind? When you ran from the Wind Demon, after . . .?"

After the demon killed my father, he meant. "No." I shook my head. "My dad took the blade away. He said it would be better if I trained with a variety of weapons, and he said that someday that sword would be needed. He was going to leave it with the person who would see that it would get where it belonged." I paused, remembering. "He didn't tell me where he was going, but it was a long trip."

"I wonder where it is?" Ken mused.

I wish I knew. But I stared at its gorgeous partner in his hand. "Why didn't you tell me before, that you had this?"

"I don't know. I didn't want to upset you at first. You were protective of his memory. And later, it felt like I'd kept quiet too long." He met my gaze. "But this is it. The last secret I have. I wanted you to know, and to also know that everything is open and honest between us." His lips pinched. "And I've been thinking that you should have it."

He offered it.

It felt as if the glade around us was holding its breath. I stood. I wanted him to see that I recognized the importance of this moment. Sho and Hitomi were watching, too. I could feel the weight of their gazes as I gripped the proffered handle and held the sword before me.

It was so light. Balanced. Natural.

And then something happened. The world lit up, blindingly white and silver for second. I felt unexpectedly rooted to the ground, and also as if a great wind was blowing up from my feet. I gasped as a *zing* of power hit me, a tingle of energy raced along my nerve endings and up my spine, down along my arm—and I almost dropped the blade when it sizzled along my fingertips and into the grip of the sword. A clear note sounded in my brain and for the briefest moment, the metal blade *glowed.*

I gasped again.

"What was that?" Sho yelped.

The note sounded again, except this time it came from *outside* of my body. I looked up and found the Yamaworu standing just past my friends. Its one eye had gone huge and its gaze moved quickly between my face and the shining blade.

And then, just as quickly, the little creature backed away and disappeared.

The glow faded and I thrust the blade back at Ken.

"Your eyes—they *glowed.* And then the sword did too," Hitomi whispered. "How did you do that, Mei?"

"I don't know!"

"Do it again," Sho urged.

I shook my head and met Ken's gaze. He looked as shocked as I felt.

"Listen, thank you for the offer, but I think the *wakizashi* should stay with you." I knew it, rather, down deep in my soul.

"After that?" His voice trembled a little. "I'd say it belongs to you."

I shook my head, knowing I was right. "I think my father gave it to you for a reason. You had better keep it."

Reluctant, he tucked it away again. He and Sho moved away, muttering, and I bent in close to Hitomi. "Did you hear the noise the Yamaworu made just now?"

She frowned. "Like a bell. Yes, Mei. It was loud. We all heard it."

"How many times did you hear it?"

She stared at me like I was losing it. "Just once."

I pressed my lips together. The little creature had echoed the sound that had happened in my mind.

I went to unroll my pack.

Maybe I *was* losing it.

7

Mei

I couldn't sleep. I didn't know what had happened with that sword. I wasn't sure I wanted to know. I kept hearing my dad's voice in my head, so I mentally ran over the weapons we had, the ones we might find tomorrow, and various preparations we could make.

I remembered the makeshift bo staff I'd forged the last time Ken and I had traveled in the forest, with Reik on the way to Ryu. It had come in handy when we met up with that swarm of Kitsune. The thought drove me out of my hammock. I swung down and crept from camp and stood breathing in the night air, listening for any unusual noises—or silences. But all the nocturnal noises sounded normal. So I drank in the sight of the stars through the canopy of trees and searched for a bit until I found a hickory tree with a low, straight branch of the right size. I used my knife to harvest it, and took it back to camp, where I sat and squared off the ends, giving the thing a few practice swings for good measure.

It should do.

With some of my nervous energy worn off, I felt like I could sleep now. I went back to my nest at the edge of camp, taking the bo staff with me, and drifted off, clutching it close.

I woke in the morning to strangely dappled light—and realized that a willow branch lay over me, the leaves stuck to my forehead and shading my eyes. Maybe the dew had weighted it down and stuck it to my skin? I pulled the leaves free, feeling the feathery imprint left behind as I sat up.

I felt good, fully energized, despite the loss of sleep. The others started to stir too, and we broke camp early, moving out quickly and quietly.

"We'll head for the cache," Ken told us, "and then angle back to meet the stream again further on. If we follow it, it will join up with another and then converge with the French Broad

River in Hot Springs."

We'd walked almost an hour when the terrain began to feel familiar. I took the lead, moving slower and listening carefully. I let my senses range out, feeling for anything unnatural or disturbing.

Nothing. Even the wildlife acted normally around us.

Still, I agitated Ken by insisting on sitting quietly near the cache for a quarter of an hour. He fidgeted, but I ignored it. I remembered my training. *The utmost caution—always—when approaching a reserve.* My dad's voice sounded insistent in my head.

At last, I stood. The others followed as I approached a short ridge, stopping at the far end of the small rise, where a landslide had left the rock open and exposed.

The slide had crushed a stand of wild azaleas, but the bushes still grew thick at the edge of the fall. Their blooms were spent for the year, but new growth flourished, healthy and green. I knelt at the bottom of the closest shrub. New shoots, reaching for sun and soil, tried to block the way, but I lifted aside a mature bottom branch—and crawled inside the suddenly visible, hollowed out interior.

Ken knelt behind me. "Is there room for one more in there?"

"Not really." I sat up in the hidey-hole, painstakingly made by breaking off and misdirecting strategic branches. "It's been a while since anyone was in here. It's starting to grow back." The stone-lined hollow dug into the ground looked undisturbed, though. I began lifting aside rocks. Reaching in, I pulled out a water-proofed packet.

"Here, Hitomi, hold back this branch." Ken peered in and then poked his head and shoulders into the cramped space. "It's perfect. I knew you were in here, but couldn't see a sign of you."

"Yes. Azaleas are evergreen too, so it's useful most of the year. It's only late in the winter when the deer get hungry and start to feed on it that you have to worry."

"Smart."

Something in his tone made me look at him. He was so close. My heart began to pound.

It was ridiculous, really, considering his butt end poked out, but the air between us felt alive. There was something so intimate about sharing that small, sun-dappled space. About having our friends so close and unable to see what we saw.

What we were doing.

Slowly, he reached out and traced a finger down my cheek, along my jaw. He leaned in and his eyes closed and he kissed me.

And I let him. Just the touch of our lips. His were so soft, his touch so gentle. But I could feel the power in him, a towering wave, held back, kept in check. I'd seen his power, his fighting skills, and his kindness. They all combined into a dangerous call, a deep, thrumming undertow. My heart heard it, responded, tried to match its song.

"What's in there?" Hitomi called.

We broke apart. And time broke into pieces. Before. And After. After my first kiss.

I was so glad it was with Ken.

I swallowed and turned back to the shallow hole. Passing him a packet, I kept my gaze averted. "Money," I said.

He passed it on. "Hitomi," he stopped and cleared his throat. "You can be in charge of this."

I kept lifting rocks. "Here's another. Dried rations. Meat and homemade pemmican. It's not bad, and it's lightweight."

"We might need it." He sent it out.

"Now we're talking!" I lifted out a large, flat package. "Hitomi is good with a bow, isn't she?"

"She is—and she's right here!" she called.

"Then here you go!" I sent it out to her.

Another small packet. I unwrapped this one to find a couple of smaller blades, more eating/skinning knives than weapons, but we were beggars and wouldn't be choosey. "That's it, I think."

"No." Ken reached into the lined hollow and shifted a vertical rock. "There's something behind this one." He pulled out a smaller packet yet and crawled out with it. I followed, and by the time I was out and on my feet, he had it open. "Another *seihoukei*," he said with a grin. "We could use this. Glad your dad was prepared."

He tried to be. I knew that much. I bit my lip. I would never know how the wind demon had caught him.

Sho nudged Ken and he looked up. He must have seen the pain in my expression.

"Sorry! I'm so sorry, Mei." He looked stricken.

"No problem."

"No. That was insensitive. I should think before I blurt things out."

"It's fine. I'm fine." I looked to Hitomi, who was caressing the curve of the bow. "Can you string that thing pretty quickly?"

She shot me a look. "Of course."

"Then you could leave the strings in their waxed wrappings. They'll weather better."

We squirreled away our new goodies and set off, aiming to intersect the stream again. The going was easy. I watched Ken for a while, but he was acting . . . normal. So I tried to do the same—and tried to focus on where we were headed. "We're supposed to play the part of hikers on the Appalachian Trail," I said eventually.

"We'll never pass for thru-hikers," Hitomi said critically. "You know, the ones that hike the whole two thousand miles in a year. We're not dirty or hungry enough."

"What?" she asked when Sho raised his brows at her. "I did some research before I shut off my micro-tab. We'll have to be day-hikers."

"Doesn't matter, as long as we find the Twisted Oak Cabin. Effie Couts lives there and Boru said she is known on the AT for her healing lotions. It shouldn't look out of place if we ask for directions."

We discussed our finds and began to map out some fighting strategies, trying to come up with ideas to make use of each of our particular skill sets. The lively discussion made the time pass quickly. Just past noon we came upon a trail marked with orange slashes on the trees.

"Not the Appalachian Trail," Hitomi pronounced. "It's marked with white blazes. This must be a local trail."

"It's following the stream," Ken shrugged. "We might as well follow too."

We stopped for a quick lunch on a sandy beach set up in a sweeping curve of the creek. It was a relief to relax a little. We knew we had to be getting close to the town. After we finished, we kept to the trail. It led us over a collection of massive boulders. I stood on the biggest one and closed my eyes, listening.

"I wouldn't be surprised if we ran into some other hikers along here," Sho remarked.

His casual comment made me remember my eyes. The Girl With the Stars in Her Eyes, the ninja from Ryu called me. *Starburst*, my father had referred to it affectionately. But my mutation was regarded with suspicion and disgust by most people. I'd grown up keeping my gaze down and a hat always pulled low, hiding my affliction to avoid the scorn and abuse.

But now I wouldn't have to go to such lengths. When I first met him, Neil had told me of a spell that could disguise my eyes, make them appear normal. When I found out that I was a ninja, like the people of Ryu, one of the best side effects, I'd discovered, had been that I could do small, nature or chi based magic, like so many of them. Hitomi had taught me how to craft a mask that would disguise my unusual eyes. Granted, it was the only thing I could do so far, but to me, it was huge. I could walk, open and normal, in the everyday world. The thought started a shiver of excitement through me.

I was just getting ready to leap down from my perch when I felt . . . something. A vibration, right through the rock.

Up ahead, the trail left the boulders and led down into a rocky gorge. Ken was already halfway down. I saw him pause in the same instant that I did.

"You felt that?" I called.

"A rockfall, maybe?" he answered, looking around him. "It must have been big."

I looked with trepidation at the loosely strewn, rocky sides of the ravine. "Let's get through this quick."

He nodded and turned to move. I was stepping down when a second shuddering thud shook the boulder. Another quickly followed. We all exchanged alarmed glances.

Sho called out. "That's no rockslide."

Small rocks jumped in time with the steady, increasingly

fast paced sounds. They drew closer, sounded louder.

"Are those . . . footsteps?" Hitomi asked, her eyes round.

A swiftly moving hawk dive-bombed Ken, screaming a warning as it swept past his head.

"Run!" I ordered. "Get up and out of that gorge!"

I ran swiftly down the path, working to keep my balance at this speed. I'd just reached the bottom when I heard it. A roar. From right above me. Deep and long and animalistic, it sent a shiver of terror running up my spine—as I'm sure it was meant to do. I spun around and looked up.

On top of the biggest boulder, right where I'd just been standing, perched . . . a creature out of a nightmare. My jaw dropped.

It was massive. Taller than a man and huge through the chest and gut. Its face extended out, nearly into a snout. Tiny, glowing eyes glared down. Its large mouth showed full of teeth that curved and pointed in several directions. One long, graceful horn curved up from its brow, the other swept down and around pointing toward the long jaw line. Massive arms nearly reached its knees and its legs, braced on the boulder, looked as broad as tree trunks.

"Oni!" shouted Sho. "Get out of there, Mei!"

I had no idea what an Oni was—and had no desire to get up close and personal enough to find out. But I was nearest. It tucked the gigantic cudgel it held into a harness across its back, then glared down at me and smacked its gauntleted hands together.

It crouched and so did I. I wasn't stupid enough to head where that thing thought I would—and if there was one thing I could do, after all of my ninja training and parkour experience—it was climb. It leaped, and I, instead of running straight ahead through the gorge, jumped up and to the right of the path, finding purchase on the rocky wall and hanging on.

It couldn't shift in midair, but it did try to swipe at me. I nimbly moved further away. With its attention fixed on me, it landed right on the path—and bellowed anger and surprise when it was blasted off balance by a great rush of air. Ken stood on the lip of the ravine, hitting it with a hard gust of his air *minding* ability. The Oni stumbled, then fell back against the rocks.

I climbed quickly higher. The monster saw me escaping, but continuous blast of air held it flat against the gorge wall. Struggling, it fought to rise, but Ken was relentless. Searching, reaching with a free hand, it grinned suddenly, then lifted a rock bigger than my head and threw it at Ken.

Ken ducked and his punishing blast of air faltered. The Oni stood and leaped for me.

He almost got me. The entire wall shivered when the creature hit right beneath me. Rocks tumbled around my head. I tucked my head and body in while it snapped at me like a dog after a treat, and held on while it slid back down to the bottom.

It shook itself and reconsidered, then started climbing after me. I heard a twang and then another and looked down to see two arrows sprout from the creature's arm.

It didn't even pause, but turned to roar defiance at the far rim of the gorge and Hitomi, where she stood with her bow strung again. She let loose and the arrow lodged in the monster's open mouth.

"Eat that, ugly!" she shouted, triumphant.

That did slow it down a little. It slid down once more and clawed at the arrow in its throat. I wasted no time climbing to the top of the rocky wall, and grasping Sho's hand where he crouched waiting for me. We ran around the edge of the gorge, met up with the other two and we all took off at a run.

Ken darted off of the trail quickly though, ducking into a thick stand of birch trees. We followed and hunkered down, watching the spot where the trail climbed out of the ravine.

"We have to defeat it." Ken looked around at each one of us. "Here. Now."

"How are we supposed to do that?" Hitomi asked a little desperately.

"We have to find a way. It's an Oni—a mountain ogre specimen. It won't stop. Now that it has engaged us, it will keep coming. We can't lead it into that town."

"Will a *seihoukei* work on it?"

Ken grimaced at my question. "It should. But none of Inaba's creatures are behaving normally." He shrugged. "We'd stand a better chance if we weakened it somehow, first. That worked with the Tengu and the Snow Woman."

"Pass them out," I told Sho, but he was already rooting in the messenger bag slung over Ken's shoulder. I took one of the elegant little weapons, then scanned the terrain, looking for something we could use against the creature.

I made a sudden, curt motion. It was up. The Oni stood on the rim of the gorge, silent now, looking around and testing the wind. It held the cudgel in its hand. I shivered. Its quiet, hunting stance was as frightening as its aggressive roar.

"We have to use the gorge," Sho whispered. "Maybe a fall will weaken it enough for the *seihoukei* to be effective."

I'd already come to the same conclusion. "But will a fall be enough?" I whispered, sliding out of my pack and leaning it up against a tree.

Sho quietly pulled his sword from its scabbard. "I'll sharpen a thick spike, sneak back and brace it below. You guys get it to go over . . ." He stood and peered from behind a tree. "There. Where the wall curves in this direction, to the right of the path."

Ken sighed. "How will we push it over? It's solid as a mountain. I could barely hold it back against that wall."

"Look." Hitomi was looking back too. "There's a sturdy oak near that curve. And a good-sized rock at the top of the path. Give me that rope from your pack, Sho. I'll disguise myself and tie a line low from one to the other, right before the spot where the canyon curves in. You guys just drive it in that direction, it will trip over the line, Ken can give it a shove with his wind, and over it goes!"

Ken sat, silent, for a moment. "Okay. It's the best we can come up with, I think. Mei and I can distract it while you guys get ready."

Hitomi stood straight, ducking behind the tree, and pressed her fingers to the scar on her forearm. Fascinated, I watched her fade away as she shifted her skin and clothing to match the tree bark.

But my attention was diverted. The Oni had begun to move forward, creeping, bent over, like it was looking for trace of our passing. It abruptly stood straight, snorting. It waved the cudgel in front of its face and rubbed an eye with its other hand.

Suddenly I saw a small rock bounce off of the vertical horn. I narrowed my eyes and saw other rocks raining down upon the creature from all directions. I frowned and followed the line of a throw—and started up in surprise. "Look! Yamaworu!"

I could see at least a dozen of the little creatures in the trees, all pelting the massive monster with small rocks. The Oni tried to roar, but it didn't come out with the same ferocious volume. That arrow must have hurt.

The creature swung its cudgel at several of the little *yokai*, but they were all tucked high in branches far above. It resorted to banging the tree trunks instead, trying to shake them out.

"Go, now, while it's distracted," Ken ordered Hitomi and Sho.

The two of them took off in different directions. "Be careful!" I hissed after them.

Beside me, Ken drew in a deep breath. Looking over at me, he tried to grin. It came out more as a grimace, but I appreciated the effort. "We can do this," he said.

I nodded as I slid my makeshift bo staff free of my pack. "There's no one else I'd rather face this with," I told him.

He flushed and we exchanged a long look, then we crept forward, to the edge of the line of trees. "Let's try to keep it there in the right area, near the edge where we want it to go down."

"Yes, but we have to give Hitomi room to work." Ken crouched down and I followed suit. "Do you see her?" he asked.

"There." She'd made it around the creature and was at the rocks close to the trail that led out of the ravine. Her *minding* talent hid her well. I could see the rope moving seemingly on it's own around the base, and . . . "Her hair!" I groaned.

"Blast," Ken cursed low. "She has trouble with her hair— especially when she's stressed."

Her disembodied hair, upswept and curled in her signature pin up girl fashion, floated near the rocks—that's what it looked like with the rest of her camouflaged so well. The Oni hadn't spotted her yet, though.

"We have to distract it." I started to rise. "Before it sees her."

Ken grabbed my arm. "Let's use the little guys' technique first." He nodded toward the rain of small missiles still bombarding the creature. He looked around. "Gather up a few of those pinecones. They ought to sting."

I quickly fetched an armful.

"Now, toss them all up," Ken instructed.

Catching on, I did. He held out a hand and caught the lot of the pointy-edged cones in a current of air. "I'll try to draw his attention away from her position."

The pinecones traveled in a fast, graceful curve, picking up speed as they went. Circling around, they approached the Oni from behind. Ken clutched his fingers into a fist and out there the spiked cones leapt the last few feet, hitting the monster in a barrage spread over his head, neck and shoulders.

It grunted and turned, away from Hitomi, as Ken had planned. Not really much more than a nuisance, but it had done the job.

Except now Hitomi had finished anchoring the rope at the rocks. I could see her, bits of her flickering in and out as she moved slowly across the open space towards the tree she'd targeted for the other end. Her disguise adjusted as she went, but it wasn't quite seamless.

The Yamaworu must have spotted her, too. They started to chatter in excitement.

The Oni stopped dead. It cast its gaze around, inhaling deeply. It started to turn in Hitomi's direction—and I squeezed Ken's arm and erupted out of the trees.

It snapped around. An evil grin grew over its face when it saw me. Without warning, it rushed me.

Shards. How did something so big move so fast?

I dodged—and the breeze kicked up by the rushing cudgel ruffled my hair, even as the *boom* of it hitting the ground right behind me jump-started my heart.

I didn't give fear a chance to latch on to me. Turning on my toes like a ballerina, I spun around and leapt atop the fat end of the cudgel. I raced up the narrowing length of it, sprung off of the creature's massive fist and landed on its shoulder. Quick as a wink, I straddled the broad neck, slid my staff under its chin and pulled.

The Oni gagged and reared back. Dropping the cudgel, it grasped the staff with one hand and me with the other. I held on and pulled with all of my strength. "Hurry it up, Hitomi!"

"Almost ready!"

Still growling and gagging, the Oni let go of the staff and grabbed me with both hands. With a mighty heave it ripped me loose and sent me sailing over its head.

But, beyond climbing, the other thing I learned doing so much parkour was how to fall. I let go of the staff, kept my orientation even as I tumbled through the air and managed to position myself so that I rolled out of the fall.

The creature recovered quicker than I did.

"Got it!"

Hitomi's satisfied shout rang out just as I was swept up in the Oni's meaty fist.

Oomph! The breath whooshed out of me as it gripped me tightly. I couldn't even scream. I flailed, my arms pressed to my sides with only my hands protruding and wiggling uselessly down by my hips.

"Mei!" Ken burst out of cover, heading toward us.

At the same time, Sho rushed up the trail and over the rim of the gorge. He wasn't alone. A handful of Yamawaro came with him. They stopped when they spotted the Oni and began to chatter and hiss.

"Let's go!" Sho shouted.

The Oni's head swung between him and Ken as it backed away. It was almost to the rope, nearly to the perfect spot for Ken to help knock it over the edge—if only I wasn't going to go down with it.

I struggled, wriggling madly. Right now I was really missing that *katana* my father had forged. It would have sliced through this monster's thick fingers like butter. Trapped, helpless and hating it, I resorted to bending over and biting the giant, greenish-tinged finger closest to me.

I succeeded only in getting a mouthful of dirt, grit and the disgusting taste of mold. I didn't come close to breaking the skin.

Suddenly, the monster stiffened. Its grip tightened further and I fought just to get enough oxygen to keep from passing

out. The creature's glowing eyes had gone flat black.
Something had changed. A scent of incense washed over me,
tangy and strong. The creature raised me higher, looked me
over. I shivered. Something else was in there, looking at me
from the Oni's eyes. Something dark and old and steeped in
magic. It glanced around, looked all about, as if taking in the
scene.

"There you are." It was staring at me again. The Oni's roar
was gone. This voice was smooth and slick, like oil over water.
"Stop this resistance. You cannot win. Your dragon friend
could not defeat me—what chance to you think you have?" The
creature stretched, rolling its neck, then glared at me once more.
"Bring her, quickly. Kill the rest, if you must."

And then it left. Just like that. The glowing eyes flashed
bright again and the Oni was back. Its grip loosened enough for
me to suck in a great breath. It shook its head and turned
toward the west, its head lifting high.

Sho rushed in, sword drawn. The creature blocked it with
the gauntlet on its other hand and took a step. Sho struck again.
Another parry with the wide gauntlet and then the Oni slid its
hand back, grasped Sho's blade and tore it from his grip,
sending it spinning. It was left facing the gorge and I was afraid
it would catch sight of the rope. I struggled again and at the
same time, Ken's shout rang behind us.

The monster turned. Sunlight flashed off of the short blade
that Ken held aloft. The short sword my father had made him.

As I watched, he released it. It hung, spinning, suspended
in midair—and then abruptly it moved, racing toward me
almost faster than my brain could react.

But my body knew. My hand opened and the handle
thunked home. I clutched it . . . and waited.

Nothing. No surge of power or . . . anything. Desperate, I
jabbed upward anyway, intending to sink the knife into the hand
that clutched me. But I felt the blade turn aside, deflected by
the creature's tough skin.

My gaze flew to meet Ken's—and we were of one mind.
We couldn't defeat it. It had to go over into the gorge. Ken
was already shaking his head in denial even as I frowned and
silently urged him to do what needed done.

Suddenly one of the Yamawaro stepped closer. It opened its mouth and let loose that ringing tone—the one that had echoed in my head the last time I held this knife.

It reminded me of how I'd felt then—how I'd felt linked to Ken and to my father and how even the forest had hung suspended around us, waiting with anticipation.

I stared into his frowning face, then closed my eyes and concentrated, focused on *listening*.

And I heard it. Felt it. We weren't alone on this trail with the Oni and the Yamawaro. I felt the intense interest of the trees, the scrubby shrubs, the squirrels hiding in a blasted out pine, the weeds straggling along the trail's edge. Even the rocks in the gorge emanated a slow, drowsy sort of attention in the battle we waged.

I gasped and my eyes flew open as something—power? light?—zinged through my limbs.

Strength, power, will—the essence of *me*—swirled in my chest, welled up and flowed out into the blade. I couldn't see it, but I knew it glowed. I felt its readiness and I stabbed upward again, and this time felt the blade sink into the meaty edge of the Oni's hand.

Energy poured from me, focused by the blade. With a crash like thunder in my head, it clashed with something large and dark and horrible—the twisted hunger that lay at the core of the mountain ogre. For a moment our forces mingled and fought, two swirling systems like cloudbanks.

Then the monster bellowed in surprise and in what must have been an involuntary reflex, opened its hand. I fell down, pulling the blade with me as I went.

Ken was ready. He blasted the creature with a ferocious punch of air. It stepped back, away from the onslaught—and hit the stretched rope and stumbled. Another push of air and it went over, falling backward into the gorge.

Sho and Hitomi ran past me to the edge, several Yamawaro following. I sucked in deep breaths, gazing up from beneath the curtain of my hair, watching their faces, listening to the roars coming from below and trying to ready myself in case it hadn't worked and the monster came bounding up again.

But Sho was pulling a *seihoukei* from his jacket. He spoke

the words in Japanese and sent the weapon speeding downward.

Ken's arm wrapped around me, helping me up. I crept at his side, limbs heavy, chest aching, and we made it to the edge just in time to see the Oni, one shoulder impaled through with Sho's sharpened stake, struggling furiously even as it dissolved from the feet up. When it had all diffused into a glittering mass of black dust, the lot of it suddenly shot skyward at an angle, as if a giant vacuum had been turned on it.

Beside me, a Yamawaro sneered after it.

"Eat that, ugly!" it said, in Hitomi's voice.

I looked up and saw her shocked expression. We all stared at each other, tired and grimy.

Then Sho's mouth twitched. Ken choked—and that was it. We all collapsed, groaning and chortling like mad while the Yamawaro looked on.

8

Akemi

The next time Akemi woke, the lights had been dimmed. Something had awakened her.

Was someone burning incense? The scent hung in the air. Voices echoed. Shouting. Not her own. Her mouth was dry, her tongue thick.

Far off, the shouts sounded again.

She considered sitting up, going to the door to investigate. But it would take so much energy. Annoyance bit deep, resentment that she'd been left alone so long. She let her head fall to the side—and saw that the IV was still attached to her arm. Raising her eyes, she looked to the mirror—

And saw the figure in it.

He watched her. A grown man, in his thirties perhaps. He had a square face and a broad jaw with a cleft in his chin. He wore a samurai's topknot and a thoughtful expression on his face.

Akemi stared. Neither moved.

And then his edges blurred. His limbs and the locks of his dark hair lengthened, swirled and he dissolved into a wisp of mist that flitted across the mirror and disappeared.

She breathed heavily, panic lending her strength. With great effort she sat up and swung her legs over the edge of the bed. The door was a mere step away, but she had to hang onto the furniture and the IV pole to reach it.

Locked.

Fighting back sobs, she crept back to the bed. Laying there, chest heaving, mind churning, the tears came. Until she calmed at last and exhaustion dragged her under once more.

9

Mei

The trail had dumped us out onto a gravel path. Our footsteps crunched as we headed west. A real roadway lay somewhere ahead—the rumble of an occasional car sounded nearer with each passing.

I moved through a fog of exhaustion. Was this what Ken felt, what all the ninja of Ryu did, when they spent all of their energy in their *minding*? I wasn't a fan.

My brain ignored the aching protest of my muscles, though. It was busily reviewing the last moments of that Oni. "There was nothing left behind," I said, addressing the group at large. "Not even a token." I gestured over my shoulder, toward the pocket in my pack that held the marked plastic square we'd picked up at the site of the battle in Ryu.

"That's the way the *seihoukei* usually works," Ken told me. He was still on high alert, watching, listening, as we moved toward town. "That's how *yokai* are usually propelled back to the spirit world, in the normal course of things. That black edge that devours them from the outside in? Like what happened to the Tengu and the Wind Demon? That's new, as I told you."

"But what's the difference between them?" I fretted.

"Intelligence?" Sho conjectured. "That Oni seemed simple enough. Tough, but single-minded."

"Rank?" ventured Hitomi.

"Hierarchy," Ken guessed quietly. "Tengu spoke of his masters. I'll bet it has to do with how close they are to Inaba."

"We have to find out the truth." I felt unaccountably impatient. "Boru thinks the answer will be key."

"I just hope that Oni doesn't rally and cross back over here anytime soon."

I shuddered. "Does it happen often?"

"If they are old and powerful enough, it can."

"I hope Boru's friend has some answers," Hitomi, trudging

alongside of me, said on a sigh.

Sho looked over his shoulder at us. "I hope she has some dinner."

My stomach growled in sympathy. My head had already begun to follow another tangent. "Did you hear what that Oni said about the dragon? That my dragon friend hadn't been able to defeat him?" Worry made me feel crankier than ever. "We should call Ryu, find out if Neil is okay."

"And if anyone has heard anything about Akemi," Hitomi added.

A surge of annoyance flared high. Would Akemi be sparing us the same kind of concern? Maybe Neil had been right. She hadn't been that good of a friend.

I shook my head. I was just tired.

"There it is," Ken said.

The gravel road had intersected a two-lane road right at the edge of the little town. We followed it across a bridge and onto a single main street.

"Smell that?" Sho breathed deeply. "Bacon!" He stopped in front of an old-fashioned Mom-and-Pop type diner.

My stomach growled again. Suddenly all I wanted was a slab of meat.

"We can't stop," Ken warned. "We need to find that witch before something else finds us." He glanced toward me. "Surely she'll have some sort of protections in place?"

"I hope so." Hitomi looked my way too. "What is it we are looking for, again?"

"We're supposed to ask for the Twisted Oak Cabin."

"Looks like the locals eat here." Sho was already heading for the door. "Let's ask."

We shuffled in. The place was brightly colored and reeked of fried food. I swallowed against the thought of a platter of bacon cheese fries. An L-shaped counter stretched across the first part of the room, with a small seating area opening up past the edge.

All conversation stopped and all eyes locked on our group.

"Just off the trail?" A woman spoke from behind the counter. She summoned a smile and gestured with the pot of coffee in her hand. "Just pick a seat and we'll get you filled up."

Sho stepped forward, inhaling, with a friendly grin. "As good as it smells in here, we have to find the Twisted Oak Cabin first thing." He raised his eyebrows at the case of donuts before him. "But I'd love to come back for breakfast."

The waitress's welcoming manner faded a bit. "Folks that head out for the Twisted Oak don't often come back into town."

There were several men sitting at the counter. The biggest one glowered at us. I watched him, wondering how he could wear flannel on such a warm day.

"My nose will lead me right back here." Sho laughed. "But would you mind giving us directions?"

"This is Effie's busy season," the waitress began. "We don't see much of—"

The frowning guy stood. "What do you kids want with that Granny Witch, anyway?"

It didn't sound like a casual question. He stared at me, his temper simmering higher. "And what is that old woman up to?" he asked the waitress. "Bringing *this* kind to town?"

This kind? Suddenly the metaphorical light bulb went on over my head. I'd become so used to being accepted among the people of Ryu—I'd forgotten to hide my eyes in public. I'd been so worn out after that fight with the Oni, I'd forgotten to use the masking spell that Hitomi had taught me.

I turned away toward the window and reached for calm. It wasn't easy. I felt tired and unaccountably cranky, but I closed my eyes, trying to visualize my chi energy the way that Hitomi had coached me.

Sho looked Flannel Dude over. Because of his *minding*, he was known for being able to size up a person, assess their character. Apparently this time he decided discretion was the better part of valor. "That's okay," he said. "We'll go."

Too late. The bumpkin pushed past him. I saw him coming in the reflection in the window. Grabbing my arm, he spun me around—and stared in confusion at the normal, but pretty, pair of eyes I'd conjured over my own marked ones. "What is this?" he demanded.

Ken stepped up. He was a couple of inches shorter than the local, but he radiated an air of purposeful menace. "Take your hands off of her."

Flannel Dude let go of me, but bristled at Ken, all thrusting chest and tobacco-stained sneer. "I saw what I saw. She's a damned *kawad*."

The sting of the nickname had not lessened for not having heard it for a few weeks. The name was slang—he was calling me a *freak* or a *mutant*. There were more than a few of us running around, those affected by the poison all of those disasters leaked into the atmosphere before the clean up could begin in earnest.

Young people, mostly. Most of us were born soon after the Rift in Japan and all of the other accompanying catastrophes. Our variations were many—oddly colored skin, forked tongues, deformed limbs, and strange eyes, like mine. Just to name a few. Our afflictions varied, but the hatred that most of the world had for us remained constant.

"Clearly she's not," Ken answered, low. He pushed between me and Flannel Dude. "But even if she was—you wouldn't be permitted to touch her."

"Permitted?" The lout laughed. "What it is to you, anyway, Long Hair?"

"Hush, Ted," the waitress scolded.

"No, Peg. You know what the freaks did to my sister—"

"We just got into town—" Ken began.

But Flannel Dude didn't want to hear it. Lunging abruptly, he pushed Ken out of the way and reached for me again, gripping my wrist tightly.

But the low buzz of irritation that had been lying under my skin since the Oni attacked flared high. I dropped low, breaking his hold. And suddenly the short sword that I still hadn't returned to Ken was in my hand. I slipped between the bully's legs, came up behind him and returned the favor—grabbing his arm and twisting it high behind him. He froze as I tightened my hold and with my other hand, brought the blade up under his chin.

He was breathing heavily, but I had barely raised my heart rate. Leaning in close to his cheek from behind, I could feel the hatred pouring off of him, and in that moment, I could almost return it.

Abruptly, I let his arm go and slid around to face him, the blade still poised at his throat. I didn't touch him, but I met his angry gaze with a fierce one of my own. As he glared down at me, I deliberately let the mask spell fall away.

He made a growling sound as my true eyes reappeared. It only inflamed the fury I was fighting to hold back.

"I don't know your sister," I hissed. "I don't know what happened to her, or who did it. I'm sorry it was something bad enough to fill you with hate and bigotry—but I'm not sorry enough to take the blame for it."

"Sorry?" he spat. "Your kind don't—"

"Stop there. That's the kind of talk that's going to cause trouble." I pointed to the older black man he'd been sitting next to at the counter. "Your *kind* kidnapped his. Killed thousands bringing them here, near starved the rest on those terrible journeys. Your *kind* beat them, worked them, enslaved them and their children—and I don't see him blaming you for it."

"Mei," Ken started.

"No!" I pointed to a couple sitting in a nearby booth, both of whom were of obvious Native American ancestry. "Your *kind* stole the Cherokee people's land near here, and killed thousands marching them over the Trail of Tears. Do you want to shoulder the blame for that?"

Flannel Dude just glared at me.

"Do you?" I shouted.

With the sword still a threat, he slowly shook his head.

"No? Of course you don't. And you know what? I would appreciate the same consideration."

I glared at all of them, at each and every person in that diner. I let them see my freakish eyes, with the large blue irises and the silver starburst pupils. "My *kind* is humankind. Just like yours."

"Twisted Oak is not far," the waitress said into the resulting silence. "Take the left at the end of this block, follow the road about a mile, then you'll see the tree. There's a track angling up the mountain just past it. Follow that and you can't miss the cabin."

"Thank you," I told her.

"Just go," she sighed.

I thrust the blade into Ken's hand, pushed past him, and went.

* * *

Maybe there was something in the air around here. I stopped a few buildings away and leaned over, putting my hands on my knees and breathing deep, reaching for calm. But Ken moved past without saying a word. I looked up to find him stalking away, his broad shoulders set and tense.

Suddenly, after all of my glib arguments, I couldn't think of anything to say.

"Don't be mad at Mei," Hitomi called. "None of us reminded her to put on her mask, either."

Ken drew up for a second and shot a look of disbelief over his shoulder. Then he stalked on again.

I admit, I didn't know how to feel about it. Ken had been unwavering in his patience and cheerful support since the moment we'd met in my old parkour group. I didn't know how to react to a Ken who was angry with or disappointed in me.

"Well, we'll all remember next time, won't we?" Sho sounded distracted. He'd stopped at the first cross street, staring at the Biwa Studios sign and the advertising posters surrounding it.

Hitomi paused beside him. "Ooh, the studios must all be in that direction—and the vid stars!"

"Uh, huh." Sho was frowning now. "These look like the films they are planning on shooting next—the ones that will be filming around here. Look at this one—The Young Samurai—"

"Enough about the vids!" Ken had stopped and turned around. Every tight line broadcast his exasperation.

"What is it with you?" I asked.

His jaw dropped. "With *me*?"

"Wait." I glared back at him. "Clearly you are mad. I just can't tell if it is because I did wear the mask, or because I didn't."

He frowned. "You know how I feel about the mask. Your eyes are a badge of honor."

"To *you*."

"I'm angry that you have to wear it at all."

My brows shot skyward. "I won't argue with that!"

His shoulders slumped. "I don't know. I just wish we'd handled that differently."

I stiffened.

He spoke very gently. "We are all different too, Mei."

Indignation blazed. "Yes, but your differences don't *show*, do they?"

"No. But I've seen how many of the *kawad* have been treated. And I know some of them have retaliated. They've banded together in gangs. I know some have been hurt so badly or grown so angry that they don't care who they hurt in return. But someone has to care. Someone has to show the haters that not every *kawad* is violent and distrustful."

Anger churned like fire in my gut. "You've seen how they've been treated, have you? Well, so have I. I've been refused service, chased out of stores. I've been yelled at, spit on. Some lunatic once tried to abduct me—because who would miss a stupid little *kawad* girl, after all?"

Hitomi's mouth had dropped open. Now her eyes started to fill with tears. But I wasn't done. I was hurt and wildly furious at the disappointment in Ken's tone.

"So you'll have to forgive me, but I'm not the person who is going to fight that fight. I *am* violent and distrustful. In fact, I thought that was what many of the ninja in Ryu liked about me. It certainly helps in *your* war—the one that *you* brought me into."

No one said a word. I didn't wait for them to gather themselves, either. I just hefted my pack and stomped past Ken.

Not until I reached the turn we were to take did I look back. Neither Ken or Hitomi had moved. Sho stared at the posters, again, a frown on his face.

Snorting, I walked on.

<u>10</u>

Ken

The locals were right. There was no missing the Twisted Oak. It stood like a sentry at the edge of a pathway leading deeper into the forest. Its trunk had been twisted by wind and weather but its straggling, wide-reaching branches were bright with new leaves.

Ken hung back, watching Mei touch the tree with reverence, struggling with his own frustration and disappointment.

Gods and Ancestors, but he was an idiot. His mother had warned him, back in Ryu, when he'd gone on a little too long and a little too glowingly about Mei Barrett one too many times.

"Remember that she is a girl," his mother had warned him. "A real girl. She has many skills, it is true, but also all the faults and foibles that we all possess—and more burdens than most."

Ken knew his mother was right—and that he'd been wrong to criticize Mei today. It was just . . . he'd searched for her for so long and the reality of her was so much more than even his foolish adolescent dreams. She amazed him on such a regular basis, she made it easy for him to put her on a high pedestal.

He told himself to stop. It wasn't a fair or comfortable position for anyone to be in. And Mei had been right on all counts—he didn't know all that she had endured in her four years surviving alone and on the run. And they should be concentrating on finding ways to defeat Inaba.

But right now all he could concentrate on was the graceful picture she made, circling the tree. The angle she stood at showed off her profile and almost made it look like the tree was talking to her.

Again, he wanted to kick himself. She was . . . incredible. Pretty on the outside and beautifully complicated on the inside. She was a puzzle that he could not resist.

Suddenly she turned away, as if she'd heard something. He

was too far away, but he looked to Hitomi, right next to her, and she didn't react. Mei started off along the path into the woods and one by one, they all followed. Ken brought up the rear.

He caught up after half a mile, when the wooded path opened into a meadow. Everyone had stopped to take in the charming scene.

The clearing was slightly sloped. A cedar-planked cabin sat back, near the far side of the open space. Its foundation was fieldstone that might have been gathered right from this meadow. It boasted a wide porch that looked to be set with comfortable furniture. A small, barn-like outbuilding stood off to the right. A cackling stream ran out of the far line of trees, passed through the meadow and continued on into the forest not far from where they stood.

"Oooohhh," Hitomi sighed. They all followed as she stepped out onto the carpet of green stretching toward the house—and they all drew up together when they caught sight of a figure by the stream's edge. She looked to be kneeling in front of a bank of bee balm.

She was only about fifteen feet away, but looking her over, he wasn't surprised they'd missed her until they drew closer. Her hair was brown, short and slightly snarled. She wore a layered mix of earthen tones that let her blend right in with the surroundings.

And she was aware of them. Raising a palm in our direction, she said in a low voice, "I'll be right with you all. As soon as I finish."

She knelt closer to the violet blooms rioting before her. Ken could see her lips moving, but she spoke quietly now, so low that he thought that only the flowers could hear her.

Or not. Suddenly a couple of bees rose up out of the blossoms. She sat back and they hovered there, mere inches from her face.

"Hello, my friends." She spoke in a more normal tone now. "I know these are lovely, but my supply of pollen is woefully low."

Sho nudged him. "Is she talking to the *bees*?"

Ken shrugged.

"How about an exchange?" She waved a hand toward the

house. "I have some pretty verbena flowering just today, up beside the deck. Interested?"

The two insects hung there. Suddenly she laughed.

He exchanged a glance with his friend. "I think the bees are talking to *her*."

The honeybees abruptly buzzed off—in the direction of the house, he noted. And the woman leaned down again. More whispers. Was she singing? She reached for a jar resting beside her and he stared, narrowing his eyes as a cloud of yellowish dust rose from the swath of flowers and hung there in the air.

The woman began to swoop the jar through, collecting the pollen that she'd obviously just bewitched from the plants.

"She's like a bee herself," Sho whispered.

"I'll take that as a compliment, young man!" The woman kept working, but her tone sounded friendly.

Stifling a grin, Ken made a motion with his fingers and a little whirlwind formed, gathered the fine pollen up and siphoned it into her jar.

"Well!" Grinning widely, she looked around at them. "That does come in handy." Twisting the lid on the jar, she climbed to her feet. "Welcome," she called. "I was beginning to worry."

Sunlight glinted off of her short bob of reddish curls, shot through with silver. A sturdy woman, past midlife, Ken would guess, but by no means old. She moved nimbly enough as she came to stand before them. "I heard that you'd run into something ugly—but was relieved to hear that you came out on top. I figured you'd be straggling in soon."

Mei stepped forward. "Effie Couts?"

The other woman nodded. "And I can see for myself who you are, Girl With the Stars in Her Eyes. You are welcome here, Mei, as are your friends." Her look softened. "I knew your father. He was a strong and lovely man."

Mei gave a nod of thanks. She looked away for a moment, then straightened. "Boru of Ryu sent us. We wish to ask for your help—"

"Yes, yes." Effie waved a hand. "I spoke with Boru several days ago, though she wasn't strong enough to scry for long—

not nearly long enough to answer all of my questions."

"Wait." Hitomi frowned. "You said you heard—how did you know what happened to us today?"

Effie grinned and gestured for them to follow her. "Oh, you'd be surprised how fast word gets through a forest—if you know how to listen."

Ken and Sho exchanged glances at that.

"Come on in," the witch continued. I don't know the specifics, but I figured you would all be hungry and tired. I have a big pot of chili simmering on the stove and cornbread warming in the oven."

Mei's stomach growled audibly.

Effie laughed. And just like that, Ken relaxed. He didn't have Sho's ability to look into someone's heart, but suddenly he knew that Effie Couts was safe.

"We'll get you all fed, then you can enjoy the Hot Springs," she said, stepping onto the rough paved walkway that led to the house.

"Like a hot tub?" Hitomi asked, following after her.

"Better. Mineral hot springs. They are what this area is known for, named for. You can ease your muscles while you wash away any *yokai* stink."

"Excuse me." Ken stepped closer. "Apologies if this is impolite, but I was wondering . . . Are there wards, protections . . ." He glanced around.

"Oh, yes, we're safe enough." She glanced at Mei. "At least from any of Inaba's creatures."

With a sigh, Ken let a few of his worries drop away. "Good. Thank you."

Effie smiled warmly at all of them. "Come on, then. Let's eat."

11
***

Mei

We washed up at a pump in the yard and I paused as Effie led us onto her pretty, wide porch. Closing my eyes for a moment, I fought back the surge of anger and irritation that had dogged my every step this afternoon. As it faded, I could feel hunger rising in its place. I felt empty and miserable. Then the warm, comforting smell of hot food drifted from the open door and I moved again, leaning my staff against the doorway and following the call of my stomach.

I shucked off my pack just inside the door. The cottage was small, but charming. Welcoming. Earth colors abounded, with green plants and the occasional bright blossom popping across all of the rooms. I stepped further in, following my friends as they moved toward the kitchen, but then saw Hitomi's eye moving around the place. I looked—and noticed the unusual number of representations of Celtic knots. From simple trinity loops to gorgeous, complicated patterns, done in paint, clay, wax and fiber—they were everywhere. I picked out a few other symbols—spiral, circle, even a couple of ying/yang icons—but they could not match the sheer volume of knots.

Sho's figure traced a rough pottery piece. "A man in town called you a Granny Witch. What does that mean?"

Effie's mouth twitched. "It's a local term—one that the mountain folk started many years ago. Usually it just means an older woman skilled in mid-wifery or water dousing.

"Which are you?" Hitomi asked.

"Neither, really. Although I can and do douse for water, my specialty is broader. I deal in connections."

"Connections between what?" I asked.

"Between people, places, bodies of water, energy . . . time. Many things." She shrugged and moved toward the kitchen, which boasted a wooden table with room enough for all of us. Handing Hitomi a stack of bowls, she turned to pull a pan of corn bread from the oven. "Come and eat while we talk. Clearly you have questions and I've got about a thousand of my own."

I sat, irresistibly drawn by the rich smell of the food. The chili was meaty, with just the right amount of spice. The cornbread was warm and crumbly. Truthfully, though, I barely took the time to taste it all. While the others talked, starting at the attack on Ryu and bringing Effie up to date on all that we knew, I merely sat, methodically shoveling food in. I couldn't get that flat, alien gaze out of my head. And there was a massive, aching hole in my gut—and I wasn't sure if the entire bubbling pot of chili could fill it.

I was on my second bowl and reaching for my third piece of bread when I realized that the conversation had stopped and everyone was staring at me.

"Mei," Effie said carefully. "What creature did you lot battle today?"

"Oni," I mumbled, my mouth full.

"Ah. I see." She turned to the others. "Tell me exactly how the fight went, please."

I let them tell the tale while I reapplied myself to the food. Effie listened carefully, then sat back, watching me. "You know, abilities related to chi energy are actually pretty rare." She glanced at Sho. "Boru mentioned something about your talent?"

He explained his gift—the ability to 'see' another person's energy and read their character.

Effie raised her brows, impressed. "That could be very useful, indeed. It could also make you a very wise man one day, if you use it in the right fashion."

Sho shrugged.

Effie sat back. "Historically, there have been a few *yokai* who possess the ability to drain a person of his life force."

"We've had run-ins with at least two of them," Ken said. "The Kappa had a—"

"Don't forget the Snow Woman," I barked.

"Two of them already? I'd call that bad luck—if I thought there was anything like chance involved," Effie snorted. "Mei—I believe that something similar is happening with you and the shining blade. You transferred your chi energy into it. Or perhaps through it."

I stopped chewing long enough to think about it. "Yes. That's what it feels like." A sudden thought struck me. "Is that my *minding* ability, do you think?"

"Perhaps. In truth, I've never heard of anyone using spiritual energy as any sort of weapon. Even just a passive transfer usually requires a talisman of great power."

"Like the Kappa's ring," said Ken.

"Or like this." I pulled the moonstone from beneath my jacket.

Effie's face softened. "Yes, I thought I felt—" Her gaze remained focused on the amulet. "That particular one took an incredibly long time to craft. It took a lot out of me, too."

Instant denial flared in my gut, making me grasp the stone. I frowned and shushed the jealous reaction. "You made it?" I forced myself to pull it off to return it. "It's beautiful. And I put it to good use, I hope, helping Boru."

"No." She stopped me from removing it. "Thank you, but it's too late for that. I'm sure you did use it wisely—and now you must continue to wear it."

I felt a gust of relief . . . but then my brain engaged. "Do you think it was the moonstone? Was that the reason I was able to do that, with the blade?" Part of me hoped not. I'd wanted to find that I did possess a *minding* skill. But another, quieter part of me—the part that didn't understand what had happened with that shining blade and didn't know what it would mean going from here—perked up, wanting it to be the stone's doing.

"No. I don't think so. That's not what it was crafted for. I spelled it specifically for a personal connection—and a personal transfer of energy. From one individual to another." She paused. "There are other charms attached to it . . . but none that could have made your trick possible."

"Maybe I should test it, you know, without the stone?"

"No. You wore it here, into the protection of my wards." She met my gaze intently. "Now you must keep it on, at all times. Do you understand?"

I stared. "No." But that jealous, greedy voice inside of me rejoiced. What was wrong with me?

She sighed. "Perhaps I am worrying unnecessarily, but you will wear it in any case, won't you? Promise?"

"Sure." I reached for my spoon again.

Gently she laid her hand over mine. "You seem unusually hungry."

"I am!" Brushing aside a surge of annoyance at her gesture, I looked to the others. "Does this happen to you every time you use your *minding* and tire yourself out?"

Ken, Sho and Hitomi all looked at each other.

"Not like this, dear," Effie said. "Have you been . . . cranky? Since the fight?"

I forced myself not to glance at Ken. "You could say so."

"Hangry!" Sho burst out. "I couldn't remember the word—but it's what you are acting like, Mei. Hungry and angry together."

I looked at Ken. "Yeah. Hangry." My voice had deepened and I could feel my face working itself into a totally unfamiliar leer.

Color rose in Ken's face and I was suddenly fiercely glad.

Effie cleared her throat. "Mei, I think that you poured your chi into that blade—and into that Oni. And I think that you brought a bit of his energy back with you."

"What?" I dropped the spoon, revolted at the thought.

"Those mountain ogres are basically just a walking appetite. They suffer a never-ending hunger."

"That sounds about right," I admitted.

"Nothing can appease them. Not food, drink, nor adventure. Strong emotion comes closest, but even that is not enough. It's a miserable existence—and it's what makes them so dangerous."

"How do I get it *out*?" I asked, my voice rising.

"We need to act quickly. Sho, I think you can help. Will you?"

He sat straight. "Yeah. Of course."

Effie stood. "Ken, Hitomi, I'll leave you to clean up. Poor hostessing, I know, but I don't want to delay." She began to move around the kitchen, taking down a jar or two, then picking up scissors and moving about the house to snip fresh sprigs of herbs.

"What can we do?" Ken was on his feet.

"Keep watch out here." Effie gestured to me. "I'm going to take these two into my stillroom."

It was a long room, pretty and organized, and filled with light from many windows. Another, longer wooden table ran down the middle and one end of the room featured a woodstove atop a brick dais. The fire was going and a kettle sat upon it, quietly steaming.

Effie sat me at the end of the table. I could feel the heat of the stove, warm on my back. Sho sat to one side while the witch set her supplies out on the table.

"I'm assuming that you've taken a peek at Mei's energy before this?" she asked him.

"Yes." He smiled at me. "I told her that she is green—every gorgeous shade of it, entwined."

I remembered. "Hitomi is pink," I told Effie, nervous.

Her mouth twitched. "Can you look again, Sho? Search for differences?"

"Yes," he answered. "But I'll need a quiet moment to prepare."

"As will I." Effie looked at me. "Can *you* wait quietly for a few moments?"

I nodded.

Sho retreated to a far corner where a stuffed chair sat on a braided rug. He settled on floor before the chair and closed his eyes. I recognized the kuji-in sign he made with his fingers—the Jin symbol that helped him focus his power.

Effie, ignoring him, went to a shelf and picked up a large bowl. Reverently, she placed it in front of me.

It was beautiful. White glass, swirled with every dazzling color of blue. Intricately carved shapes circled the outside—more Celtic knots—but the interior was smooth and somehow . . . waiting.

"This is very special," she murmured. "Crafted with the cleanest desert sand, fine volcanic ash and tempered in the purest glacial water."

I watched her work, pouring ingredients in. Sea salt. Rosemary and thyme she crushed in a mortar. Fresh ginger she ground right into the mixture.

My stomach growled. "It smells wonderful."

"It's for cleansing, not for eating," she answered, abstracted. "Sho, are you ready?"

"Yes." His tone sounded distant. "I'm looking. There's something . . ." He frowned. "Mei, can you stand up?"

Nerves growing, I stood and faced him. His eyes were closed, but I knew that didn't mean he wasn't looking.

Abruptly, his eyes opened. He climbed to his feet and moved toward me, focusing on my middle. "Mei . . ." He took my hand and his eyes drifted shut again. "She's right. There's something . . . else, there. Three of them, I think. Little, wiggly black spots. I can feel how hungry they are . . ."

"How small?" Effie demanded.

"Small," he answered vaguely. "Like little hungry worms . . . and what they want more of is . . . you, Mei."

"Well, they won't have you," the witch declared.

"Get them out!" Tears started and I let them flow.

She pushed me into my seat again and draped a filmy fabric over my shoulders. Fetching the kettle, she held it aloft above the bowl. "Make a tent over your head to catch the steam when it rises. Breathe it in, as deeply as you can."

She poured the hot water into the bowl and fragrant wisps rose. My stomach growled again and Effie snapped her fingers. "Quick, cover your head, grip the bowl, lean in and breathe."

I did as she said, but drew back in surprise when my hands circled the bowl. "It's cold! How can it be cold?"

Effie made a grim face at me. "Trade secret. Now, breathe!"

I obeyed, making the tent and sucking in the moist, good-smelling steam. One deep breath, and another, and another.

"Now, rise up a moment." Effie held a covered earthen bowl in her hands. Removing the lid, she began to sprinkle a brownish/grey powder over the liquid in the bowl. "This is that marvelous, magical mushroom powder that Boru and her friends in Ryu make—the stuff that makes your *seihoukei* so effective against *yokai*." When there was a layer of the stuff over the surface of the liquid, she poured more water in. "Again," she said. "Breathe it in."

I could taste the new tang in the steam. I pulled it as deeply into my lungs as I could.

"Listen, Mei. I'm going to hold on to you and attempt to drive that dark energy out. It won't hurt exactly, but it's not going to be comfortable. I need you to hold your position and keep breathing that mist in."

Her strong fingers gripped my shoulders and I instantly felt a little better. Not so alone. She wasn't sharing her energy with me, nor I with her, but somehow we were together. Connected.

"Help me with the words, Sho," Effie whispered. "The words you say when you cast your weapon at a *yokai*."

He said the simple, Japanese words, coaching her along, repeating the phrase that helped banish a *yokai* back to the spirit world.

"Take her hand again, while you say them." Effie's voice sounded strained.

We were all three together now, and something new was happening. The words were taking shape. I couldn't see it, but I could *feel* it, a growing ball of power pressing against me.

"Great Goddesses, Mei," Effie gasped. "Stop fighting me. Take the spell. Let it in. It's a *gift*. A cleanse. It will help you rid yourself of that Oni."

"Oh." I held that mental image in my head—a picture of me accepting the glowing sphere from Effie—and abruptly, I had. It was inside me, settling in my chest, a great hot, growing searchlight, lighting me up from within.

I gasped, but Effie gripped me tighter. "Keep breathing the steam. Let it work."

I could feel that it was working. The light was spreading inside of me—and suddenly I could feel those dark shadows darting and racing away from it.

Horrified, I gasped. "Gross! We have to get them out!"

The thought of those wrigglers working inside of me, eating at me from the inside out . . . I shuddered, and kept breathing, willing the steam and the spell to rid me of the horrid, hungry things. The light was still moving, expanding, searching out every small crevice and crack. I felt full, exposed and more than a little panicky.

"Hold on," Effie said grimly. "They've got nowhere to go. This will not be pleasant—but let it happen."

"Let what—"

I stiffened and sat straight up. Nausea rose. The fabric fell away from me as my face burned and hurt, then my ear, and my hand. My stomach clenched—and then—

A little, black, slimy *thing* crawled out of my nostril. I could feel another oozing from my ear. The third slipped from beneath the fingernail on my right index finger.

"Ugh!" I flung the gross thing from my hand, wiped frantically at my nose and ear. The black blobs were dissolving even before I touched them, and soon they were hanging together in the air, melding into one amorphous blob.

"Say the words," Effie urged. "Again."

We all said them and like before, the bits of Oni residue hung still in the air a moment before they were propelled skyward.

I sat back in my chair, blinking, and then I clutched my middle. "Shards, Sho! Why did you let me eat so much?"

* * *

Later, we sat on the porch and watched the evening come into the meadow. Hitomi had brewed a pot of restorative ginger tea and I sipped mine slowly, hoping it would help settle my stomach.

Next to me, Effie laid her head back on her chair and sighed. "That was both easier and more difficult than I thought it would be. Sitting up to drink again, she eyed me over the rim of her cup. "I think we should discuss it, Mei."

"Yes." But now that I was free of those dark shadows, I couldn't forget the one that had fallen over the Oni while he had me in his grip. "But I have a question." I told them all of those few, chilling moments when it seemed that something else had been alive inside of the creature. "It was different from those little shadows that were inside of me. For a short time, something alive and aware was wearing that Oni like a puppet." I swallowed, fearing I knew the answer already. "It was Inaba, wasn't it?"

"Likely," Effie sighed. "He knows the stories about the Girl With the Stars in Her Eyes, too. Now that he's made his move, he'll keep sending his minions after you." She saw the look on my face. "You're safe here." A shadow crossed her face.

"Inaba's creatures will not be able to cross my wards."

"But will he be able to . . . do that? Take me over, like that?" I shuddered.

The witch leaned forward. "No. I don't believe he will. You've enough worries, but I don't think this should be one of them." She sighed. "It's a complicated matter. And it's why we should discuss what happened today. I want to know everything I can about it."

I nodded.

"To tell the truth, I was surprised that the Oni's dark energy had not made further progress with you. Once it was in, and with the amount of time that passed before we figured it out and intervened, I feared that you might be more . . . corrupted. And then, I wasn't surprised at all."

"I don't understand."

"Energy is a fluid thing, always moving, adapting. It flows inside of us and outside—and between us, too, linking us with the world."

I nodded. I'd experimented with mediation under my dad's instruction and also with Sho. I understood the concept that the Ninja believe—that all life is connected—and I'd glimpsed the waving lines of energy that make up the living life force.

"Boundaries are important. They define us. But our connections are equally as important and they help to shape us too."

"So even though I am connected to that Oni—as we all are—his energy crossed a boundary—and that caused the problem?"

"I believe something like that happened—but now that I've connected with you so closely, I can scarce believe that it did. You have the strongest barriers and defenses that I've ever seen or sensed. Once I understood that, I couldn't imagine how that Oni got past them."

I thought back and then told her how it had felt, when I'd pierced that Oni with the knife—and with the light. "Like clouds or weather fronts colliding—and mixing, at least in the contact zone."

"That explains it, I suppose." She leaned toward me. "But you'll have to be careful, using that skill, if that . . . blending . . .

is to be a side effect."

"And will those defenses you mentioned protect me against Inaba—against him invading my mind?"

"I've heard of Inaba seeing through his minion's eyes, but I'm willing to bet it is a different concept altogether, dealing with strength of mind rather than energy transfer. From what I've heard, it only works for him on weak-minded creatures. That Oni may be all muscle on the outside, but he's all appetite on the inside. Not much room left for brainpower."

"If it were that easy, then Inaba would have just taken over a Scout and got access to Ryu long ago," Ken interjected.

I hadn't thought of that.

"Yes. He's right. I think that they are two separate issues. I just don't believe that even Inaba, with all of his dark magic, would be able to invade your mind—or he would have done it by now."

I breathed a sigh of relief.

But Effie still looked frustrated. "I'm on new ground here. My special gift is all about seeing and understanding connections, but in all of my years I've never seen or heard of anything like this. And I've never known someone so self-contained and . . . separate."

I lifted a shoulder. "I've had to be self-sufficient for a long time. Maybe it's as simple as that." I frowned. "And in any case, wouldn't those strong defenses be a good thing? Maybe they are a part and parcel of that *minding* ability, a means of protection if I am making use of my chi energy that way." My shoulders slumped. "If that even is what is happening."

"Yes. That's a good thought. In that case your strong barriers might be useful—but clearly more work needs to be done, to make sure you are protected. There are so many things here that we just don't know. And also . . ."

"Yes?"

"It's just that we all *need* those connections. And considering all of the whispers and legends surround The Girl With the Stars in Her Eyes—I fear that you might need them more than most." She set down her cup and blew out a frustrated breath. "Oh, I have to think about this—and I'd like to talk to Boru about it, as well."

"Yes, we should check in." Hitomi agreed. "We've much to tell them and I'd like to hear how things are, there."

"Not tonight, though." Effie stood. "I'm too tired to scry for long and I need to marshal my thoughts." She waved a hand. "My bedroom is next to the still room. There are two others. Plenty of beds and couches. Sleep where you are comfortable and I'll see you all in the morning, yes?"

We bid her goodnight. When she'd gone, Hitomi came and took her seat, then stretched out a foot to nudge me. "Are you tired, too? After all of that?"

"Shards, no." I said with a groan. "My mind is awhirl and I'm still too full to even think about lying down."

"That *was* an impressive intake," Sho said from the chaise where he had stretched out. "But I wish Effie had not been so worn out."

"We never asked her about the Elementals," Ken said suddenly.

"No, but did you notice how quiet she got at dinner when we spoke of them?" Sho asked. "She knows something."

And I'd heard the slight emphasis she'd used when she spoke of us being safe from Inaba's creatures. As if there were other things we might not be safe from. But I didn't say it out loud. Didn't they have enough to worry about?

"Tomorrow, we ask." Ken sounded determined. "We came here looking for answers, but all we have so far is more questions."

I noticed that he didn't look at me as he spoke. Fine with me. Maybe the Oni's irritability had left me, but I still wasn't sure if I was ready to forgive and forget.

"I want to go back and look at those movie posters, too. There's something funny about them and I want you guys to look too. I'm not sure if I'm imagining it . . ." Sho heaved himself from the chaise. "But you know, *I* only had one piece of cornbread earlier. I'm going to go see if there's any left—and then I'm going to find a bed. Come on, Ken, let's each go claim a mattress. It will be a nice break from our nylon hammocks."

Ken started to follow, but stopped in the doorway. "Are you guys coming in?"

"Not me," I answered. "I'm going to sit here and listen to the creek babble and the frogs sing." I froze suddenly, clutching the arm of my chair. The words brought back a memory—one of laughter and camaraderie, from when Ken and I had first traveled together on the way to Ryu. Biting my lip, I met his gaze directly for the first time since the Oni had gone from me.

He remembered too. His grin told me that much. It set off a yearning deep in my inner recesses. I did my best to ignore it—and I certainly wasn't going to let it show. I returned his nod, though, and felt a little better as he moved on into the house.

"Want more tea?" Hitomi asked.

"No, but thank you. It did help a little."

"Mei," Hitomi ventured after a few minutes, "why does that man from the diner hate you? Hate all of the *kawads*?"

I shrugged. "Clearly he has some ugly personal experience, but mostly? People just need someone to hate. To blame, I guess. I mean, I know we are all getting back to normal, but I still remember wearing the masks when I was a little girl, don't you?"

Hitomi pulled a face. "We didn't need them in Ryu. Boru's wards cleaned the air. We only had to wear them when we left the village."

"You were lucky. My memories are vague, but I know it made everything so complicated. Fearing the very air that we all need to survive?" I shook my head. "We were lucky the filters were developed to set us all free. And that's just the air, not the devastation in the islands and the coastal cities."

"Yes, but why blame you? You are more a victim of the Rift and the destruction than anyone. All of the *kawads* are. Why not sympathize with them instead of hate them?"

"Well, we've only just learned that Inaba is behind all of the destruction. Most people only think it happened randomly, a natural event caused by the Ring of Fire." I sighed. "Haven't you noticed? People don't really deal well with randomness. They like meaning, purpose, a story. And now the *kawads* are growing up—and they are resenting the slights, the insults and the isolation. They are fighting back, joining together. Some of them take it too far, or use their differences in ugly ways." I met her gaze. "They are giving them a story."

"The gangs are mostly in the big cities, aren't they?"

"Yeah. There are not that many in the Southeast, yet. The only gang I ever ran into was in Winston-Salem, and I think they were only there because they were after me." I raised my brows. "That was the night I met Reik." I felt a little twinge at the thought of our troubled friend. "I hope he's all right."

Hitomi shook her head. "Reik knows how to take care of himself. You've got plenty of worries, but that doesn't need to be one of them."

"I think he's more vulnerable than you think, actually," I said.

She thought a moment. "You might be right. But he's tough too, and he's got his mother looking out for him."

I nodded.

"We'll ask if they've heard anything from him when we scry home tomorrow," Hitomi said with a yawn.

Home. I felt a pang. A home was supposed to be my reward for killing the wind demon. Home. Stability. Friends. My eyes drifted toward the cabin, where Ken slept.

Things were different now. And instead of resting, I was chasing bigger monsters.

We sat for a while longer, talking a little about what might be going on in Ryu, and eventually just listening to the night.

As it grew later, Hitomi started to yawn. "I'm for bed," she said at last. "Are you coming in, too?"

"No. I want to sit here a while—and then I think I'll just take the couch."

"Okay," she said dubiously. "If you want to waste a perfectly good bed . . ."

I shooed her on and laughing, she went. And I was left alone with my thoughts.

12

Mei

Unfortunately, my thoughts were terrible company. I gave up on them and sought out the couch earlier than I had planned. There were plenty of pillows and a soft afghan, and the couch was plush and comfortable—but I still slept fitfully. I tossed and turned and eventually woke with a startled gasp, though I could not remember what had frightened me. Finally, I gave up on sleep, too.

Leaving my boots behind, I went out in bare feet and the shorts and t-shirt I slept in. The grass was soft beneath my toes and the stars were bright overhead. I felt better immediately.

After a while I gave in to the babbling invitation of the stream. Moss made the ground springy and even softer here, so I sat and leaned against a maple and idly ran my fingers through a bunch of overgrown clover at the water's edge.

Perhaps it was the fresh air, or the cheerful camaraderie of the creek, but I must have drifted off, for I was suddenly dreaming. Rialka was there in my dream again, and I was so glad to see her. She looked as beautiful and serene as ever as she took my hand. Approval and encouragement flowed into me with her touch, and I drank it in like water.

She led me along a stream—it looked like the one beside me—and then she bent her knees, smiling and waving a hand over the lush growth on the bank. She introduced me to the patch of clover—and it spoke to me, telling how it grew from the smallest seeds, finding a perfect home next to the burbling water. I dreamt it grew tall and taller—and it talked of the shining sun and the gentle breezes, of the life coursing through it, pushing it higher and helping it to burst with sweet, white blossoms. It caressed my hand and told me not to fear, but to wake up—

And I did, blinking in surprise and straining my eyes in the dark—and trying to understand what I was seeing before me. It took several long moments before I could make it out and wrap my brain around it.

Small and transparent, hard to make out in the gloom, a tiny, winged sprite hung in the air before me. It stared at me quite intently.

Still blinking, I returned the look. But it spooked when I leaned forward—zooming backward and frantically morphing as it went, so that the sprite disappeared and it became a clear, swaying flower, a transparent, flittering butterfly and at last a graceful seahorse darting in circles. Its panicked movements calmed, however, when I made no further aggressive moves. It hovered there, neck swaying, eyeing me cautiously, and waiting.

"It's a summoning."

I turned to find Effie Couts standing a few feet away. No reaction from the creature—it wasn't afraid of *her*. I disentangled my hand from the clover and stood. "What is that? Is it made of *water*?"

"It is. It's here for you. You'll have to go." She shook her head. "He doesn't deign to see many. It's an honor, for all that it's a danger, too."

"What? Who? What is all of this, Effie?"

"I can't tell you much. He calls himself Neelus." She stepped closer. "You'll be frightened—but you must not let it show."

I thought back to Boru's words—they seemed so long ago—back to the original reason we'd come to see Effie Couts. "Boru said you have knowledge of Elementals. That's what you're talking about, isn't it?" A thrill of fear and excitement shot up my spine.

She just gestured. "Follow the sentry. It will show you the way."

I looked back toward the house, but she made a sharp gesture. "No. Not your friends. Just you." Turning, she moved slowly away.

The little creature, still a sea horse, began to move. I hesitated, not sure I was ready to meet an Elemental face to face. But the sentry was moving and did I really have a choice?

The little shifter hung over the middle of the creek and I was grateful that the faint reflection of moonlight made it easier to pick out. I trailed along on the bank, moving carefully and once it was sure of me, it began to idly transform. I had to watch closely, so as not to lose it, but I marveled as it shifted easily to a little sparrow, a sprite again, and then a dragonfly.

The stream narrowed as we went and the forest began to close in. I had to work a little to keep up. It was a relief then, when the sentry darted through an arched opening between trees and I moved branches aside to follow it into a little clearing.

Here was the ending of the stream—a small pool at the base of a large rock formation. The water ran dark and deep and brimming, filled endlessly by the little creek. A narrow ridge rose behind it, stretching out into a low hill.

I wasn't the only person who had found the spot. A faint path led through the clearing to the side of the pool. A small shelf had been carved from the largest stone and a cup sat in it. I was thirsty, but I didn't drink. I didn't know if there might be a price I'd have to pay.

The sea horse hung above the pool, swaying slowly in the scant light. We regarded each other for a long moment, then it moved gracefully around the jutting edge of the rocks and disappeared.

Swallowing, I followed. My nerves were on edge and growing worse. The Elementals I had glimpsed back at Ryu had made my hair stand on end. They were almost alien . . . and utterly powerful.

Suddenly I remembered the discussion my friends and I had had, about avoiding the Elementals' attention until we knew more about them. Ugh. Well, it wasn't as if I'd sought this out. I hoped it wouldn't be one more reason for Ken to be annoyed with me.

I pulled up as I circled around the rocks and saw what was on the other side—an arched entrance carved into the hill. The transparent dragonfly zipped into the darkness beyond and then back out, beckoning me.

Despite myself, I hesitated. But I'd already made the decision. And in any case, without the help of those two Elementals back in Ryu I would likely not have defeated the wind demon that had murdered my father and hunted me for so

long. Now I was expected to face off against a greater evil—
and defeat the villain who had set that creature after us in the
first place—and I couldn't do it without some serious help.

Breathing deeply, I moved past the arched doorway into
darkness.

It took a long time for my eyes to adjust. I stood in utter
darkness and waited. The air was still and quiet. I couldn't
hear the night noises from outside any more, although I had
only gone a few steps beyond the doorway.

Eventually my sight adjusted and I began to pick out details.
The cave was small. I could just make out the extension of the
deep pool ahead of me. No sign of other visitors in here,
though. The fine sand floor lay undisturbed. A carved stone
bench sat at the edge of the water, and the sentry waited above
it, its message clear.

I approached, feeling loathe to leave footprints in the
smooth sand and worse about putting my dirty feet into the
pool. But the bench was situated so that my feet dangled in the
water—and after a moment, I forgot to feel bad. The water was
hot and strangely . . . heavy. This must be one of the mineral
springs that Effie had mentioned. I sighed and leaned into the
hard back of the bench, trying to let the soothing warmth relax
me.

Not much chance of that. I sighed. There was too much at
stake—and too much I didn't know. I tried, though. The water
was so warm and the heat was rising—

I sat up. The *water* was rising—but only around me. It
encased my feet and climbed up my legs, reaching my knees as
I stood.

I tried to walk away, to lift my feet one at a time, but it was
like they were planted in concrete. I couldn't walk or move or
even jump up onto the bench—and the water had reached mid-
thigh now.

I freaked out. For one long moment I thrashed and twisted
and yelled. It wouldn't stop and that relentlessly rising water
was going to rise and rise and cover my mouth and nose and
drown me.

Gradually, reason asserted itself. Don't show fear, Effie had
warned. And too, I'd been led here—surely it hadn't been to

kill me. Easier to let Inaba and his minions do the job. I struggled to calm down, to fend off utter panic. And once I did, the thought struck quickly—the Kappa's gift!

Hayate, a Kappa whom Ken and I had met on the road to Ryu, had given me a boon in exchange for the help I gave him. It was the gift of the ability to breathe underwater, he'd said, and it would last for thirty minutes.

But how to trigger it?

I couldn't help but suck in deep breaths and lift my face as high away from the water as I could—but then it was up and over my head and I was held motionless, encased in a clear, watery cocoon.

I held my breath until I grew dizzy and desperate—and then let I out a curse, unclenched my fists and took a great breath.

The first one felt cool and misty and tasted faintly of algae, but after that it was just like breathing normally. I couldn't tell the difference. Relief swamped me. And at the same time, the fierce hold on my limbs relaxed and I could move inside of my bubble—though I could not break it.

I didn't have much time to marvel at it—for at nearly the next instant a large, resounding crack sounded. Everything outside was blurred, but I could see enough to watch a large, ragged rift open in the far cave wall—and to notice the water in the pool begin to drain away. Another large crack sounded and my bubble and I dropped with stomach-fluttering speed into a crevice below.

All of the water from the pool rushed with me into the dark. We moved fast, curving and falling, joining up and being carried along with what must have been an underground channel or river. It felt like a bizarre amusement park ride, but I was protected from rough walls and jagged turns as I sped along to an unknown destination. And then, I was abruptly ejected into a broader body of water—and I bobbed feet first to the surface of an underground lake.

I craned my neck, trying to see. Pinpoints of light shone from far above, but I couldn't make anything out. For several minutes I floated peacefully, stretched out, staring upward and wondering how big this cavern could be—and then the cocoon bumped against something large and solid—and popped like a bubble, dumping me into the surrounding water.

It caught me by surprise and I came up sputtering in the warm water to find that the large object was an island of sorts—a large, stone dais dissected by a circle of carved pillars and topped with a graceful, domed roof.

I dragged myself up and rolled onto my back, grateful to be warm rather than cold and shivering, and waiting for the next development to reach out and shock me.

Nothing happened, though, and eventually I climbed to my feet and gawked.

The cavern was immense. Smooth water stretched away in every direction. More pillars, massive brothers to the ones encircling me, supported a grand ceiling made of many arched sections. Pictures in carved relief covered each one, fantastical images of sea creatures, elaborate boats, unfamiliar maps and old, blurred writings. Those tiny lights scattered amongst the carvings, so that the whole place was lit with a dim glow.

Dripping, I made my way around the circle, taking it all in. By the time I'd come around again, I was drying off and wondering how long I would have to wait.

Impossible to tell how long I waited in the silent, never-changing spot, but it felt like forever.

And then I heard it. A whisper of a sound. I strained, looking, turning in every direction . . . and at last I saw it. A large swell in the water, moving rapidly toward my platform.

It came closer and moved in to circle the dais—and I caught a glimpse of the creature producing it. Roughly humanoid and unnervingly large. Abruptly it dove deeper and the swell disappeared.

I held myself ready, not sure where it might be, and then the hairs on my neck stood up. I spun around and saw the swell was up again and headed right for me.

It came straight on. I grasped a pillar and braced myself—and at the last minute the water rose high, lifting the creature upright and allowing it to step lightly onto the stone right before me.

I stared unabashedly, even as my pulse and breathing quickened. Taller than a man—perhaps seven feet—he was hairless and grey all over in several mottled shades. The face was sharply angular in the cheek and jaw, in direct contrast to the long, sloping forehead and extended skull. Two, thick, spiraling tentacles sprouted from the back. One curled forward to drape over his shoulder and I blinked my eyes against the softly glowing luminescent bulb at the end.

"Well," he said, staring unblinkingly at me. "You're smaller than I expected."

My heart was pounding, but I couldn't help but sigh. "Why does everyone say that?"

I couldn't help but stare, either. The two main tentacles were surrounded by a wealth of smaller ones, of varying thicknesses. The effect was similar to a thick head of hair. Many ended in a tiny, shining globe but others were entangled around a fascinating collection of small, bright objects. I could see ancient coins, a small lover's eye miniature, a jewel-encrusted broach, a poker chip and a tiny compact disc. I almost couldn't look away, there was so much to discover.

Nodding, he took a turn around me, measuring me in the same way, until he stopped and took up a position in the center of the platform. "You are welcome, Girl With the Stars In Her Eyes."

Relief swamped me, but my body was still reacting to his presence, as if he generated an electric field that threw all of my systems into overdrive. Still, I managed to bow my thanks. "My name is Mei."

He returned the gesture. "I am called Neelus."

I drew a deep breath and forged right in. "Forgive me, Neelus, but I have to ask . . . Are you an Elemental?"

"I am." Three graduating fins sat where his ears should be. They waved gently as he spoke. "I am the caretaker of the unseen pools, the hidden lakes, the underground rivers and buried streams."

I pressed my lips together to keep from smiling—he was so serious. "Are there so many of them, then?"

"They are countless—and valuable beyond most creatures' imaginings. The quiet, sacred spaces nourish the shy and fragile creatures, and guard many secrets. They slip along underneath the surface of the world, and connect the known with the unknown."

A clue as to why he and Effie were acquainted. I looked around. "Is that what this is? A forgotten place?"

Nodding, he looked up at the gorgeously carved ceiling. "The race of dwarvish creatures who created this spot have long since disappeared. The stories they depicted are long forgotten. Yet, it is beautiful still, and my home when I am needed in this region." He tilted his head. "I have forgotten my manners." He flicked a finger and a chair rose fluidly out of the stone behind me. "Would you care to sit?"

I did, actually. "Thank you." I took the seat and ran a finger along the arm. The surface was smooth and not made of stone, as I had supposed. It had a slight give—and I had a sneaking suspicion that the material was not ice . . . but some sort of solidified water. "How?" I asked, marveling.

"I am Elemental," he answered simply.

"And the . . . transport . . . that brought me here? Did you create that as well?"

He inclined his head and said formally, "You did very well with it, too. Many are completely unnerved—and thus proved unworthy."

I flushed. "I had an advantage. Perhaps it was unfair."

"The Kappa's gift? No, that only raises you in my esteem. There is barely a creature in existence who could wiggle such a favor from a Kappa."

I felt a little defensive towards my little green friends. "Perhaps most do not treat them in the correct manner, then."

"You are undoubtedly correct. Many people can only fear what they do not know. You are different, in a multitude of ways." He inclined his head. "It is why you are here."

I remembered Effie's words. "Others have come here—but not many?"

"No, not many."

"Why have I?"

He had stumps of vestigial horns instead of eyebrows on his sloping brow, but he still managed to look surprised. "Direct." He waited a moment. "I shall return the favor."

"Thank you." The truth was, I was completely at his mercy, utterly unnerved over it—and struggling not to let it show.

"You wear the moonstone pendant."

I pulled it out from beneath my t-shirt, trying to decide if I was relieved or disappointed. "*This* is why you brought me here?"

"No. In fact, it is the stone that brought you."

"The *stone* brought me here," I repeated.

"I assisted in the creation of that particular talisman. It was no easy process. In return, I laid my own enchantment on it. It brings me people or objects that are powerful, interesting or important."

My mouth quirked. "Which am I?"

"All three, it is to be hoped."

"No pressure, then." I don't think he understood snark when he heard it.

"On the contrary." He studied me. "Those shoulders seem very slight to bear such a burden. And by all accounts, you are in no way ready to take it up."

I sighed. "That's another thing I keep hearing."

Was that a hint of a smile?

"I confess, I am glad the moonstone brought you. I could not summon you on my own. We have been forbidden to interfere. And unlike many of my brethren, I hope you will prevail in your trials ahead."

I scowled. "Brethren—you mean other Elementals?"

He inclined his head.

"And they *want* me to fail?" I found it incomprehensible. "But if Boru and Rin and the others at Ryu are right, then Inaba's tactics are destroying large parts of the planet and poisoning the elements."

"True. Inaba is an anomaly, a creature that has refused to follow the natural order. But for many years the havoc he wreaks has—like him—been confined to his own spirit realm. His few interferences here have been overlooked. No longer. He has grown powerful and incredibly destructive. Now the Great Mother is awake."

"The Great Mother?" I whispered. I remembered the eyes that I'd thought looked back at me from the mountain, at that battle on the edge of Ryu. I'd been both awed and terrified— and just meeting that gaze had knocked me nearly unconscious.

"She rules over all—earth, air and sea—and the creatures

therein."

"Mother . . . Earth?" It came out so low I wasn't sure he heard me.

"That is one of her names." He cocked his head. "In Shinto, the spirits of your dead live on—yes?"

"Yes."

"After a number of years, many let loose their ties and become one with the Great Ancestor—a being of great might and knowledge. Our Great Mother is similar. Her power is enormous, far beyond the scope of mere human imagination. She is part of us, of every living thing that lives or has ever lived—as we are all part of her. She rules over all in this physical realm, although few enough know of it. Even your *yokai* must bend to her, when they take their physical forms in this world."

I nodded, like my mind wasn't blown.

"Normally, she sleeps. But Inaba threatens the balance. He has awakened her. She knows you, now. Rialka chose you. The Mother's children—the trees and plants and animals—have approved it. She bade us Elementals, her direct descendants and her aides, to give you help, once. But now we are to step aside. She has decreed that *you* will be given a chance to stop Inaba and his desecrations, without interference. Should you succeed, all will be well enough."

A pit opened up inside of me. "And if I don't?"

"She will wage war. It may be that she will only destroy Inaba and his followers. But there are voices whispering of the damage your race has brought, counseling against the chance to allow further pollution, destruction and contamination. There are those who believe you should all be purged."

My blood froze. "Purged? As in, eliminated? All of us?" The irony was like a knife in my gut. Large portions of the population refused to acknowledge that I was human at all, and now I was to be made responsible for the entire human race?

"It is true that the Earth existed for millions of years without humans, and could well thrive so, once again."

I staggered to my feet, walked over to lean against a pillar.

"Rest assured, though, that I am not of that camp. I find your people to be a source of endless fascination. And I am not alone."

I guessed that was supposed to make me feel better. Head shaking, I stared wildly out across the water. "But . . . what if I mess it up? What if I can't do it, but there is someone else out there who can?" My shoulders hunched. "There have been others. There *are* others. What if I am not the *right* Girl With the Stars in Her Eyes?"

"Masayu Barrett?" When he spoke again, it was with stiff formality. Turning, I found him, straight as an arrow, before me. "May I?" He held a webbed hand out between us.

I stared at it in fascination.

"May you, *what?*"

"I wish . . . I wish only to touch you. Briefly. I am forbidden to do much, but I can answer that question for you, at the very least."

I closed my eyes. Considered. Finally, I nodded.

He placed his wide, webbed hand on my head. His eyes closed and I was momentarily distracted as his eyelids shuttered from the sides, instead of the top. We stayed in position for several minutes, but I felt nothing.

Suddenly his torso lit up with a series of small, glowing lights. His hand tightened on my head and the lights ran faster, like crazed runway illuminations.

Then, just as suddenly, he let me go.

Moments passed.

"Well?" I asked at last.

He took a step back. "Mei Barrett."

I waited. "Yes?"

"Loving daughter, loyal comrade, formidable warrior, maker of beautiful washi, friend to ninja, kappa and the flowers in the field—you already know the answer to that question. In your heart, in your gut—you know that you are Rialka's daughter. Her champion. And that this fight is yours."

I sighed. He was right. I'd dreamed of Rialka for years before I'd stepped into her temple on Ryu and felt her warm welcome. Deep down, I knew I was the one who must try to help her finally defeat her ancient enemy.

"Now ask the question that really haunts you," he commanded.

My shoulders slumped. I knew what he was asking. Knew he'd seen the longing that I'd pushed deep since that last day at Ryu. "Will I ever get a chance at a normal life?" I glared at him. "Does any scenario in this situation play out so that I can just be . . . me? The girl who makes washi and loves to climb high and has a home and—"

"Has feelings for a young man?"

Warmth rushed into my face. I didn't answer, but lifted my chin. And waited.

He didn't answer right away. He stared upward while I continued to wait—and then he blinked and looked down at me. "Yes. Should you fight and win—once Inaba is defeated—your life will be your own again."

"And if I don't fight?" I asked softly.

He made a face. Clearly he'd seen enough to know that that wasn't really an option—even though I'd let go of my focus, my determination during these last days out here.

"You would never find peace. Inaba would never rest, never stop searching. Worse would be the torture of your own making—the grief and regret that would be far heavier burdens than the ones you carry now."

He tilted his head, expectant. "Now, ask the next question."

I drew a deep breath. "How can I win? I've been fighting one way or another my whole life—but this? I don't know how to fight this fight. I've never felt so helpless or unprepared."

He nodded. "You fear the answer more than the question—because the answer is that you *cannot* win." His hand slid sharply through the air, cutting me off before I could say anything. "You cannot win alone. And you cannot win at your current level of knowledge and skill."

Shuddering, I pleaded, "Then what should I do? I am used to training, learning. I'll do anything that's necessary, if someone will just *tell* me."

"I am not permitted to say much—but this I will tell you. Rialka and the fates and Nature have conspired to bring you this far—and now you must seek out the knowledge that you need. Help is coming. Be alert and listen well when it arrives."

I nodded. "Yes, I can do that."

"You are blocked in ways that will hinder you—and prevent

your victory." He frowned. "I should send you back. I've already said too much."

I swallowed my disappointment. "Of course." I bowed. "Thank you for your kind attention."

The harsh planes of his face softened a little. "One more thing I will offer, in return for a trade."

I reeled a little in surprise. "Trade? What could I have that would tempt you?"

"A promise." He nodded toward my pendant. "The moonstone will soon need a new bearer. Only promise to give it where you think it will be used wisely."

"Yes. Of course I will."

"Thank you—and now you must listen." He ran a gaze over me and I thought it might be fondness shining from those large, wide eyes. "Weapons and techniques and shields are all very well, but a true warrior learns to understand his enemy. Anyone may risk their life in battle, but few will risk their true selves."

Instinctively, almost involuntarily, I hunched my shoulders. My true self? I wasn't even sure who that was.

He sighed. "It will not be easy. You have much to learn before you are ready." He lifted his head, as if listening. "You must go to the Shihan."

I knew only that the term loosely meant Teacher. "Where?"

He frowned. "Tell Effie that I have said so."

I lowered my head, unwilling to push him and appear ungrateful. "I will. Thank you."

"Remember," he said intently.

"The Shihan. I will tell her."

"Now, I will send you back by a slightly different route." He swept a hand high and suddenly water from the lake was running up and over the platform and pooling at my feet. It started to climb—and I suppressed the shudder than ran through me.

"It will be easier this time," he assured me. "You still retain the Kappa's gift."

Privately, I doubted it would be easy, but I held steady as the water climbed. When it reached my chest, Neelus leaned down toward me. "The quickest way is through the spider's gate. Tell Effie I said to send you through."

There was no time to answer. The water was closing over my mouth and nose. The Elemental still stared at me through the film of water, though, so I nodded.

His form wavered as he drew close and I gasped involuntarily when he thrust his face inside the bubble.

"No one can overhear us here. And this is for your ears only. I should not say any more at all, so I ask you not to share this advice."

I nodded, not wanting to open my mouth.

"For centuries I have watched humanity. I have observed many truths that you all bear out time and again. This is one. It is perhaps one of the most difficult things for you to do—to open a heart that has been walled away—and yet this is exactly what you *must* do." His great eyes blinked sideways at me. "Do not forget."

I shook my head. He withdrew his from the watery envelope. From outside I heard his muffled goodbye.

"I wish you well."

I started to move. I held up my hand in farewell as my cocoon slipped down into the water and I was on my way.

<u>13</u>

Mei

The journey back was rougher, and along smaller channels. This time, when my protective bubble popped, I found myself surfacing in a small, rock-lined pool, located inside a barn-like structure. Limbs heavy with fatigue, I climbed out and stumbled to the door.

The eastern sky shone orange. It was just past dawn. Cheerful bird song greeted me and I blinked as I realized I was in the small outbuilding just beyond Effie's cabin. I couldn't comprehend the magic that had made that possible, but I was just grateful I wouldn't have to trek that long way from the grotto. Nearly sobbing with relief, I dragged myself to the house.

Effie and Hitomi were awake and in the kitchen.

"Mei! Did you sleep outside?" Hitomi beckoned me with a cup in her hand. "Coffee and tea are ready. Come and have something."

But Effie knew. She took one look at me and rushed over to drape an arm across my shoulders. "I'm afraid Mei's had no sleep at all. And she will need it now." She steered me toward the back of the house. "You can take the other bed in Hitomi's room. Sleep yourself out . . ." She met my weary gaze. "And then we'll talk."

Unable to even express my thanks, I fell into the bed and was gone before they left the room.

* * *

I awoke to the smell of bacon and sat up, my stomach rumbling. Glancing out the window, I saw that it looked to be late morning. Surprised, I stretched. I'd been so tired, I thought I would have slept longer. But my fuzzy head was gone, as well as that dragging feeling of fatigue.

The door cracked a little, then widened as Hitomi saw I was up. "She's awake!" I winced as she bounded in and bounced on the bed. "Finally!"

"You didn't have to wait," I chided. "You should have had breakfast without me."

"We did," she laughed. "And lunch and dinner, too. You've been asleep a full day!"

"What?" I blinked at her.

"It's not unusual," Effie said from the doorway. "It's draining—the proximity of an Elemental."

I just stared. I didn't think I'd ever slept so long before.

"Take your time, get yourself together, then come out. We'll talk after we eat. Hitomi, come and help me finish up?"

I was bathed and back in my travel/training gear when I emerged a while later. Everyone had gathered at the table and Effie was just setting a platter of golden French toast in the center.

"Eat first, talk later," she ordered.

I was happy to oblige—and happy also to grow pleasantly full after a normal plate of toast and bacon. "No more Oni, for sure, then," I said, sitting back and patting my stomach.

"Neelus would never have granted you an audience, were you still contaminated."

The others all pushed their plates away as well, watching me with wide-eyed curiosity.

"Well?" Sho raised a brow.

"How was it?" Hitomi asked.

I searched for the right word. "Nerve-wracking," I settled on at last.

"Tell us," Ken leaned in.

So, I did. And they were a satisfying audience, gasping and commiserating at all the right parts. They let me talk nearly uninterrupted, all the way until I got to the part about the Great Mother.

Effie groaned then, and dropped her head in her hands. The others just looked shocked.

"As in . . . Mother Earth?" Some of the color had drained from Hitomi's face.

"Mother *Nature*?" Sho asked.

I shrugged. They had been raised Ninja in Ryu—where living in harmony with Nature was part of their culture. I wondered if this was another case in which they casually knew so much more than I did, like with the *yokai*.

"This is not good news," Ken said. "She might be sometimes called Mother Nature, but she is more than just blossoms and rainbows."

"Indeed, she is." Effie looked up. "There is as much devastation in the natural world as there is beauty. Volcanoes are natural. Hurricanes. Viruses. Disease. The Mother respects adaptation, survival of the fittest, and the balance that leads to the widest avenues for Life."

"She knows your name," Hitomi breathed.

"It is as well that she and her Elementals will not involve themselves," Effie said firmly. "They are often quick-tempered, impatient and quick to judge—and heedless of the far-reaching results that might affect *us*, if it looks like a better solution to *them*."

I choked and nearly brought up my bacon. "Far-reaching. One word for it—if we fail they could wipe out the entire population."

Effie sat straight. "That is not due to the Elementals, Mei— or to you, either. Inaba set us on this path as soon as his dark magic started causing global catastrophes. We are permitted to flourish on this Earth, but he destroyed an entire nation and ripped apart several coastlines. Meddling on that scale is interfering in *her* sphere. Do you think she was not going to take notice?"

"She's giving us a chance to handle this ourselves," Sho mused.

"Yes, and it's not *your* fight, Mei, but *ours*," Hitomi emphasized. "Everyone in Ryu."

"And all of our allies in JanFran and beyond," Ken added.

"Even those like me, who have only lately learned about Inaba's selfish and evil intents . . . we are working to help to stop him, too." Effie smiled at me reassuringly.

Ken nodded. "While you were asleep, Effie has been showing us how she's working on a tracking spell. She's been working long distance with Noff to develop a weapon we could use."

"A tracking weapon?" I asked.

"Yes. Ryu is still fighting off those Kitsune, and scouts all over are reporting more contact with *yokai*. We cannot win every battle. But we could tag a powerful yokai before we call retreat."

"Tag it—and track it—back to Inaba, you mean?" I sat a little straighter.

"Yes. We need to get a better idea of his location, his movements. How is he controlling so much from the spirit world? We'd always assumed he had a witch, an interpreter who has skills like Boru, but people have reported sightings of him in JanFran—and in the ruins of Iga too." He shook his head. "Is he even in the spirit world now? Has he found a way back—a way to stay? It's what he's wanted for so long. We have to learn more."

"We're not ready yet," Effie sighed. "Something like this takes a lot of experimentation—and it's not always easy to get a *yokai* to agree." She grinned. "I hear there a few of those young Kitsune getting more than they bargained for, when they are captured at Ryu." Shrugging, she rose to pour more tea. "But we hope to be ready—"

I knew why she'd stopped. "When I'm ready," I finished for her.

"When *we* are ready," Ken corrected.

I was caught up in the whirl of thoughts in my head. I'd told Ken—and everyone—that I'd accepted my role as Girl With the Stars In Her Eyes, back before that battle at Ryu. But Neelus was right. I'd been waffling, avoiding the issue, since we'd left the village. I couldn't do it any longer. And I didn't have to. Now, I had something to focus on. Training to get to. I could see ahead. My old determination was rising—and I welcomed it back with relief.

It was time to get back in the game.

I turned and looked them each in the eye. "I have an idea how we can start." I told them about what Neelus had said about going to Shihan.

"The Teacher!" Effie's eyes lit up. "Even I have heard of him. There's nothing he doesn't know about spiritual energy and how it behaves. It's the very thing. Just the stories that are told about him . . ." She stopped and reached over to lay her hand on mine. "Mei, if we are right about your new talent—it's going to take a very delicate balance. You'll have to learn to protect yourself and open your channels at the same time. It will be difficult work. But I know you can do it."

I gripped her hand back. "I know how to work hard."

"And the Shihan is the perfect person to teach you—but he is difficult to find." She slumped back. "Will your people in Ryu know?"

"We can ask," Ken aswered grimly.

I sighed. "I suppose we can hope he's in JanFran. Then we can also work on finding Akemi."

My friends exchanged glances.

I tensed up. "What is it? What don't I know?"

"We contacted home while you were asleep. They've heard from Neil," Hitomi whispered.

"Did he find her? Are they all right?"

Ken spoke up. "He was smart about it. He worked with the people in JanFran, but they hadn't had any word or sightings of the Snow Woman since she left Inaba's compound and showed up in Ryu."

"And no word of Akemi, either?" Their faces had already told me the answer.

"Not yet. Neil convinced the watchers there to help him infiltrate the compound. He took some of their people in with him, as part of his disguise. Scientists. And others."

I sucked in a breath. I'd heard the villagers in Ryu say that no one had ever made it back out of Inaba's stronghold.

"He got a quick look around. Mei, they found confirmation that Inaba did cause the Rift. Somehow he combined dark magic and spiritual energy with thermonuclear energy. That's where the altered *yokai* are coming from. He's still trying to find a way to anchor a spirit here on earth."

"So he can subvert Rialka's spell and come back through," I said blankly.

"It looks like he's changing methods now. Maybe because of how we've defeated the altered *yokai*. Maybe they are not as resilient as they were before he tinkered with them."

"There's a lot more experimentation going on in there that we didn't know about and still don't understand. Neil didn't find any sign of Akemi, though, and then he was found out. He had to fight his way out, but he says he did a good amount of damage in the process."

I heaved a sigh of relief. "He's home safe, then?"

"For now. He says he's heading north in search of the Snow Woman—maybe he'll find that Akemi is still with her."

"But there is no way to know, for sure," whispered Hitomi.

We all sat in miserable silence for a moment.

Effie cleared her throat. "I think you should call Ryu and discuss these latest developments."

I pressed my lips together and nodded. I'd like to see how Boru was doing.

Effie did the scrying this time—and she used a big wall mirror so that we could all comfortably see. After she'd whispered the words and called Boru's name, it was only a few seconds until the other witch's face loomed close in the flame.

"Better than teleconferencing," I muttered.

"More reliable—and less likely to be hacked," Boru answered with a grin. "Mei, I'm glad you are okay. Is everyone all right?"

We all answered her in a loud chorus.

"Good. Now tell me everything!"

I did, spinning my tale and relaying my instructions.

"The Shihan . . ." She mused it over. "Listen, all of you, I can't say much, but know that we've sent you some help. Keep your eyes open for it. But the reports from JanFran are disturbing. Something is going on. The pace of this fight seems to have suddenly escalated. Training with the Shihan might be what you need to get you ready in time."

"Effie thought it was a good idea," I offered.

Boru exchanged glances with her friend. "It likely is, especially after what happened with that Oni. And if Neelus says so . . ."

"Do you know where the Shihan is?" I asked.

Boru shook her head, her expression . . . odd. "No."

"What is it?" I asked.

"Rin is not going to like it. Nor the rest of the Council. They want you to come back here for further training."

I stiffened. "I don't have to answer to or explain myself to them."

"I know," she assured me. "And I agree that you should go ask in JanFran. There are people there who are acquainted with the Shihan." She pursed her lips. "Still, I might delay a little, in sharing this—and by the time I do, you can be well on your way." She grinned, but it faded quickly. "Rin has her hands full at the moment, in any case."

"With what?" asked Sho.

"That four-tailed Kitsune. He's proven to be a formidable enemy."

"What's happened?" Ken demanded.

"He's keeping us on our toes," Boru admitted. "He learns quickly and he's inventive. They've had some larger reinforcements come in, too." Her smiled looked tired. "We had a Nue visit us for several nights."

Sho gasped. "Inaba has *yokai* so powerful and ancient cooperating with him?"

"What is it?" I asked.

"An old, old type of *yokai*. It has the head of a monkey, the body of a raccoon dog, the tail of a snake and the limbs of a tiger."

"It visited in the night, just as the old stories say," Boru told us. "It came with dark clouds and strange winds and hovered over the village, above the barriers, but it brought malaise and bad dreams and terror. People grew ill. Others felt hopeless or confrontational. Not the sort of thing we need, in a siege situation."

"What can be done about it?" Ken asked, frowning.

"We've defeated it," she answered with satisfaction. "With thanks to Reik."

"Reik?" we all chorused.

"He's back?" Hitomi asked happily.

"No, but he contacted us and told us how we could defeat the Nue. Thank goodness."

"How did he . . . seem?" I asked. I noticed Ken's sour look when I did.

"As tired as we feel. He wouldn't say where he was. Or if he planned to return."

"Then why warn us at all?" Ken asked roughly.

"He still cares about us," Hitomi insisted indignantly.

"Don't be too hard on Reik," Boru continued. "He's walking a line balanced between two worlds, which is never easy."

"It's his *mother* that he worries for and left us to pursue," I reminded Ken. "What would you do for your mother? What would I have done if the wind demon had taken my father instead of killing him? If he was under Inaba's control?" I shuddered.

"We're not giving up on Akemi," Sho said firmly. "Why would we give up on Reik?"

I caught the worried glance Boru and Effie shared.

Ken backed down. "So you've held the barriers?" he asked Boru.

"So far. I have help. And I'm getting stronger, every day. We'll be okay."

"And Akemi, as Sho mentioned? What is to be done?"

"Leave her to Neil and to our JanFran compatriots, for now. Rin has sent scouts to the north, too. You have your own fight to worry over. The best way you can help her and us too, by the way, is to arm yourself." She looked at me. "Go. Find out all you can, keep training, learn how to protect yourself and how to fight the real enemy."

I sighed. "Will you keep us updated, when you learn anything? I hate to think of her out there, all alone."

Boru's face softened. I knew she was thinking that I knew about being alone. They were probably all thinking it. And they were right. I wouldn't wish it on anyone, even Akemi.

"We've got to figure out how to get all the way to JanFran," Hitomi said. "Fast."

Effie and Boru exchanged looks. "There are ways, and then there are ways."

I remembered the Elemental's words then. "Oh—Neelus said to tell you to send us through the Spider's Gate."

Beside me, Effie paled and clutched my hand. Boru suddenly looked a little sick too.

"What is it?" I asked. "He only said that it was the fastest way."

"He wouldn't have said it unless it was necessary," Effie

breathed. "But this could be a problem."

A noise sounded in the background behind Boru. She glanced over her shoulder, then looked back at Effie. "You can tell them how to handle it, can't you?"

Effie swallowed. "Yes. I will."

"Listen to Effie carefully, all of you. She knows what she is doing." She lifted a hand and pressed it against the mirror on her side. "Take care of yourselves, all of you."

"You too," we all chorused.

And as she faded away, we turned to her friend.

14

Akemi

They'd removed her IV. Brought her soft pajamas and nourishing meals. They'd given her a screen. It was pre-loaded with books and vids, but had no connection to the outside world.

Akemi couldn't concentrate enough to read. She couldn't relax enough to lose herself in a show. She still felt so exhausted, but she couldn't let herself sleep the days away.

The screaming still woke her, occasionally. Sometimes she heard it during the day. She should be learning what she could, finding a way to escape. But her *minding* talent, the premonition of danger—and the incredible physical timing it gave her—was useless here. Every second she spent here she was in mortal danger, and all she could do was sit at the edge of the bed, watching the door, waiting for someone to come in.

She didn't know why. The people who came in were garbed in plain white and they gave nothing away. They would not answer her questions. They barely spoke at all. They gave her no clue as to where she was or why or what they wanted from her.

She'd never been treated like this. She didn't know how to react. It infuriated her to be ignored.

She paced her anger out in the room, but she was so tired she could only make a couple of passes. Instead, she perched on the edge of the bed. She tried to calculate how quick she would have to be to slip out of the door when one of her silent jailers entered, but who knew what waited her outside? She was in no condition to fight yet. Right now she breathed hard just from walking to the adjoining bathroom. So she waited and she tried to pretend that she didn't know they were watching.

The scent of incense would intensify occasionally, and she would feel unseen eyes on her. Several times a day she caught the telltale flicker from the corner of her eye. He was in there, that man in the mirror. Not all the time, but sometimes.

He was there now. She'd seen the wisp drift across the edge of the long mirror. Her knee jiggled with the knowledge. Anxiety and fear and anger built.

"I know you are there!" It burst out of her at last. "Why don't you show yourself? Why don't you *do* something, *say* something, *ask* something!"

The stillness held—and then a fine mist showed in the mirror and slowly coalesced into a figure. The same man, but he was far more gorgeously dressed this time, in a finely embroidered kimono.

"Your pardon," he said formally. "I rather thought you were frightened of me."

"What are you doing? Why are you watching me?"

"You are a lovely girl."

Akemi froze.

"And do you know, after all of these hundreds of years, I am glad I am still able to enjoy the pleasures of simple beauty. Truly, it is a vast relief."

She didn't respond.

"Do you know who I am?"

Even as she watched, his image dissolved into a wispy trail that danced from the far corner of the mirror to a spot closer to her. If she'd had any doubt as to his identity, that—and the comment about hundreds of years—would have cured her of it.

She nodded, then waved a hand toward the mirror. "How do you do that? You are a spirit, are you not? Like Rialka. How can you scry all the way from the spirit world?"

His mouth twitched, as if he could not hold back the smile of pride. "*Only* I can do it. It takes a great deal of power to manifest this way. "And I am spirit, yes, but also so much more." He heaved a sigh. "But I waste my breath. You, being who you are, will only be frightened, not impressed."

He was wrong. She was impressed. And a little envious. She would certainly like to possess a unique power. Something only she could do. It would go with her eyes—which had been unique, until recently. A power like that would show the doubters that *she* was special. Chosen.

Chosen to defeat . . . him.

He had melted away again and flitted across the mirror in a whirl. His eyes emerged first and she was caught as the rest of him formed again.

"I'm not afraid!" she bit out.

He laughed. "Are you not? Good." He eyed her appraisingly. "Such confidence comes from a happy upbringing, I suppose. You've been treated differently since you first opened those intriguing eyes of yours, haven't you? I suppose you have never once doubted your own destiny."

Akemi lifted her chin. "Doubts are for others." She did not doubt—not for a second. Because if the doubters were right, then she was just like them. Not special at all.

He laughed in delight and she wondered if she'd revealed too much. "We have that in common, at least." He swooped closer. "Interesting though, because my childhood was not a happy one—yet not once in all of these years have I doubted my own potential, superiority or power." He drew back. "And power has its privileges. He rose up high and gazed down at her. "I like you, young one. I'm not sure what I am going to do with you, but I like you. And so I shall reward you."

With that, he popped out, and Akemi was left to wonder whether to be relieved—or afraid.

15

Mei

"There must be an element of urgency, if Neelus told you about the gate." Effie had been muttering for several minutes now as she made her way through the house. "But what is it? Why risk it?"

"Mei." Ken beckoned and I stepped over to the kitchen where he stood in the sunlight coming through the windows.

"What's up?"

His stance shifted, and then shifted again. I watched bemused as he silently held out a zipped plastic bag.

"What is it?" I asked.

"It's just . . . something I collected for you."

I stared, questioning.

"It's silver fir needles, the soft, fine kind that only come with new growth, near the tops of the tree. Effie has some growing here and I thought you might want to use it as decorative element . . . in your washi."

"Oh." It came out softly. Sudden moisture blurred my view of the delicate little needles. He was one of the few people who knew about my papermaking—and how it made me feel connected to my mother.

He flushed. "Maybe it's stupid to even think about now, with all that we have to worry about. You can just toss it, if you want."

"No! You are right, they would make beautiful washi." My heart ached, that he would think of such a thing. "I'm going to keep these safe in my pack. Thank you, Ken," I said softly.

We abruptly moved apart as Effie pushed past us deeper into the kitchen. "So risky. But why?"

Bemused, we followed as she picked up a jar here, rifled through packets of dried herbs there.

We exchanged glances, pulled firmly back into the here and now. "What is the spider's tunnel, Effie?" Ken stood in the doorway of the stillroom after she crossed in.

I looked over his shoulder. "And who or what is the spider?" I added.

She stopped suddenly, turned and dumped her load of supplies onto the table. "Both good questions." She nodded. "Both important." She motioned us in. "Gather everyone. Sit down, I'll explain."

We called the others and all took seats, waiting expectantly.

Effie looked around. "Do any of you know what ley lines are?"

The others all shook their heads, but I frowned and tugged on a wisp of a memory. "I remember . . . something. Back when I was trying to figure out what the wind demon was, I did a lot of research into supernatural stuff. They are . . . not real, right? Invisible lines that run all over the globe? But they are just . . . pretend, not real any more than latitude or longitude lines?"

"Oh, they are real. You can't see them, but you can feel them. They are lines of *power*," Effie emphasized. "Sorcerers and witches have long used them for navigation and communication across distances. You can imagine what an advantage that was, back before the telegraph, the telephone, let alone the sort of instant global access that is available today."

"Where do spiders come in?" Hitomi shuddered.

"Maybe they crawl along the lines like they are webs," Sho suggested.

'No. There are certain spots, places where a couple, or even several lines cross. These are places of great power—and if you know how to activate it, they can act as a gateway."

"A gateway—to a tunnel," Ken said. He looked at me. "And there is one near here?"

"It's within a day's journey." She made a face. "And that is close enough."

"Where does the gateway—the tunnel—go?" I asked.

"Exactly where you need it to go," Effie said with a sigh. "The other end connects to the west coast. In the morning you emerge just outside San Diego. Travel in the evening and it comes out onto the Kitsap Peninsula, near Seattle."

"And the spider?" I pressed.

"She guards the gate."

"Is she Jorogumo?" Ken asked.

Effie nodded. "She began that way—but she is a special case."

I was watching the horror flash across Hitomi's face.

"A *yokai*?" I asked.

She nodded.

"How bad is it?" I shuddered. "Worse than the Oni?"

"This one is." Effie's tone was growing grimmer by the moment.

Sighing, I waited.

"After a spider lives for many years, it becomes a *yokai*. It gains magical powers and the ability to shift shapes. They begin to feed off of human prey instead of insects and build a nest in caves or in empty houses in towns," Ken began.

"They like to live as young and hot women, and lure all the good looking guys in—and then they eat them," Hitomi said indignantly.

"They can go for years before the people around them catch on," Sho continued. "They've found lairs with hundreds of drained bodies piled high."

I looked to Ken. "Have you ever fought one?"

He shook his head.

"This one is out of the ordinary, even for a Jorogumo," Effie broke in. "Even long ago, she was a threat. She was a very successful *yokai*, beautiful and long-lived. She barely remembered being a spider, it had been so long. But she grew cocky. She made the mistake of preying on a beautiful youth who was a favored descendant of Tsuki-yonni, the Moon God. When the Moon God discovered the boy's fate, he was furious. He'd watched the Jorogumo for many years from his perch in the sky and knew how to punish her. He stole away her beauty and cursed her to remain a hideously ugly, gigantic spider. She could only take human form if she drank the distilled tears of the stars."

I made a face. "Do I want to know?"

"It's dew," Sho said. "Right? I've seen it referred to that way in the old plays."

Effie nodded, but I dropped my head in my hands for a

moment. "Let me guess. It's not exactly easy for a spider to distill dew."

"No. You've guessed it," Effie nodded. "She guards the gate and demands a dose of distilled dew as payment to use it."

"But you've been through?" Hitomi asked. "You have the ability to get or make what she wants?"

I thought back to the way she spelled the pollen from the flowers.

Effie's eyebrows raised high. "If you lived within a few hours of a dangerous monster's lair, you'd make sure to have what she needed, wouldn't you? Any witch worth her salt would be prepared. I collect the dew and I made an . . . arrangement with a local, uh, businessman, to distill it into an effusion of local whiskey."

"What is it like, using the gate?" Ken asked. "Stepping in here and ending up across the country?"

"It's jarring," Effie admitted. "But it's not the gate that should worry you—it's the gatekeeper. She's tricky and dangerous and the last time I went through she was . . . on edge. Different." She stood and began to organize the supplies before her. "There must be a reason that Neelus wants you to go through that way. I'll give you the dew and I'll mix up a few other things that might be useful, too."

"Thank you," I said, standing, and then looked around at my friends. "In the meantime, let's try to figure out how we might fight off a giant spider . . . just in case."

16

Sho

"**C**ome on!" Sho jumped from Effie's small car and dragged Hitomi out with him. He wanted to see those posters again. He hadn't been able to forget the Young Samurai ad. There had been something about it . . .

He slowed as he approached the corner where the ads were posted, all together. Two men stood across the way, wearing long coats and neck cloths and boots. They might have been related, or perhaps it was just the matching, short, wide sideburns and thick heads of curled hair that lent the illusion. One scribbled in a book, but the other held Sho's gaze steadily as he approached.

"They must be filming a period piece here in town," he said quietly to Hitomi. There was something else about them . . . something beyond their looks . . . but he couldn't quite put his finger on it . . .

"Oh?' She stopped as the reached the spot and began to scan the posters. "Oooh, look! They are remaking Galaxy Tours! I wonder who will play Captain Joe?"

"That's not the one I wanted to show you." Once he was distracted from the strangers, Sho's eye was immediately drawn to the Biwa Studios sign and the prominent ad for The Young Samurai. There was something *wrong* with it.

"Look." He directed Hitomi's attention. The scene showed a training courtyard before a wide stair leading to a fanciful old-style Japanese home. A young boy in somber training gear stood, looking fiercely proud, with his blade at the ready as he faced a much larger, more flamboyantly dressed adversary. Men and boys were gathered around, looking on in encouragement and excitement.

"The last time—"

There! It happened again. A flash, as for an instant, the image somehow . . . changed.

"Did you see that?"

"See what?"

Sho glanced over his shoulder, to see if the men behind them were paying attention, but they had gone.

He turned back and caught the briefest glimpse of the change again.

He took a step away, keeping his gaze fixed on the poster, then took a step sideways.

There. "It's like one of those illusion cards for kids. Tilt it one way and it's a puppy and the other way it's a dinosaur. Or a kitten and a flower. Whatever."

"I know what you mean." Hitomi moved her head around, then stepped back and forth. "But I can't get it to work for me."

Sho stared at the altered image. It showed the same courtyard but a very different scenario. In this one an execution had just occurred—an armored Samurai had beheaded a kneeling foe. Men were gathered again, watching, but the proud boy's shoulders were hunched and he was leaving the scene, fear and disgust on his face. An older boy watched him go, openly mocking him.

"Here." Sho grabbed Hitomi and put her in his spot. "Stand here and tell me what you see."

She described the first scene.

"And it doesn't change?" They shifted her position several times without results.

"It's probably just me," Hitomi assured him. "It takes me forever to see the other image in those optical illusions too, you know, like the one where it's a young woman and an old woman at the same time?"

"Maybe."

"Hey guys!" It was Mei, calling from further up the road. "Here's our ride!" She pointed as an old, refurbished van pulled in next to them. It bore a logo for naturally cured, organic wood chips.

Sho looked back to the altered scene on the poster. What did it mean? It was important. He knew it, somehow.

"Let's go," Hitomi urged.

He followed, but slowly. Just before he reached his friends he glimpsed the two men in old-fashioned garb again. They stood across the main street now and both stared at him boldly. He nodded. They glanced at each other. Then Sho's attention was drawn by Effie as she pulled him in to say goodbye, and when he looked again, they were gone.

17

Mei

I whispered the words to spell my mask into place before I met Effie's friend, Old Burnsy. He seemed kind and just a little bashful, meeting all of us at once, but he assured us he was happy to give us a ride all the way to Nashville, Tennessee.

"I make the drive once or twice a month, depending on business and the weather. Got several restaurants who will only use my wood to smoke with," he told us proudly. "Plus I package up chips for several of the vendors in the big Farmer's Market." He adjusted his cap. "Be happy to have company on the drive for once, although three of you will have to squeeze in the back with the wood."

"We are just grateful for the ride," I told him. "We'll sit wherever there is room."

"Let's load up then, and move out. I like to get there a bit after the lunch rush."

We gathered our things and although we had already said our goodbyes at her cabin, I stopped to hug Effie. "Thank you for everything."

She made us promise to keep in touch—and to come back to visit. I noticed Sho was barely paying attention, and kept looking back to the corner where the ads hung. "Did you get another look at them?" I asked as he climbed in.

"Yeah."

"Did you figure out what was bothering you?"

He shook his head, then settled down next to a wrapped pallet of corded wood and let his head sink to his knees.

I motioned Hitomi to go ahead and sit in the front seat next to Burnsy. "Is this your first time on a highway?" I asked her.

"It is!" She bounced into the seat and flashed the driver a smile. "How fast does your van go?"

"Fast enough to get us there in just over four hours—and slow enough not to attract unwanted attention from any troopers." With a grin spreading over his wrinkled face, he started the engine and we set off.

I leaned against a stack of burlap sacks of wood chips and set my pack on top to serve as a pillow. Ken settled into an empty spot past the sliding door.

I felt a twinge. I knew he didn't approve of my disguise—but I wasn't willing to forego it.

"You still tired?" he asked as I leaned my head against my pack.

"A little," I admitted. I was grateful he was willing to take the first step to normalize things between us.

"I think I'm glad the Elementals are taking a back seat," he mused. "They wear you out." With a glance toward Burnsy, he leaned in. "They've given us a chance and we'll make the most of it. You're not alone in this. We'll be fighting with you."

"I know." I shot him a smile. "I'm glad we are in this together."

JanFran. It felt right to be headed there at last. It was where Inaba kept his stronghold, where her parents had met, where she'd been born and her mother had died several years later. She'd left the city as a frightened child and now it felt as if all the pathways in her life were leading her back.

In the front, Hitomi and Burnsy were engaged in a discussion about smoking meat and Southern food in general. At the moment he was trying to explain collard greens.

"Listen, this will be Hitomi's first time in a real city, right? I mean, bigger than Asheville?"

"Oh, yeah." His eyes lit up. "I'd forgotten. She'll be excited."

"I was thinking, on our way out of town—could we stop and take her to a Mexican joint? Do you know any with good tacos?"

He wrinkled his nose. "Tacos?"

"I asked and she said they were at the top of her list." I raised a brow at him. "Anyway, what's with the sneer? Don't tell me that you're a food snob."

He shot me a similarly incredulous look. "You did eat my mom's cooking, right? Of course I'm a food snob—I'm used to the good stuff." He grew sober. "Still, we'll need to keep a low profile. And be on the alert."

"I know, I know. But why not make her first day in the big city a special one?" I shrugged. "I mean, we have to eat."

"Not tacos," he muttered. He wore a light, distant look on his face and I wondered if he was thinking back to his first days out of Ryu, on his first scouting mission. "Let her enjoy herself, but the rest of us should keep an eye out. Who knows when we'll run into more of Inaba's minions?"

"Agreed." I yawned and tried to get comfortable.

"I'm just glad it's not burgers," Ken muttered. "Some of those fast food places?" He shuddered. "I make it a policy to never eat at several of them."

"That's it!"

I jumped as Sho's head popped up. He stared between the two of us, wide-eyed.

"That's what?" asked Ken.

"A policy against it. Against The Young Samurai! I knew I recognized the name, but I just couldn't remember . . . I heard my parents discussing it once, with a gathering of theater people."

"What did they say?" I didn't understand his intense interest in the vid ads, but I knew better than to discount almost any odd occurrence.

"They said it was a play that they would never produce. Nor would many other theatres. It had some sort of taboo associated with it. They urged the others to avoid it, as well."

"What taboo?" Ken looked interested.

"I don't remember. I was young. I barely remember the conversation." Sho frowned. "I need to find out more. If we scry home tonight, I'll ask them."

He sat back, brooding, and I settled back into place too. We'd reached the interstate and I dozed for a time, letting the hum of the wheels on the road soothe me. Several times I jerked awake, but everything was calm, so I went back to sleep.

I didn't awake fully until we left the interstate. The stop and start of city driving let me know we were close.

"Look at all of the people!" Hitomi gawked out of the window, but glanced back at us, all alight.

We were in the tourist section of the city, and heading for

downtown, based on the skyline. Outside, hotels and restaurants and theatres lined the street. We stopped at a light and Sho stood up to look out of the high, back windows.

"Look at that old theatre," he said reverently.

"It's beautiful. And it looks like it's been there for a good, long while."

"They must be having a Hitchcock event. It's a smart idea to have the guy in costume. He looks just like him."

"Who does?"

"That guy. Right there, near the entrance."

I cast about but didn't see him and then the light changed and the van moved away. "Aw. I missed him. I have actually seen The Birds. I watched it, thinking I might learn something about the wind demon, way back when."

Sho looked at me strangely. "You didn't see him?"

"Nope."

"Almost there," Burnsy called. "We'll stop at the Farmer's Market first."

We gathered up our belongings. Hitomi exclaimed over the buildings and the number of cars and the busy atmosphere. Open places like this had grown immensely popular once more, once we all started spending time outside again.

Burnsy pulled up at the glass-window-fronted main entrance of the market. "All right. Delivered right on schedule." He grinned. "Now the lot of you jump out and go enjoy yourselves in the market. I have to go 'round back to the trade entrance."

"You don't need our help to unload?" asked Ken.

"Shoot, no! I do this all the time. Got a system. You kids go and enjoy yourselves." He grew serious. "And be sure to keep in touch with Effie Couts. She could use some nice, young people in her life."

We sent him a chorus of thanks and climbed out.

Hitomi eyed the building and the people streaming in the entrance, then squared her shoulders and looked at the sky. "So. We head northwest out of the city, right?"

"Right." I spotted a sign and nudged Ken. "But first, let's go in. Look." I pointed to a prominent sign listing the restaurants featured inside the market. "Mexican food."

Her eyes grew big. "Really?" She grinned. "Tacos?"

"Tacos," I said firmly.

"Forget tacos," Sho said. "Look at the sign. They have burritos as big as your head!"

* * *

It was while we were enjoying the food that I felt the first prickle. I sat a little straighter and began to stealthily scan the open seating area. No one person or thing stood out. But I felt it. Someone was watching us.

Ken caught on to the subtle change in my attitude. But he was good—the best I'd ever seen. He casually shifted so that he could cover the part of the surroundings that I could not.

I couldn't narrow it down. Everyone appeared happy and relaxed. No one was overt in their attention. I eyed a group of teenage boys gathered by the restrooms, but they were only interested in the girls exclaiming over the bakery case next door. A large, blonde guy with a partially shaved head and a heavily muscled form caught my eye, but he appeared to be happily intent on the burrito in his hand as he left the counter and moved on.

"Everyone almost done?" Ken started gathering the trash.

"Mmm hmm . . ." Hitomi shoved the last of the soft taco in her mouth and sighed. "Thanks, guys! That was so good. I love tacos!"

"Not every place has food as fresh and home-cooked as this one," Ken warned. "You're going to have to learn to discriminate, out here."

"I'll be careful to develop my palate, Ken, in between fighting *yokai*," she said with a roll of her eyes.

"Ha. You laugh, but there is some truly terrible stuff passing for food out here." He sighed. "All those years of complaining about my father's ever present mushrooms—who knew I would actually miss them?"

I laughed, but then I tensed as a commotion broke out among the boys by the bakery. I watched as pushing, shoving and a few testosterone-fueled insults spread through their group, but it faded as someone took charge and settled the dispute. I sat back, moving my hand away from my knife—and then I saw it.

A tiny shuriken—a ninja star. It stuck out of the top third of my cup.

"Shards," I whispered. *Gods, but I'm an idiot.*

Ken froze when his gaze followed mine and found the foreign object. We both turned to scan the room at once—but I knew it was too late. Whoever it was, they'd made their point—and their presence known.

Gingerly, I pried the weapon from my cup. At least it had hit above the level of tea inside. Then I wondered if it the throw had been so deliberate—and so skilled. I ran my finger over the sharp corners and edges. It wasn't star-shaped, like so many shuriken, but a hexagon. "Look at this." The middle was solid—and marked with a vividly painted eye. *My* eye.

Ken silently asked permission and I handed it over. He examined the six sides, each illustrated with a different martial arts weapon.

"That's a yumi, the tall Samurai bow," said Hitomi, leaning in to look.

"Yes, and a katana, a bo staff, a dagger, a shuriken and a pair of sai." Ken frowned over the thing.

"What does it mean?" I looked from one face to the next.

Sho shook his head. Ken shrugged.

"I've never seen anything like it," answered Hitomi, "and we've all practiced with different weights and shapes of shuriken, in preparation for using our *seihoukei.*"

"Clearly it's meant to be a message," I said irritably. "But what—and from whom?"

"Wait." Sho was frowning. "I've seen that before. The image. With the weapons and the eye."

"It's nagging at me," Ken agreed. "I was beginning to think the same thing. But where?"

Silence reigned, but then Ken's eyebrows shot high.

"Wait," Sho repeated. He and Ken looked at each other.

"Obsidian's Eye!" they chorused.

"Huh?" It meant nothing to me.

"Really?" Hitomi frowned.

"What is it?" I asked.

"It's an old guy on the Ryu Council," she said with a shrug.

"It's a *position* on the Council. The old guy just happens to be the latest one filling it," Ken corrected.

"Oh, yeah, now I know who you mean. He wears an arm band and this image is embroidered on it." Hitomi looked proud of herself for placing it.

"He has a matching tattoo underneath, on his arm," Sho said. "I've seen it when we sparred at the training grounds."

"But who is he? What does it mean?" I was still lost.

"The Obsidian's Eye is the only position on the Council that is filled by an outsider," Ken told me. It is always filled by a member of the Kuroshi family."

"You remember the story?" Hitomi asked. "The final battle, when Rialka defeated Inaba and banished him to the spirit world? There were others there, more than just Rialka's ninja clan members who had come for her."

"Yes, the earth mage, and the daimyo's men—the samurai soldiers of the man who Inaba tried to blame for his own crimes."

"Just as we are the children of the ninja there that day, so the Kuroshi are the descendants of the daimyo's men. They were struck by the same blast of magic, given gifts that day, too, and passed them on as Ryu's ancestors did."

"Different gifts," Sho said. "They were given great strength and all the many skills of a warrior or combatant."

"How nice for them," I said with a roll of my eyes. "Some of us have to do it the hard way."

"The Obsidan's Eye is the link between our people."

"And you think it is him, shooting ninja stars at me?" I asked skeptically.

"Put it this way," Sho said with a grin. "As a message, it could have been worse. That thing could easily have killed you. It didn't. That throw took skill, so whoever managed it could have taken us all out easily and quickly. They didn't."

"They could have just come and talked to us, too," I grumped.

"They didn't," Sho repeated with a shrug.

"Clearly there are eyes on us," Ken broke in. "Let's get moving. Maybe we can lose them."

We gathered up our packs, and moved out.

18

Akemi

The building shook, just before a massive boom nearly jolted her from her bed. In the distance the shouts rang out again, and this time screams, curses and unearthly roars accompanied them. Akemi huddled between the bed and the side table, her *minding* warnings going berserk in her head. No one came to move her, to check on her, to reassure her. But gradually the noise stopped. She stayed put until morning, however, pulling the pillows and blankets from the bed and dozing upright until morning came and with it, her silent, white-garbed attendants.

Still no words. No explanations. But they moved her to a regular bedroom. It was far more comfortable and grand than the hospital room she'd been in, with a carpet and lovely furnishings, books and a tall, four-poster bed. She had a closet full of clothes in her size and a full array of make-up that kept her occupied for a couple of hours.

She had a window, although it opened up onto the smallest square of garden she'd ever seen, with tall walls and a wired mesh across the top. It was so small and narrow, it only got sun at noon. She had no idea how the plants thrived.

There was no screaming here, at least. And her strength was slowly returning. But her door was locked again, and her visitors were even fewer. They fed her fine meals and left her alone.

Except for Inaba.

She forced herself to say his name after his third visit. The mirror from her previous room had been moved into the small parlor off her bedroom. He came sporadically, always accompanied by that smell of incense and one sumptuously elaborate outfit after another.

He never asked about Ryu, her family or friends. He never referred to the centuries-long fight between him and her people.

He brought her small gifts. Tiny, sweet cakes. Calligraphy supplies. A set of ebony hair sticks, pointed and hollow, carved with interesting patterns.

They talked of fashion through the ages, which she enjoyed, and which rulers had possessed the best palaces, a conversation which he appeared to take pleasure in.

She gathered her courage and asked him if she could leave her room. He watched her for several long moments before he answered. "You may not venture out. It is not safe."

"I can take care of myself," she grumbled.

He laughed. "There are creatures in my palace who would eat your tender flesh for a snack before they came to my table for dinner."

She lifted her head. "Can you not protect your guests?" she asked snidely.

"Oh, yes. But it is the ones who would befriend you who would pose the most danger." He shook his head. "Oh, to be young and innocent once more. You are a beautiful girl. You have trained all of your life, I assume, and possess certain skills of fighting and stealth. You are a lovely vessel, filled with potential, and so, many will hate you for it."

She knew that his words should not warm her.

He looked steadily at her. "Have you not tasted this truth yet, in your few years?"

She thought of the doubters, of the hostility shown by some of the people back home. Her mother had said it was all born of jealousy—and Hitomi had chosen to believe her. "I guess I have."

He nodded. "I knew it must be so."

After that they talked of history and politics and science— and she gradually realized that he was steering the conversation toward men and woman who had changed things, who had opened new worlds or steered thinking in new directions. She thought he numbered himself among such people—and the thought occurred to her that he might number her there too. She was simultaneously alarmed, flattered, and suddenly yearning.

What was he doing? Was this just a way to convince her that he was not the villain they all believed? Did he think that he could convince *her* and send her back to carry the message?

She thought about that. He must know it would never happen. She knew the stories about him. For centuries her people had witnessed his crimes. He explored dark magic. He experimented with dark creatures. He thought nothing of abducting innocents to use to practice on, or of sending horrific monsters out amidst unknowing people, just to test his theories. He'd kidnapped sorcerers and scientists to try to advance his own knowledge. He'd corrupted whole families, turning them to servitude with fear and threats and torturous persecution.

Or had he? This Inaba seemed so cultured, so knowledgeable, so calm and even-tempered.

The Council and people of Ryu would never believe her account of him.

But he thought her smart and strong enough to make the attempt.

That illicit glow grew warmer in her chest.

19

Mei

The weight of that unseen gaze stayed with me as we moved through Nashville's streets. I saw Hitomi hunch her shoulders and rub the back of her neck several times as we made our way through the busy downtown section of the city.

"That's a dangerous tell." Ken spoke up the next time she reached for her nape. "Now, whoever it is, they know you can feel them watching."

"I *can* feel it, like an icy claw," she complained.

"But he doesn't need to know it," I advised. "Now he'll be more alert, more careful. Better to keep him guessing. Do you know? Or are you oblivious? Give yourself every advantage."

"Okay. Yeah." She nodded. "I get it."

"Look," Sho interrupted. "A bus is pulling in up there. This line heads west through the city. Let's hop on it and maybe we'll ditch our unknown friend."

"Good idea," Ken agreed. He started forward. "Oops, everybody sprint!"

We took off and hopped aboard just as the driver reached to close the doors. I took one side of the bus, watching the sidewalk closely. Hitomi took the street side and Sho headed for the back while Ken dealt with our fares.

I saw nothing unusual out there. The delay as Ken paid for all of us gave a young woman the chance to slip on as well, but she headed for a seat near the back doors and pulled out a tablet.

Ken finished and moved to take a seat. His gaze was fixed on the girl and he chose a spot where he could see her easily. I noticed Sho was also gazing at her with appreciation, so I took another look.

She was Asian, and pretty. Young and dressed in that sort of casual street style that looked edgy and pristine and must cost a fortune. She carried a designer weekender bag, as far from my slightly worn, functional backpack as could be. She was fully made up, had her hair curled—and exhibited not the least bit of interest in any of us.

Sho caught me watching him stare. He gave a little shrug and turned back to focus on the street behind the bus. I turned to my side again, but there was nothing out there except people going about their business. I closed my eyes. Could I still feel the attention from our unseen watcher? Maybe. But it felt as if it had faded, or grown distant.

Good.

A few silent minutes passed, then Sho straightened. "Hey, guys. Come here a second."

I headed back. Hitomi did as well. We flanked Sho, who gestured out the window. "Look."

"Where?"

"At the bookstore. Tell me what you see."

"Pretty," I said. It was set back from the road and appeared to have a Shakespearean theme. **Much Ado About the Page**, the sign blazed in fancy script. The curb featured a solid wood screen covered in flowering garlands, a couple of rocking chairs and a glass-fronted bookcase.

"Do you see him? Quick before we move on. See the guy in the rocking chair? I swear, he signaled me a moment ago."

I shifted to the side, trying to see what he described. "I must have just missed him."

"What?" Sho frowned.

"The chair is still moving. He must have just left."

A wild look in his eye, Sho pulled Hitomi closer to him. The bus was moving again and we were leaving the store behind. "Quick. What do you see, Hitomi? Who is sitting in that chair?"

"In the rocking chair? No one." Hitomi glanced at me. "But I can see it still rocking slightly, just like Mei said. Did we just miss him?"

Sho grabbed her chin and pointed her face back. "There! You don't see anyone sitting in that chair? The one right next to the bookshelf?"

"No."

He slumped into his seat.

"Who do you see, Sho?" I asked gingerly.

"Shakespeare! Or a guy in a Shakespeare get up. Plain as day!" He frowned at our blank expressions. "First the two guys at the signs in Hot Springs. Then Hitchcock. Now Shakespeare. And none of you saw any of them." His gaze grew distant. "It must mean something."

"If you are seeing things that we cannot," I said slowly, "then it probably has something to do with your *minding*."

"Yes. That makes sense. But I don't get it. Are they trying to tell me something?"

"I don't know, anymore than I know what this means." I drew the shuriken from my pocket. "And I don't like not knowing."

"I'm with you." Exasperated, Sho flung his head into his hands.

We sat with him while he pondered. I let my mind wander too, while my fingers turned the little weapon around and around. Had my father ever mentioned anything like this? I didn't think so, not the odd shape or the symbols.

"Mei, look." Hitomi nudged me and pointed to the monitor to one side of the back doors. It had been running commercials and the occasional fluffy news piece, but now the anchors looked more serious and though the sound was off, headlines scrolled beneath them.

A growing number of encounters with strange creatures along the ravaged west coast. . . . Reports of increased **kawad** *gang activity, and established gangs extending their reach outside the major urban spots . . .*

"You know anything about that?" The other passenger had looked up from her tablet and was eyeing us carefully.

Hitomi and I exchanged glances. "No."

"Do you know if there any of those *kawad* gangs here? In Nashville?"

I shrugged. "We're not from here."

She sighed. "Me neither."

Ken moved closer. "Have you had trouble with the gangs?"

"Not me. But I'm afraid my brother, Teague, might be mixed up with them. That's why I'm here. To find him."

Ken took the seat next to her and they put their heads together to speak in lower tones. I felt a stab of pain at the sight and turned away to keep the image from burning itself into my retinas—or onto my heart.

"Boys are stupid," Hitomi said in disgust.

I sighed. "He's free to be as stupid as he likes."

"Yeah, but . . ." Hitomi narrowed her eyes. "Too bad I had to leave my bow behind."

"Hitomi!"

"Yeah? Too bad I can't cast my *minding* onto other people. I'd give her a big, hairy wart on her nose. Or sprout pimples all over his face."

Despite myself, I laughed. And then, for the first time since it happened, I let myself relive that quick kiss, back at the cache.

It had meant something to me. Because it was my first— yes. I'd never let myself get close enough to a boy to feel anything like this before. These three were my first friends, the first people I'd really trusted since my father's death.

But the kiss was special because my feelings for Ken went beyond friendship. I'd been drawn to him from the first, when he was just a new kid in the parkour crew back in Raleigh. And the attraction had grown stronger as I got to know his easy manner and quick wit, as I experienced his loyalty and saw his skill and dedication, watched him show his love and devotion to his family, his village and their cause.

He had feelings for me, too. Surely that sweet gift of silver needles had meant that he did. But I had no real experience with judging this sort of thing. His feelings might be more casual than mine. Or they might have changed after our disagreements over the mask and the kawad problem. Or after seeing me in Oni mode. My face burned just at the memory— and my real fear slipped out. Ken might have a change of heart because he's discovering that the real me is not as heroic or exciting as the girl he imagined for so long.

The thought caused a miserable tightness in my chest and a surge of panic in my gut. I'd taken the risk and allowed myself to care for him—and now I needed Ken. I didn't even want to think about doing this without him.

"Hey!" Hitomi had been studying the map next to the vid screen. "Our stop is coming up. The last one before the bus turns around and heads back east."

"Okay." I gathered up my pack, missing my makeshift bo staff. It would only draw the wrong sort of attention, though, so I'd left it at Effie's, too. "Time to head out," I called. I didn't look toward Ken. I didn't want to see him take his leave of that girl.

20

Ken

"**G**uys, listen." A foreign urgency filled Ken as he hurried to catch Mei and Hitomi. They stood, heads together as they faced west. Sho lagged behind with the girl Ken had just befriended on the bus.

"That's Duri." Ken waved his hand and paused to admire her profile as she spoke to Sho. "You know the place where we were headed, the wildlife management area nearby where we were thinking of camping? She knows something about it."

"Enough to tell you all to be careful," Duri said, moving closer and directing a blinding smile at him.

He basked a moment in that soothing warmth. Her presence was so . . . calming. And yet exciting too. Only the thought of Mei watching him made him break contact and glance her way.

She didn't look happy.

He shook himself. "Look, Mei." He pointed—and saw her focus sharpen as she turned and saw the gym situated up the street.

"Perpetual Motion," she read aloud. "It's a parkour gym?"

"Yes." Duri stepped forward, all business now. "It's where my brother and his friends hang out." She headed for the brightly painted building.

Ken started after her—but Mei reached out to grab his arm.

"I mean, normally I'd love to spend time in there," she said, low and fast. "But seriously, we've got a job to do. A big one, remember?"

Hitomi frowned. "Yes. Come on, let's get to where we're going."

"I think we need to stop here," Ken told her urgently.

"Why? What does this gym have to do with the place we need to find?"

"The guys that run this place are helping the parks department design an outdoor parkour trail up there. Duri's brother went to help out—and she says he hasn't been seen since."

"Oh." The girls exchanged glances.

"The brother's closest friend was there too—and he keeps talking of some 'creature' that they spotted up there."

"He keeps talking about big spiders," Sho added, joining them.

Mei sighed. "Then I guess we'd better talk to him."

They all trooped after Duri. She barely glanced at the gym as they entered, but Ken saw Mei pause and take a long look around. It was an impressive space, large and open. And extremely busy at the moment. A big sign hung over the registration desk.

Welcome to the PM All-Nighter Jam!

A massive scaffolding area, swarming with kids, took up one corner and a big, square tower with an observation deck sat in the center of the space. There were stairs in the middle of it and several other more interesting ways to scale the outside.

Mei paused at a spot where a series of vaults had been set up. An instructor took a flashy pass through the course, to the whoops and yells of his students. He broke it down into a simpler line and sent the first volunteer through. The boy made it, albeit without the same grace, but still he basked in the same sort of cheers and encouragement that the instructor had received.

Ken saw some of the tightness melt away from Mei's shoulders at the sound and knew she felt comfortable here. He guessed she was enjoying the positive atmosphere and missing her old crew. They'd been a laid-back, accepting bunch, like so many parkour enthusiasts. It was easy to understand why, after being alone for so long, that she'd found friends in that community.

"Ken?"

He turned to find Duri beckoning him to the registration desk. He fought a surge of annoyance at the sight of the young men gathered around her.

"Colin?" He heard one answer as he approached. "Yes, he's here. Over there."

He indicated a teenager not far away. Alone, the boy

gripped a bar and steadily lifted himself in one chin-up after another.

"Maybe they shouldn't bother him," one young man said. "You know how upset he's been."

"Hey, wait." A redheaded guy with a faux-hawk stared over Ken's shoulder. "I know you," he said to Mei. "Don't you run with the parkour crew in Raleigh?"

"Oh, yeah." Mei colored. "I used to, but I'm uh . . . moving."

"Sorry to hear that. That's a good group. I've run with them a couple of times when I was in town to visit family." He turned to the guy at the desk. "She's good, Tim."

Tim shrugged.

"You'll be careful with Colin, won't you?" the red head asked Mei. "He's missing his friend."

"His friend is my brother," Duri spoke up. "I want to talk to him and to the people in charge of setting up that trail and to anyone else who might know something about Teague's disappearance."

The casual atmosphere instantly changed, with some of them exuding sympathy and some withdrawing completely.

"Go ahead and talk to Colin," the guy at the desk said with a sigh. "I'll fetch Lawrence, the owner, to talk to you, too."

Ken stepped out ahead as they moved toward the boy. He had experience dealing with people who had encountered something they couldn't quite believe in. And he recognized a strong desire to please Duri, too.

Mei, he thought, stopping suddenly. He wanted to impress *Mei*. Not Duri.

Didn't he?

"Colin?" He called out as they drew close. "Mind if we ask you a few questions?"

"Hi." The boy lowered himself and turned to face them, his expression wary.

"Hi." Ken kept his expression friendly. "We'd like to talk to you about what happened up at the new parkour trail."

Colin's face fell. "Lawrence and the rest of them don't want me talking about it anymore."

"This is Duri." Ken motioned her forward. "She's Teague's

sister. She needs to hear your story."

Like those were the words he'd been waiting to hear, the boy lit up. He grabbed her hand. "I'm so glad you are here! You have to go the police. They'll do something if it's you. They'll listen when *you* say he's missing. If you file a report they'll have to do *something*."

Duri stroked his hand. "Yes, of course I will. I just got into town and I came straight here to talk to you."

He looked dazedly happy to hear it, but then, abruptly, the boy's excitement faded. "Wait. Maybe you shouldn't be here. It's not safe here, either."

"Tell us what happened up there, Colin." Ken nodded encouragement.

"You won't believe me," the boy groaned. "No one does."

"Tell us," Mei urged. "You'd be surprised what we'd believe. We've seen some weird stuff."

Slowly, he began to tell his tale. The two friends had traveled up to the site in the wildlife management area. "They have hunting and fishing there, but hiking and bird-watching and biking too. The parkour course is going to be amazing—if we get to finish it. We were digging postholes to anchor a floating chain when we heard someone calling for help. It came from the woods."

Ken exchanged glances with the girls. "Was it a woman's voice?"

"No. It sounded like a guy. You know, a young guy."

That was a surprise, but Ken just nodded.

"We thought it must be a hiker or biker. You know, just an accident. Every day. Normal."

"It wasn't?"

"No. When we went in, the forest was quiet. Dead quiet. No birds or bugs making any noise, you know what I mean? None at all." He shuddered. "Spooky."

"You went in on foot?" Ken asked.

"Teague walked. I was riding my uni-scoot." He gestured toward the far wall where a self-balancing one-wheeled vehicle waited. "It's rigged for off-road. The only thing we could hear was the roll of it over the leaves."

"Teague was behind me," he continued. "I heard him make

a noise."

"What kind of noise?" Mei asked.

"Like he was surprised—like a surprised grunt. At the same time, something hit my head and bounced to the ground. I looked up—and only saw his feet kicking as he went straight up into the trees."

"*Straight* up?" Mei asked.

"Yeah, like something hauled him out of there."

"And that was the last time you saw my brother?" Duri interrupted.

Tears welled in Colin's eyes, but he kept his composure. "Yes. I took some of the guys back up there to look for him, but there was no sign of him."

Duri nodded as if she were merely filing the information away. "Here comes the owner. Perhaps I'd better go and speak with him."

Ken watched her walk away. He only stopped when he realized Mei had encouraged Colin to tell them the rest of what had happened that day.

"It had to have been something big that pulled Teague up like that," he insisted. "Something strong."

"Colin," Mei spoke low. "You said that something hit you on the head, and then bounced on the ground?"

"Yeah. It landed in front of me. I bent down to pick it up. And that's when I—I froze—because something big was *behind* me. I knew it. And I didn't wait to find out what it was. I just leaned forward and sent my scooter shooting out of there. About a second later I felt something huge hit ground right behind me—right where I had been."

"You didn't see it?" Ken hid his disappointment.

"No. I kept going, and if I'd turned to look it would have slowed my scooter. But then I hit a slope and went tumbling down arse over elbow. I could hear whatever it was coming through the brush behind me. When I landed, my uni-scoot crashed up against me. I picked it up and ran full on. I knew that thing was close, but I ran as fast as I could—and then I busted out into a clearing where some people were setting up a target range. Whatever it was—it didn't follow me out of the brush and trees."

"No one saw it?" Ken asked.

"No—but they heard it. A bunch of them thought it must have been a bear, because it sounded so big. They took their guns and explored a little, but didn't see or hear anything else."

"It could have been a bear, I suppose," Ken said thoughtfully—but he doubted Colin would buy it.

He was right.

"It wasn't," the teenager said flatly.

"How do you know?" Hitomi asked.

"Because it didn't make any wuffling sounds or anything else a bear makes. It was dead silent. And fast. A bear would not have lifted Teague like that." He paused and motioned us in closer. "And because it followed me here."

"What?" Mei reared back. "You've seen it here?"

"Well, not all of it. Not exactly."

"*What*, exactly?" demanded Mei.

"I saw it move, in the shadows. I heard it again, in the alley between this building and the next. No one believes me. Or they don't want me scaring people away. Even the police said they would come out and look—but they didn't." His lip curled. "But I'll show them. I ordered a camera to rig in the alley back there. It will be back. And this time I'll keep the proof."

Ken straightened. "What sort of proof?"

"I had proof. Now it's gone. A foot."

"A foot of what?" Hitomi sounded confused.

"An *actual* foot. The monster's foot."

"Tell us what happened," demanded Mei.

He nodded. "I was taking out the garbage—back to the dumpster in the alley. I help out around here—these guys have been good to me."

Ken nodded encouragement.

"I had just dumped the garbage. I heard a noise. A weird, clicking sound." He stopped for a moment. "When I put the lid on the dumpster down, it was there, hanging above me in the shadows. It was so dark, I couldn't really see, but I could feel the mass of it up there. Close."

"What did you do?"

"I ducked. I felt the whoosh when it made a grab for me

and missed. Quick as I could, I threw a rock a few feet away and then another into a pile of crates further down the alley."

"Did it fall for it?" Mei asked with a twinge of approval coloring her tone.

"Yeah. And I used the opportunity to haul butt for the door. It heard me, though, and came back quick. I only got away because I tricked it—did a sweet push off the opposite wall and went through the door when it was reaching for me over there. I made it inside, slammed the door—and caught its foot."

"Ugh." Hitomi grimaced.

"You sliced its foot off with one slam of the door?" Mei sounded skeptical.

"No. Not at the first slam. It tried to force its way in, but every time it thrust out, I slammed back. It made the weirdest noises! And I yelled my head off. When the guys came running, it started pulling away at the same time as I slammed—and the end of its foot just fell off."

"What did it look like?"

"Just a nub. I think it must be a bug or spider of some sort. It was like it had a hinge at the end of its leg and just a rounded end as a foot. But it was disgusting because the blood was thick and nasty green."

"Ugh," Hitomi said it again.

"Do you still have the foot?"

"No. Lawrence and some of the guys thought I was pulling some sort of prank." He flushed. "Like I would joke about something like that while Teague was still missing."

Ken clapped a sympathetic hand on his shoulder.

"They tossed it. And now I don't even have the evidence," Colin sighed. "But I did get a picture. It's on my tab. I'll show it to you." He glanced around. "But we'll have to do it somewhere else or in the back or something. I can't let Lawrence see me showing it around."

He beckoned and the girls started right after him. Ken hung back. "Hey, Lawrence is waving at us to come and talk. Want me to handle it?"

Mei waved back.

"And I'll just fill Duri in on everything too," he called.

Mei came to an abrupt halt. "Why would you do that?"

Ken thought about it. He frowned. They had to be careful, didn't they? Except . . . "I think she would want to know."

Saying it out loud convinced him further.

Mei looked at him oddly. "What makes you say that?"

He considered. The thought just hung there, right in the front of his mind. He struggled to look past it—and found something else. "Her brother. This could be the same creature that snatched her brother."

She nodded thoughtfully and continued to stare at him.

Ken turned back to find Duri smiling at him—and he felt warm and tingly, knowing suddenly that he'd done the right thing.

21

Akemi

"Have you wondered why I trusted you with these?" Inaba was dressed in gorgeous, icy blue silk robes today, trimmed in sparkling silver. He gestured and the sharp ebony hair sticks rotated slowly off of my makeup table and rotated above it.

Akemi rolled her eyes. "Did you think I was stupid enough to try and use them against *you*?"

He cocked his head. "No."

"But you thought I might use them to threaten the ever-silent servants? Pretty obvious, as tests go." She laughed a little. "I hope that not being an obvious idiot means that I passed."

"Perhaps they represent more than one sort of test," he said thoughtfully. "Now, I must go. I will return tomorrow afternoon. It would please me if you would wear them." He let them fall back down to the table. "And also the brown leather corset in your wardrobe." With a flick of his fingers, he faded away and Akemi was left staring at the empty mirror while her heart pounded.

The next day she wore the hair sticks, the corset—and the layered black tunic and tights that went with it. It covered her completely, but was fitted and slightly padded at the joints with overlapping, scale-like embellishments. It made her feel . . . powerful.

When she wasn't feeling like a bundle of agitated nerves, actually. Was he going to allow her to finally leave these rooms? Who would escort her? What was out there? Would she find a way to escape—and should she take it? Did she even want to?

She shook her head. Surely this was another test.

Roaming from room to room, she was pleased with how much stronger she felt now. All the rest and rich food had done her good. Abruptly, she straightened. The smell of incense drifted through the room.

She whirled, but the mirror was empty.

"*Akemi.*"

"Yes?" Where was his voice coming from?

"Go to the other room and look out into the garden."

Swallowing her nerves, she went. The sun shone outside. She yearned to feel it.

She jumped suddenly as a huge creature materialized in the center of the garden, taking up nearly the whole space and crushing a couple of flowering bushes.

Huge, horned and massively muscled, the creature blinked and shook itself, as if it was just as surprised as she. Its skin was green and its eyes shone white as it turned and saw her through the glass. It visibly bristled—

And then its shining eyes dimmed and went flat and black. She knew, somehow, that the creature was gone. It was Inaba in there.

"How are you doing that?" she breathed.

The creature raised a fist and the glass in front of her retracted into the floor. "A delicate blend of technology and magic," it said in Inaba's smooth voice. "Not perfect, but occasionally useful." The monster stepped through and extended an arm. "Would you care to see my court?"

Sucking in a breath, she reached up.

The halls were sterile and white at first, but then they crossed through a set of electronic double doors and the passageways widened. The floors here were stone, and the walls covered with some sort of woven textured material.

The silence gave way also. She could hear the murmur of far off voices, but nearer sounded a shrill, squeaking noise. Inaba took a turn to the right and it grew louder. As they approached an arched doorway, she saw a gorgeous antechamber, with two walls of painted screens and one open to the outside—and the creature making the sound.

A long, thin creature that looked remarkably like a tiny dragon—made of worn and ragged cloth. It snapped ferociously at the wooden staff holding it pinned to the floor, and each snap was accompanied by a squeak of anger.

"Stealth, I told you, did I not? I want to hear his secrets, not that his kitchen staff is being terrorized." It was a woman who held him down. Young and lovely, she wore wide legged black pants, a ragged pink tunic and a wide, green cinch-waist belt that hung with several weapons. Her staff's blunt end rested on the frightened creature, the other end looked sharp enough to cut glass and the middle was fashioned of double, white handles.

"Yes, Tsubaki. I hear you. Secrets. I will get them," the little dragon whined.

"Get back there, then. The dinner party approaches—and it is already afternoon in that part of the world." The girl, catching sight of their approach, let the creature go and snapped to attention. "My lord!" She bowed deeply. The tiny dragon disappeared.

"Tsubaki." The monster next to Akemi nodded its head in regal fashion while the girl straightened and shot her a look of suspicion and dislike.

"Do you need me to dispose of this human for you, my lord?"

Akemi glared at her. Inaba merely chuckled. "Thank you, but Akemi is my guest."

He swept on, carrying Akemi with him out the door. He paused next to a lush tree, thick with green leaves and many petaled pink flowers. It was the lone spot of green in a zen garden full of stone and sand and rocks, but the air was fresh and cool and she breathed it in gratefully. Inaba stood still a moment and she had the chance to enjoy the tree's luxuriant growth before they moved on along a covered passage. She glanced back to the warrior girl as they went.

Tsubaki lifted her chin in challenge. Akemi's *minding* surged in warning, but she had to satisfy herself with an answering grin as they walked away.

The covered walkway edging the border of the garden was long and wide. Akemi had to take two steps to the creature's every one, but still, she drank in the novelty of being outside—until they reached another set of beautifully painted screens. They slid open and Inaba led her into a large, grand hall.

She actually stopped, gazing around in awe. The space was

cavernous, huge and constructed of all lavishly decorated and carved stone. Rows of columns supported an immense, painted roof, and each one told a story in its layers of stone. Bright red banners hung from on high. Smaller columns topped with stone lanterns were interspersed throughout the vast room.

And everywhere were *yokai*.

The alarms were a constant ringing in her head, but she could not help but stare. Scores of them milled about. Small and large, beautiful and horrendous—and every one of them bowed low to Inaba—and directed a seething hate at her.

She clutched her head.

"Do not be alarmed. You are under my protection." Inaba began to walk forward, down the middle of the cavern. "For now."

He led the long way toward the front of the hall. There, two plain pillars, painted vivid red, separated an alcove from the rest of the wall. A massive mirror, elaborately framed, took up the entire back wall. The whole, smaller space was lit by a multitude of varied candles.

As Inaba stepped close, a groaning noise started up—and the floor of the alcove opened up. A round dais rotated upward—upon it a massive throne.

"You may stand here." Inaba left her standing before the dais on his right side. The creatures gathered closer as he ascended and took the throne.

"What tidings?" he asked.

Akemi rubbed the spot behind her ear. Beyond her *minding's* anxiety she could hear something low and . . . rumbling.

A figure stepped forward to face the creature on the throne. He looked like a human monk and kept his whole body bowed low. "Biwa Studios reports timeframes on schedule."

"Good." The monster containing Inaba nodded.

The monk straightened then, and began to back away. Akemi started. He had no face.

A hag-like creature stepped up. She stared at Akemi and wiped drool from the side of her mouth.

The rumbling etched up a notch.

"What of the Chimi?" Inaba asked.

"They are poised in the marshes and along the coast." She bowed. "All are ready."

"Very good."

The hag withdrew and silence fell. Except for the . . . growling. It was growling she heard, vibrating in the small spaces in her ear. Inaba sat, waiting.

The growl erupted into a full-fledged yowl. Akemi's *minding* shrieked at her and she ducked just as a large form swooped at her head.

Rising up, her fists clenched, she watched the creature bank high and land on a ledge near the top of a pillar. It settled and glared down at her—and she had to forcibly hold back her gasp. A Nue!

"What insult do you offer us, Lord Inaba?" The creature's voice sounded gravely, the monkey's face on its hodgepodge body looked angry. "Why bring this human here among us? She reeks of *minding*. She's obviously a spawn of Ryu."

A wave of muttering agreement swelled across the hall.

"She is indeed from Ryu," Inaba answered.

Akemi refused to shrink before the howls of protest and cries of anger. She knew enough to know it would be the end of her.

"You cannot be thinking of making her part of your court?" the Nue protested, his snake's tail lashing back and forth.

"That is exactly what I'm thinking. She could give us singularly unique advice." Inaba leaned down and looked at her with a question in those flat, black eyes. "If she wished it?"

She wanted to scream. To cry. To run. To stay. He'd put her in an impossible situation. If she denied it, they would rip her apart. But did she want to deny it? She'd come so far down this path—perhaps too far to turn back.

She nodded.

The Nue leaped from its high perch. Landing before her, it began to pace. "She must meet the challenge, as we all did— and prove her worthiness."

Shouts of agreement.

"Let me fight the Ryu human, Lord Inaba. My honor demands it."

Surely not here? Not now? She had no weapons.

Frantically, she scoured her memories, searching for what she'd heard or learned about fighting such a powerful and old *yokai* as a Nue.

"No." The room fell silent at Inaba's answer. "How did those newspaper men say it? I think you've been scooped. I believe that Tsubaki issued Akemi's first challenge."

The Nue snarled in frustration, but fell back with the rest of them when Inaba raised a hand. They all parted and the warrior girl Tsubaki stepped into the empty space formed down the middle of the room. She bowed her acceptance and began to walk forward, her staff twirling.

Inaba leaned forward. "You said you could fight. You told me you could take care of yourself. I heard you. Now it is time to see if *you* have been paying attention."

Akemi stepped out of the alcove. Without hesitation she strode toward the approaching woman. She would only have one shot at this.

Tsubaki never paused. Her staff was raised and when her strike came, it was *fast*.

But Akemi's *minding* told her where it would land and she was already inside the strike zone on the downswing. When the staff hit the floor, she threw all of her weight into a punch to the girl's jaw.

It came as a shock, and Tsubaki actually stumbled back and fell. Akemi took the chance to dart in close again and rip a weapon off of her wide belt.

It was a *kusari fundo*—a thin chain bound between two weights. Not highly effective against a staff, but better than nothing. She swung it experimentally and the tension in the room went up a notch.

Tsubaki didn't seem to care. She struck again as soon as she was up—and this time Akemi was on the outside of the blow when it landed. She wrapped the chain around the double handle and yanked hard—and the staff separated as she'd hoped. She reached out and snatched up the sharp half before her opponent realized what was happening.

Akemi didn't kid herself though. The staff was not her weapon, as it clearly was Tusbaki's. She fended off a few blows, moving backward all the while, toward the entrance they'd come in. Cries of foul play from the yokai rose up around them when she stepped out onto the covered walkway, but Inaba was suddenly there and nodded to show he would allow it.

Tsubaki looked suddenly alarmed. She doubled her attack, and it was all Akemi could do to parry her blows. She gave it up abruptly and turned and sprinted. When she reached the lone tree outside the alcove, she shifted her grip on the spear and held the blade high, aimed for the spot where the trunk began to split into branches.

"Forfeit!" she demanded, panting. "Or I stab this into the heart of the wood!"

Tsubaki glared hatred and disbelief—but stepped back and let her staff fall.

Inaba stepped forward. Akemi bowed and offered up the half-staff. With a shake of his head, bid her rise. "To the victor goes the weapon—and a spot in my court."

Akemi hefted the staff, but then turned and handed it to the warrior girl. "I think I'd rather have this." She wrapped the weighted chain around her forearm.

"I wasn't sure if you had picked up on the fact that Tsubaki is the *yokai* spirit of the tree," Inaba said.

"Tell her to change her name, or at least shorten it." Akemi tossed her head. "And maybe don't dress to match your tree," she told the girl herself.

Inaba opened his mouth to speak, but sudden light flashed in the creature's eyes. They blinked back and forth between shining white and black several times before the black held sway. He leaned down to speak so only Akemi could hear. "Don't imagine the testing is over yet."

The black blinked out then, and the *yokai* all melted away. The white clad human servants came from the alcove and began to lead the bemused creature away—and two of them also took her arms and escorted her back to her rooms.

<u>**22**</u>

Mei

The pics were exactly like Colin had described—except he'd forgotten to mention the foot was hairy. I let Hitomi handle the sympathetic gross-out while I studied the other pics of insects he had saved for comparison. He was right—the thing did look like the nubby end of a spider's foot.

"Colin, you said something hit you on the head and you bent down to pick it up."

"Yeah." He'd gone suspiciously quiet.

"You still have it, don't you?"

He flushed. "Don't tell the guys, will you? It's the only real proof I have left."

"What was it?" I asked.

"Do you promise not to tell?"

"I do promise."

He reached in his pocket. Staring about to make sure no one was watching, he motioned for me to come closer. Hitomi and I both inched toward him.

His fingers unfolded and we saw the small, plastic spider in his palm, shining lurid, neon green.

We exchanged glances while he tucked it away again.

"Listen, hang on tight to that, Colin, okay?" I told him. "Don't tell anyone you have it, not even Duri or the police."

"Really, not even them?"

"Not yet, okay? Not until I tell you. Can you do that?"

"Yeah. No one else knows."

"Don't lose it," I cautioned him.

"I'll keep it right here," he assured me.

He wanted to head back to speak further with Duri, so Hitomi and I huddled to consult.

"It definitely looks like a Jorogumo is mixed up in this, doesn't it?"

Hitomi sighed. "Yeah. And we're going to have to stop

her, aren't we?"

"What else can we do?" I waved toward the busy gym at the end of the hallway we were tucked into. "Let all of these guys become spider food?"

She groaned. "Why is she hanging around here? Why couldn't we just give her the dew and be done with it? Head to Seattle and face the real work we have to do? All of that is going to be hard enough."

"I know." I sank down against the wall, right next to a collection of mops and brooms and a life-sized, stand-up cut out of a scruffy, European guy hawking a brand of parkour shoes. "Because nothing is ever easy?"

"You can say that again."

"That plastic spider—it reminded me of something."

"The cube? The one we found back at Ryu?"

"Yes. It was right where the Wind Demon fell in battle, and the Tengu that Ken and I defeated dropped something similar too, when it was defeated." I sighed. "You know what that means?"

"Inaba. He's mixed up in this."

"It does seem so. And maybe that little spider figure is important."

"You think that's why the monster followed him here?"

"Why else?"

"Listen Mei . . ." Hitomi hesitated. "You don't think . . ."

I raised my eyebrows and whispered, "Duri?"

"You had the same suspicion?"

"Yeah—but I was afraid to mention it."

"Why?"

"Because what if I start to think that every other girl that Ken shows an interest in is a *yokai*?"

She laughed.

"Ken and Sho are acting strange about her, don't you think?"

"Well, I've never been around when they were near 'outside' girls, you know? But I never would have expected them to . . . hover . . . like that."

"Yeah. Me neither." Ken and I had traveled together when we first got to know each other. We'd laughed and talked—and argued—but how he was acting with Duri was . . . different.

Maybe he just liked her better.

"She did say she'd just got into town," Hitomi said slowly. "Do you think it's a lie?"

"Maybe. Or it could just be semantics. Maybe she just got into town from the woods where she was busy eating that poor boy."

"You don't think she's really his sister?"

"Does she seem all that upset to you?"

"No, not really," Hitomi mused. "And if it was your brother, wouldn't you have headed to the authorities first? Or at least by now? Why is she hanging around here?"

"Scoping out her next meal," I said darkly.

"So, what do we do?"

"Keep our eyes open? Watch her. And we've got to find a place to stay tonight. It's getting late. We'll head out early and then see how the boys act when she isn't so close anymore."

* * *

Lawrence made things both easier and more complicated when he invited us to spend the night at the gym, along with the participants of the all-nighter jam.

"Everyone will be up late," he warned. "The pizza doesn't come until midnight—and it will give folks a second wind. They'll train and play until the wee hours, and then they'll collapse to sleep in the pits or on the mats all over the gym."

He invited Duri too—and she accepted. Why did no one else find that odd? He gave her the bed he kept in a high loft for the nights he stayed over to work. Hitomi and I rolled our eyes at that—and again when he and Ken and some other guys made a show of helping her up to the loft. If we were right, then she could have probably jumped up there from ground level.

We were invited to hang our hammocks on the next level down from the loft. It was not much more than a landing, but it had convenient vertical bars bolted to the edges and it was big enough for our two rigs. Colin insisted on staying in the loft— to protect Duri. Sho and Ken planned to bunk on the gym floor beneath our level.

Neither Hitomi or I were tired yet, though. Not surprising,

considering we'd spent most of the day riding. She begged the use of the computer at the registration desk. Sho came down and whispered that he was going to ask discreet questions about Teague and what the others thought about the situation—but ruined it by adding that he thought Duri would like to know.

And Ken—he never descended from the loft, staying up there with Duri and Lawrence the whole evening.

It drove me a little batty—and spurred me into doing something I wouldn't normally do.

I dropped the spell and let my eyes show.

Careful to keep them mostly hidden beneath my hair, I climbed the ladder to the loft and beckoned Ken over. "You want to get some training in?" I asked. "Together?"

He glanced back at Duri and my blood started to boil. He gave no indication that he'd even noticed the change. "Maybe later."

I took out my frustrations on the scaffolding. Their set up was fabulously complex—and when one of the young kids saw my eyes—he adjusted his shorts and rolled out . . . a tail. I grinned at him, gave him a high five and we hit the bars. He was insanely good, as one might expect, and I had a grand time climbing, swinging, balancing across and dive rolling from the bars. For good measure, I practiced my flags for a while until my shoulders ached and I was pleasantly tired.

I joined in on a circle then, as a girl and her friend staged a trick-off, clapping and whooping it up with everyone else. I indulged in some midnight pizza. And then I smacked the spell back into place, climbed up to the loft, stuck my head over and reminded Ken that we had an early morning.

Startled, he looked up from where he and the others sat talking. He blinked at his watch and agreed. A couple of minutes later he climbed down and joined Sho in setting up a spot to sleep.

We weren't the only ones bedding down. The music selection had turned from raucous to a softer electronic vibe. Groups of people gathered to work on particular skills, but others had curled up in corners or sacked out on stacked mats.

I sat and prepared the set of cargo pants I meant to wear tomorrow. Just good planning to trick them out for possible action. Effie had given us all a few potions to use if things went sour with the gatekeeper. But was the gatekeeper here with us already? I didn't know, but I wanted to be ready. I tucked her gifts into pockets and also lined my special compartment with other small tools I liked to carry. Then I climbed into my hammock and swung there a while, thinking over the day and missing the stars overhead, the wind in my hair and the leaves rustling above.

There was no sound from the loft above us. Lawrence had left when Ken did and now he worked with a group gathered around the p-bars. That left Duri and Colin up there, I thought. I was pretty sure I would wake up if either tried to climb down in the night, but at the thought I decided to get up and adjust my hammock so that my leg rested against the wall with the ladder. Now I'd feel the vibration if anyone tried to sneak down.

After that, finally, I drifted off.

* * *

A good notion, after all, because it was a vibration that woke me—a small buzz against my knee every time someone took a stealthy step down the ladder. I rolled over, turning my face away, but toward the spot where they would have to cross to continue down to the next level.

All movement ceased, but I kept my breathing even and soon enough they were climbing down again, slight and slow. Someone was being careful.

My heart began to pound as the shadow crossed my field of vision. Duri.

Of course. She paused at the next ladder. I could feel the weight of her gaze. Then she slipped over the edge and disappeared.

After a moment I carefully rolled out of my nylon nest. Pulling on my shoes and my cargo pants, I crept over and placed a hand on the ladder's bolted anchor. Again, I could feel each step as she climbed down. Then the vibrations ceased— but something told me to wait until I peered over.

Agitation grew as the seconds slipped by. Finally, I took the risk—and I was glad I had waited. She was just now leaving the ladder below. I narrowed my eyes, thinking she would bend down and wake Ken, but she stepped over him without hesitating.

The gym was dark and quiet. Everyone slept. It was difficult to follow her as she moved away, and once she passed beyond the center tower, I lost her completely. Moving stealthily, I slid down the ladder in two leaps, landing silently on the mat next to Ken's feet.

He didn't stir. No one did. The whole place was eerily silent. Giving in to my nerves—and my wishes—I bent down to shake him awake. But he slept on. Sho, too, refused to wake. Frustrated, I looked up. Would Hitomi have awakened, if I tried before I came down?

A rattle sounded—loud in the silence. I froze. It came again, and then again, faster and louder.

It was the door at the end of the hallway we'd been in earlier. The door to the alleyway.

Taking a couple of steps, I peered down there—and nearly jumped out of my skin when I spotted a dark silhouette in the shadows. It didn't move. Neither did I. Frozen, I waited while the door rattled again. Someone—or something—wanted in. The shadow was taller than Duri. Who was it? Would they open the door?

Seconds passed—and then I realized. It was the standing cardboard cut-out of the shoe guy. No one was down there.

Where was Duri? Crouching down, I scanned the gym but saw nothing. I inched back and shook Ken again. I patted his face, pinched his arm. This wasn't natural.

Fine, then. I could handle this on my own. I looked around for his pack, hoping to grab a *seihoukei* or two, but it wasn't near him.

Another rattle—and this time I heard a soft snick at the end. I moved quickly back to the hallway and saw a strip of soft light that meant the door was standing slightly open.

I drew my knife. I hadn't seen a thing, hadn't caught so much as a glimpse of movement. Duri could not have snuck past me. Could she? Had she opened the door? Gone out? Or was she somewhere inside the gym—waiting?

I couldn't ignore the image of a Jorogumo chasing Colin in that alleyway. My gut was telling me that only an idiot would go down that hall—but what was the alternative? I had to make sure such a monster didn't come in to a building full of sleeping victims.

I inched my way down on silent feet. Even before I reached the slightly open door, I could hear—it. Something large. Something quick. It sounded like it was scurrying on the side of the building, around and above the door.

A horrid thought struck me and I moved closer to the door, waiting for my eyes to adjust.

Nothing.

I hoped I was wrong. But I leaned a little from side to side, adjusting my perspective—and that did it.

A bit of reflected streetlight outlined a massive web stretched across the entire doorway.

For several seconds I only breathed, trying not to panic.

I reached into one of my deep pockets and gripped the canister there. Thanks to Effie, I was somewhat prepared for this—but I needed a plan of action.

My mind raced. Could I fight this creature myself? Not like I had another option. Was it Duri? Or was she still inside? Was I facing two of them? If I was, then it would be better to split them up—and keep the creature outside from getting in.

Before I could think too much about it, I tucked my blade in my boot and pulled out the canister. Green lid. Good. I plucked a small, thin rod from my other pocket, then stood, breathing deeply and visualizing what I meant to do.

I eased the door open further. No reaction from outside. The scrabbling noise continued over the door. Maybe it was finishing and anchoring its web.

Now.

Like a dancer, I moved quickly, one motion flowing into another. I shoved the tool into the lock, then kicked down on it, breaking it off and jamming the tumblers. Facing the canister outward, I sprayed the web.

For a moment, nothing happened. Then a green spark flew out of the middle of the web. If it had been any other situation, I would have enjoyed watching the gradual spit and dazzling green glimmer as the web started to dissolve in a sparkling display from the center, outward.

The motion above stopped, but I kept going. I reached

behind me and grabbed the life-sized parkour shoe guy and launched him through the dissolving web and into the alley.

The creature leaped after it. Oh, good gracious gods and ancestors—it *was* a spider. A huge, hairy, many-eyed monster.

I slipped out of the door and pulled it closed behind me. The lock was demolished. Good. It wasn't getting in that way.

But neither was I. I took in the narrow alley. Wherever I was, that thing could climb the wall next to me, drop down and pin me—and the battle would be over before it started. But the crates that Colin had mentioned were still stacked about twenty feet away. I took off for them, intent on using them to get to the roof where Spider-zilla and I would be on more even ground.

But the Jorogumo had other ideas. It had already caught on to my trick with the cardboard figure and turned back. Now it took a gigantic leap and landed right in front of me.

Slowly it turned to face me. Its odd clicks and chittering sent shivers down my spine. It waved its striped front legs at me and I saw that one of them was indeed missing a foot. A multitude of eyes stared down at me—two large in the center and several more, smaller orbs ranged above.

All of those eyes. That's probably why it recognized my feint right when I tried to dodge past it. It snagged my leg with a loop of spider web and tugged. I fell and it began to drag me in.

I rolled over on my back and stared into the two biggest, multi-faceted eyes, shrank from the sight of the beckoning, wiggling mandibles besides its mouth. Struggling, I allowed it to draw me closer . . . closer. *There*. Judging that I was in range, I suddenly I sat up and pulled my knife from my boot, cut the web and aimed a powerhouse kick at its eye.

Screeching, it let me go. I was instantly up and running for the crates.

It didn't linger. Still making an unholy noise, it came in pursuit and threw a line of web at my feet, connecting my boot to a loose crate. I fell, but rolled, cutting myself free again, but it jumped over my head, throwing another loop and catching my knife hand, hooking the other end to the alley wall and immobilizing that arm.

I switched hands and cut through again, but it was slowing

me down and sooner or later it was going to get both hands at once. I needed to get on that roof where there would be fewer anchors for it to make use of.

But it was ahead of me now, perched on the side of the wall and blocking my way. Its legs bent as if it was poised to jump.

I knew it was over if it landed on me. I'd never break free of all of those legs. So I did what I had to do—and waiting for the exact instant before it launched itself—I threw my blade at it, as hard as I could.

It caught my motion and shifted in midair, avoiding the knife, but missing me and leaving the way clear.

But I was only on the third crate up when it came back and landed at the bottom of the stack—and now I had no knife. It climbed up, rearing back and reaching for me—and I surprised it by slipping down a level and kicking at its soft underbelly with both feet.

I heard the air whoosh out of it. It must have hurt, because it slipped and scrambled down. I turned and climbed quickly to the top of the pile.

The *too short* pile.

I couldn't reach the roof. One crate—shards, *half* a crate more and I could have pulled myself up and over. The Jorogumo sat at the bottom, taking in the situation. I swear it gave me a spidery smirk. Resting its front legs against the bottom crate, it waited to see what I would do.

I jumped. And again. I tried to get a good hold of the edge, but it was too far. My fingers only barely touched and slid away. I jumped a third time, then looked down to see the creature starting a more careful ascent.

Something whizzed over my head. I ducked, but it would have been too late, had it been aimed for me. Instead, I stared up at a large shuriken stuck in the side of the building, still quivering.

What? Who? I wanted to look around, to scout out just who it was who followed and tossed these things at me, but there was no time. With a cry of gratitude and relief I jumped up, landed a foot on the weapon and pushed up to reach the roof.

Behind me, the spider surged upward. It had no intention of letting me get far. But I turned, reached down, and hanging precariously, I yanked the ninja star from the wall.

Just as I'd thought—though it was decidedly bigger, it was marked in the same way as the one from the market. I didn't pause to think or analyze. Instead I pulled up a bit to steady myself, then took a swing at the creature as it reached for me. The weapon's sharp blade sliced right through one of the monster's furry, striped front legs.

Roaring back, it screamed at me in a high-pitched register that made my ears and teeth hurt. Instead of retreating this time, pain and anger goaded it up and toward me. Without thinking, I raised my arm and threw the shuriken straight down. The blow struck hard and true and cleaved one of the giant eyes in two.

It fell back, legs folding in as it tumbled down the crates. When it hit the ground it crumpled into a ball, rocking and keening. I took the chance to scan the alley and surrounding rooftops, but saw nothing.

"Come out!" I shouted.

No answer. No sound at all, save for the creature's crying. Sighing, I stood, then turned and ran across the roof to the front of the building. Shimmying down the drainpipe, I paused at the locked front door to sort out my lock picks and had it open in seconds. I let myself in, then locked it again behind me.

The gym still lay dark and quiet. Everyone still slept. I struck out for my friends, but paused as a small noise sounded from behind the registration desk.

I reached for my knife before realizing it was still on the ground outside. Closing my eyes, I hoped I could get it back. But for now, I crouched down and crept in the direction of the desk.

Another noise—a small moan. Utterly silent, I eased toward the table that had been set up there—until Duri rose out of the dark and turned to face me, surprise written all over her face. She had red sauce smeared across her mouth and a pizza box in one hand.

"Oh, hi," she mumbled. "You hungry, too?" She lifted the box. "There's plenty left."

23

Akemi

Something woke Akemi—and at first she was only irritated. She hadn't been sleeping well, despite endless hours practicing with her new *kusari-fundo*. Her head had been in overdrive since the fight in Inaba's court—and he hadn't returned to her rooms since.

She had no idea what it all meant, but she knew the next time she went out—if there were a next time—it wouldn't be so easy. That Nue waited. She could feel it. She'd racked her brains—she'd known she'd heard Reik talk of battling one—but what had he said? How had he defeated it?

She'd remembered finally, when she'd tired of endless repetition with her chain, and sat down at her makeup table. She'd picked up the hair sticks Inaba had bid her wear that day. And the thought suddenly occurred to her. Maybe he really hadn't sent her out unarmed?

She'd run a finger over the carved holes in the sticks—and she'd finally remembered. A hollow arrow, that's what Reik had said he'd needed to defeat the creature. It had made a whistling sound as it flew, hit the creature in flight—and acted like a special, single purpose *seihoukei*.

She'd picked the stick up, launched it at her sofa cushions— and smiled at the high-pitched whistle it let out before it stuck in the pillow.

She'd been sleeping with them ever since, and wearing them all day. Now her *minding* woke her with a sound like a gong and a rustling noise whispered in her bedroom—from up high— and she slid a hand under her pillow to grip them tight.

"I know you are awake, human. You stink of fear—as well you should."

"I guess you just stink, then."

It shrieked an angry response. "Too stupid to know you will never survive in this court. I would normally enjoy sitting back and watching one of the Oni eat your liver, but I cannot. It is ridiculous that I should have been defeated by your pasty human villagers and their *tree*. But now your death will buy back a bit of my honor."

Akemi slid off of the bed, letting the sound of the creature's grievances cover her movement. The lights were all out. She could only vaguely see the Nue's dark form in the corner of the ceiling, but she heard the scrape of its tiger claws when it launched for her bed.

Wait for it. As it pounced on her pillow, she let loose one hair stick, then the other. Their whistles sounded loud in the dark. The first one missed. She cursed as she heard it bounce off and hit the floor. But the second one struck true. The Nue screeched in terror and anger—and then it was gone.

Shaking, she stood. She turned on all of the lights. The door into the hallway stood open. She contemplated it, fingering the hair stick, for a long while.

Then she gathered up her chain and her stick, pulled a chair to the middle of the sitting room, sat down and faced the door. And waited.

She awoke, still there, in the morning. Sunlight and the scent of incense. The door was closed. Inaba was in the mirror.

"Come, child," he beckoned. "I have questions for you. And a job."

24

Mei

We set out early the next morning. I was relieved to be on foot again, and even more relieved to be heading out of the city and into the suburbs where we encountered more trees, grass and growing things. But mostly I was happy that Duri had not come with us.

It had been a near thing.

Duri had followed, pizza in hand this morning, as I'd worked hard to force Ken, then Sho, awake. Hitomi had popped right up, and so had all of the rest of the females in the gym. But all of the guys had been slow to stir. We left them to it and had all trooped cautiously out to the alley. Duri had trailed along.

The Jorogumo had gone, but a trail of green ichor meant that it likely still lived. Duri had stared thoughtfully at the slime, then tossed the pizza aside. Both boys rushed to reassure her. I turned away to look for my knife. Combing the alley, I found it and tucked it away with a sigh of relief. My father had forged that blade especially for me, and it had seen me through four years of danger, isolation and loneliness after his death.

Sourly, I thought I would have missed that weapon more than Duri appeared to miss her brother. She never mentioned him. Nor did she ask what had happened in the alley, although she did go along with Ken's assumption that she would travelling with us to the park site.

Colin, thank goodness, had come to the rescue. He'd called in his police contacts to speak with her. The officers had rolled their eyes at our story and grown annoyed when we tried to show them the green trail, but they were eager to ask Duri about her missing brother. They wanted to know his habits and friends and had asked her to come to the station with them to make a report. She'd sighed and rolled her eyes, but agreed— and she'd also promised to meet us later at the parkour trail site.

"Oh, good," Hitomi whispered in my ear as we set out. "I can't wait."

"I almost fell out when I saw her rise up with that pizza in her hand," I answered quietly. "The whole time I was fighting that Jorogumo I half-believed it was her."

"I still half believe it. Or at least, I still think she had something to do with it. When has Ken *ever* been difficult to wake? He sleeps with one eye open and pops up like a daisy. I'm the one who's a stump in the morning."

"Could she be working with it? Putting the victims to sleep?"

"Jorogumo do traditionally prey on young men. Young *handsome* men."

"Maybe there are two of them?"

"Historically, Jorogumo are solitary creatures."

"But how could she have made it past me down that hallway? Or beat me inside the building?" Frustration rattled me. "We're missing something."

Hitomi gestured to the boys where they walked ahead of us. "Should we ask them?"

I bit a lip. "Let's wait a while. If she is influencing them, maybe it will fade with time and distance?"

Hitomi shrugged and we walked on. The weather was pleasant now but it was going to be a hot day, I could tell. Ahead, the boys stayed uncharacteristically silent.

"Tell me again why we don't just *fly* to JanFran?" Hitomi said suddenly and with plenty of snark.

"You know why," I sighed. "How many scouts died years ago? Registration. Passenger lists. It's just too easy for Inaba's people to track us when we travel like that."

We walked on.

"Hey," I turned to Hitomi after a while. "Do you feel anything?"

"Like what?"

"Like eyes." I gestured. "How's your neck?"

"Fine." Her eyebrows shot up. "Oh! The shuriken that was thrown in the alley? You think somebody's still watching us." She glanced around. "Creepy."

"Maybe creepy. Or maybe not."

"Really? How is that not—"

"Shakespeare!" Sho shouted and came to a sudden stop.

"Do you see him again?" Cautiously, I glanced all around.

"No. But Shakespeare, Hitchcock—and I'd just figured out that the first two guys might have been the Grimm brothers— but I haven't given them a thought! Not them, not those weird, changing images on those movie posters, none of it!" He frowned. "Not since I sat down on that bus . . ."

"Next to Duri," Hitomi said darkly.

He frowned at Ken. "Was it the same for you?" His eyes cast about. "It's all fuzzy. All I can remember thinking about . . ."

"Was *Duri*?" Hitomi asked.

"Yes," nodded Ken. "The poor girl. She needs help."

"Yes, yes," Sho said impatiently. "But I should never have got so wrapped up in her problems that I forgot about my own—especially *this*."

"But it's her brother who's gone missing," Ken reminded him. "Surely she's scared and worried—"

"I haven't seen too many signs of it," Hitomi muttered.

"She's just being brave," Ken sighed.

Sho raised his eyebrows at me.

"Let's keep going," I said, stepping out. "Maybe distance will help," I said low. "He spent more time around her."

"I'm just so relieved to see the effects can fade," Hitomi breathed.

So was I. Seriously relieved. But I was also curious about what Sho had just said. "Sho." I beckoned him back to walk with us. Ken never even glanced around. "Do you really feel so strongly about these odd sightings of yours? I admit, it's weird that we can't see what you did, but you said it was a problem."

"It is," he said earnestly. "I can feel it. It's important." He sighed and shot Hitomi a look that asked for help. "You might not know exactly what I'm talking about, but sometimes, with your *minding*, you feel an urgency—like you have to use it. Hitomi? Do you know what I'm talking about?"

She nodded. "Yeah. I went to Asheville with a group one time and we were dawdling on the way back, just sitting and resting near a stream. The others went on and I lagged behind, adjusting my pack. Suddenly I knew I had to hide. No time to run. I was already bent over my pack, so I just leaned down and made myself look like a dead log. Right then a mountain lion jumped down from the trees." She shrugged. "Maybe it's instinct. Or part of the magic. Or maybe my subconscious had heard it moving or something . . . but sometimes you have to listen to your *minding*."

"Yes—that's it. I have to discover the *truth*. That's what my *minding* is telling me."

"The truth about what?" I asked.

"I don't know!" He was clearly frustrated. "Which is why I can't ignore it."

"And you think Shakespeare, Hitchcock and the Brothers Grimm are trying to tell you that truth?" Hitomi didn't bother to hide her skepticism.

"Yes. No." He rolled his eyes. "All I know is—I have to pay attention."

"We'll help you," I promised.

But there was nothing to be done now, so we walked on in silence. Ken still forged out ahead, never even looking back. I frowned at his back for a while, then tried to distract myself. "What happened with that mountain lion, Hitomi?"

"Oh." She smiled. "I confused the crap out of it. It could smell me, but couldn't find me. It knocked my pack about for a bit and I just sat there, not daring to move a muscle. Then it just lay down, like it was going to take a nap."

"What did you do?" I asked, fascinated. I'd grown up in the North Carolina Mountains. I knew those cats were not to be messed with.

Hitomi checked her watch. "Why don't you ask Ken?"

"Well, Ken?" I called.

"Ah, what?" Clearly he hadn't been paying attention.

"Don't you remember when you helped me escape that mountain lion?" She quirked her mouth at me. "Ken saved my bacon, in the end."

"How?" I asked.

He frowned. "I . . . I remember."

"Tell Mei," Hitomi urged.

"I . . . I spun up a water spout and aimed it right at the cat. It screeched bloody murder and took off for the hills," he said absently. He stopped walking.

We kept going.

"Wait!" he called as we went around him. "I . . . something's not . . . There's . . . What's wrong with me?"

Hitomi and I looked at each other and shrugged. And kept walking.

He started after us. "Wait! Seriously. That is the first thought I've had in . . ." he checked his watch, "twenty-four hours—the first one that hasn't centered around—"

"*Duri*," Hitomi sighed. "We know."

"I'm glad you are coming out of it, finally."

He looked at me, a little wild-eyed. "Finally? Wait. This is not right." He thrust a hand through his hair and I felt a corresponding *swoop* in my stomach. "Why was I—Where was my—What *is* she? Is she the Jurogumo?"

"I don't know," I admitted. "I thought she was—but now . . . I'm not sure. But I am sure that she's no regular human."

"She's creepy," Hitomi said with a shiver.

"She's dangerous," Sho said darkly.

"Well, she's not the creature I fought in the alley."

"Shards—yes!" Now Ken looked shocked. "You fought that giant spider—and I barely spared a thought for it!" He grabbed my arm. "Are you all right?"

"Yes." And I was a little gratified at his dismay. But I was also caught up in my train of thought. "Do you think that there are two of them?" I frowned and moved away. "She doesn't seem the type to cooperate—with anyone, let alone another spider woman who might steal her . . . prey."

Heroically, I did *not* glance at Ken.

"Well, the legends all speak of a single creature living alone," Hitomi mused.

"Wait—were you not caught up in her—spell or whatever?" Ken sounded a little hopeful.

"Nope—it was only the guys who fell for it." Hitomi sounded a little smug.

He flushed a little. "Well, that does go along with the legend of the Jorogumo."

"She had you all in a deep sleep, too," I told him. "Every guy in there was hard to wake, but the girls were fine."

"And that is *not* included in any of the stories I've heard." He sighed, frustrated.

I shrugged. "Maybe we are wrong. Or maybe she's just another *yokai* who is not acting as they've always acted for millennia."

"Inaba," he sighed.

"It could be. I don't think we know enough yet."

"If it is true, if she's the Jorogumo, or is helping it, that means that making it through the gate is going to be a fight, not a negotiation."

That sobered us all right up. We went on and it grew warmer and more humid. I took off a layer and wished my pack was full of ice—or at least that it didn't stick to me. We all agreed that none of us was very hungry for lunch, so we sat in the shade of some trees next to a storage facility and ate granola bars.

Ken still seemed distraught and withdrawn. At one point, I saw him approach a downed tree at the side of the road.

"Hey!" I said sharply as I stood to look at what had caught his attention. "Not those ones! Those are poison."

He stopped, his knife poised over a group of mushrooms. Nodding, he sighed and put the blade away, then strode back toward the road without a word.

Hitomi shot me a glance and followed him. They sat, talking quietly while Sho and I ate in silence, both absorbed in our own thoughts. I was tucking the wrappers away until I could find a disposal when I felt a prickling down my spine and the almost familiar weight of attention on us again.

"Guys," I stood and stretched, "I think our watcher is back."

"From yesterday?" Frustration colored Ken's tone—as if he didn't need one more thing weighing him down. "How did they find us again so soon?"

"I don't think that—whoever it is—that they ever left," I began, and then realized that he and Sho didn't know about the shuriken that has appeared last night. I hadn't wished to tell the whole story with Duri there. Quickly, I explained.

"How do we know this lurking, ninja-star-throwing

unknown is an *ally*?" Ken was clearly skeptical.

"Well, so far the only thing our mystery guest has done is alert us to their presence—that is what that little stunt in the farmer's market was, right?"

"I guess so," he admitted.

"And their next move was to save my butt in that battle last night. That shuriken showed up at exactly the right place at exactly the right time. Without it, I don't know that I could have beaten that Jurogumo."

"I don't believe that for a second." Somehow Ken's compliment lacked his usual warmth.

"No, I mean it. I hope whoever it is, they do turn out to be an ally—because if there are two of these spider creatures, we're going to need all of the help we can get."

"If it is the Obsidian's Eye, he'd be good to have in a fight. He might be older, but he knew what he was doing." Sho shrugged.

"If it's him, why not show himself?" Ken asked.

"Who knows? Maybe he knows something that we don't."

Ken nodded, thinking. "Okay. Let's go over it. Plan some moves. We have the few tricks that Effie gave us—"

"Minus one," I reminded him.

"Noted." He had started to sound more like himself. "But we still have some valuable weapons . . ."

The rest of the afternoon felt more normal. We left the suburbs behind and struck out on a windy, old country road, passing ancient farmhouses and the occasional church. The area was thickly forested on either side, where it hadn't been cleared, and I heaved a sigh of relief to be away from the hustle and noise and back in a more natural environment.

The afternoon had just begun to slide into evening when we stopped to consult Ken's map.

"We take the fork ahead," Ken pointed. "It's a smaller road, but it cuts directly west toward the park area instead of meandering south."

Sho was staring at an old, hand lettered sign. **Parable Pond**, it read in faded script. He looked at the sky and then down the wooded lane the sign indicated. "I know we still have a ways to go but I, for one, am not eager to arrive at the parkour park in the dark of night." He glanced at Ken.

"Yeah," Ken agreed. "I'm not too eager to see Duri again, either."

"Ugh, that's right. She'll be waiting for us," groaned Hitomi.

"If we wait it out here tonight, maybe she'll finish her business and be gone by the time we get there tomorrow." Sho sounded hopeful.

"If she is any one of the things we suspect, she'll still be waiting for us," I reminded them.

None of us looked happy at the prospect.

"I think we should make camp here." Sho set his shoulders, as if ready for a fight.

"Is this related to what we talked about earlier?"

He nodded. "It is. Somehow. I'm not sure how, but I feel strongly that we should camp at this pond."

"Then we will." I shifted my pack. "I wouldn't mind an early night." I glanced at Ken. "Or the remote possibility of missing Duri altogether."

"Thanks," Sho said softly.

I grinned at him and nudged Hitomi. "We promised. We meant it. Let's stop and see if anything comes to you—and let's all keep alert, too."

* * *

Someone cared about this pond. From the rounded end, where we were set up, it looked like an enormous dinosaur's footprint, complete with three long toes stretching out ahead of us. Someone had mowed all of the edges for several lengths— even between the toes. Our tarps and hammocks hung beneath the shade of a pretty little grove of mixed hardwoods. On the right side of the pond, midway up, someone had placed a wooden two-seater swing.

Hitomi sat there now, humming and pushing herself with one foot. She'd surprised us all by pulling out potatoes and onions she'd bought at the farmer's market. Assembling them in foil packets with some smoked salmon, she'd left them to heat in the fire and gone to enjoy the swing. Sho was wandering the edges of the pond, and Ken sat down next to me on a fallen log.

"Hi." He stared out over the water.

"Hi." I waited. A while. It didn't matter, though. Sitting quietly together felt . . . familiar. Nice.

"Mei . . . I'm sorry."

I frowned at him. "For what?"

"For this whole thing with Duri. I didn't mean to—"

"Ken!" I poked him in the shoulder to shut him up. "It's not your fault. She's a *yokai* . . . or something. You got tangled up in her magic. That's all."

"Yeah, but I should have . . ." the sentence trailed away.

"What?"

He shrugged. "Resisted, I guess."

"Listen, at least she didn't leave bits of her behind, like hungry little piranhas, to eat you from the inside out." I shuddered at the memory. "Are you holding that Oni against me?"

"No!"

"Good. Then don't be so hard on yourself."

He sighed. "Okay." He let his legs swing over a little until our knees were touching. I shifted too, until our thighs pressed close. He reached for my hand and I took his, letting the warmth that came from his touch steal all through me, comforting and spine-tingling at once. We sat then, not speaking, just watching the sky darken and the fireflies rise blinking into the dusk.

_____25_____

Sho

Sho wandered along the edge of the pond and wondered what randomly firing synapse had prompted him to choose this place. Had it really come from his *minding*—or had it been his cowardly and extreme reluctance to run into Duri again?

The aroma of roasting fish wafted his way. He heaved a sigh and turned to head back to where Hitomi was moving to check the campfire—but he stopped when he heard voices raised in argument.

He turned his head. They came from the forest—and were they speaking in Japanese?

"Sho!" Hitomi waved, beckoning. He nodded and held up a finger before turning to track the escalating bickering. He stopped, suddenly. A path led through the thick woods—a path that had not been there a moment before.

He hesitated. The sun was sinking—but his *minding* was prickling him again—and he had to know.

His footsteps fell silently on a bed of pine straw. The path curved several times, skirting big trees and thick clumps of shrubbery. It finally ended at the edge of a wide-open space. But not a completely empty space. It took several seconds before Sho realized what he was seeing.

It was an old drive-in theatre. There was the giant screen, missing a few rectangular panels. Weeds and high grass choked the parking areas. Posts stuck up in rows, their speaker boxes missing or tilting precariously.

He'd stepped out of the woods into the middle edge of the space, and he could hear the voices echoing from his right. Stepping in that direction he spotted a smaller stage there, to the side of the big screen. Colors and light flashed in the gathering twilight and almost involuntarily he moved toward it.

He marveled as he drew closer. The place must act as a children's theatre or perhaps a community stage. It was small and only just a step or two above the ground. The backdrop consisted of a set of large, tiered steps, like a giant coliseum. Two entrances gaped darkly in the mock stone of the tiers and lush foliage framed the sides and back of the structure.

The stage itself was fronted by a slow moving stream that ambled from the forest and divided it from several rows of wooden benches grouped to match the curve of the stage front.

It was a beautiful setting, picturesque and empty—save for the production going on right now. Sho drew closer, fascinated. The figures onstage wore masks and elaborate, colorful kimonos. They were indeed speaking Japanese and Sho suddenly realized they were performing a play in the ancient Noh style.

Utterly caught up in the performance, he moved forward and took the front, center bench. The actors were incredibly skilled. Even masked they displayed so much in body language and inflection, in the smallest movement and tilt of a head. After a moment he recognized that they performed a version of the famous *Matsukaze* or *Wind in the Pines*.

"Beautiful, is it not?"

Sho jumped. A man sat next to him, older and Japanese and dressed in simple robes. His heart pounding, Sho gave the elder a respectful nod and turned back to the performance. Two of the main characters—sisters—were trying to catch the moon's reflection in the water.

"This version was written by my son, Zeami," the old man complacently. "It was quite popular in its day."

"Zeami?" Sho's mouth dropped open. He turned, the play forgotten. "You—your son was Zeami Motokiyo?"

The elder inclined his head. "Of course, he did base this play off of a small piece that I did, years earlier."

"I . . . You . . ." Sho scrambled to his feet and then bowed low. "You are Kan'ami Kiotsugu?"

"I am. Or, I was. Depending on several factors and points of view."

Sho stared. The man was a legend, one of the most famous Noh actors, authors and composers in ancient Japan—hundreds of years ago. "It is an honor, sir." He looked up, trying to show his respect and awe. "But how? How is this happening?" He thought of his earlier sightings. "And why?"

"You are needed, Sho. A group of us has chosen you. We need you to be our voice, our arms and legs, our warrior in this realm."

"We?" He swallowed. "You mean Hitchcock?" He leaned in and his voice lowered to a whisper. "Shakespeare? That was really . . ."

"Yes. And you were correct. Those were the Brothers Grimm. All of us and more, we were willing to show ourselves, to expend tremendous effort to try and contact you—to get your attention."

"Why?" Sho felt overwhelmed with awe and confusion.

The elder's eyes crinkled as he smiled. "Because you are a story-teller, Sho. Like us."

His heart swelled.

"Because you can see into the hearts of others, but we have seen into yours. And because you have a unique power that could help divert a great evil."

"Inaba?"

The elder nodded.

"How? What can I do?"

"You can see truth, which is a very powerful thing. Your *minding* is more powerful than you know. But perhaps I must answer your first question before I can fully explain. How am I here? I died many hundreds of years ago. I suppose that you might be surprised that I have not passed on, sloughed off my spiritual individuality and become one with the Great Ancestor."

"Uh. Yeah." Sho knew that the spirits of his ancestors lived on in the next world, watching over family members for years until they eventually blended into the common spirit—the Ancestor. "I hadn't worked my way to the specifics yet, but, yeah."

"You honor your ancestors at Bon and other festivals, do you not?"

"Of course."

"Why?"

"Because it gives them ease and . . . joy?"

"And nourishment, of a sort," the elder explained. "Souls

require this energy before they can achieve a proper state of rest and salvation. As mortals, we write the names of our passed family on the ancestral tablets. We offer rice, reverence and respect for several decades, and this gives them the sustenance which they need to eventually move on."

Sho nodded.

"This is one path through the spirit world to the next. Many follow it. It feels right and good for them. But the spirit world contains many creatures—it is a population as varied as the one in this world. There are many layers to that place and many variations. You have heard of hungry ghosts or angry ghosts?"

"Yes. I know they are feared."

"They are spiteful, malevolent souls, men who die violently or lonely or disgraced. Sometimes they are spirits whose families neglect them, and do not give them the honors they need and deserve."

"Is Inaba a hungry ghost?

"Not quite. That one was hungry even before he died, and that has not changed. But hungry ghosts are not the only other creatures in the spirit world. Many *yokai* dwell there. And some souls do not use their gathered energy to pass on to the next state of being. Some are tied to this world for reasons of their own. Some are comfortable there and carve out their own niches to stay within. Others, like myself, learn to travel between worlds so that we may be where we are needed. But this requires a great deal of energy."

"I think I understand." Sho thought back. "My friend Boru says that it costs spirits greatly to contact her—and that it deeply drains the mortals who are able to hear them."

"That is true."

"So, after all of these years of your descendants honoring you, you've built up enough energy to travel between worlds?"

"No." The elder sighed. "My own direct descendants have long since lost track of the connection."

"So how do you—" Sho waved a hand.

"There are other ways for spirits to gain power, Sho. There are trades—often with *yokai*, who are not always subject to the same sorts of restrictions. Some families perform extra rituals and offerings to help their ancestors. And there are . . . different paths. Inaba, for instance, long ago conscripted several families into his service. For countless generations they have served and revered him. They do his bidding on this earthly plane. He gains influence here through their efforts and special powers in the spirit world due to their near-worship of him."

"But how do you—" Sho began again, then he stopped and glanced toward the stage.

"Yes. You have a quick mind." The elderly spirit nodded in approval. "Yes, I gain power when my work is performed, when my name and history are shared and taught to new generations." He smiled. "In this day and age, I get a zing when someone reads about me in an online history of theater."

Sho grinned. "Well, that adds another big plus to being famous, doesn't it? If you are talked about after you die, it powers your afterlife."

"In a matter of speaking."

"Well, I'll be happy to tell everyone I know about you and your long career. And I'll see that we put on your plays, back at Ryu."

Kan'ami Kiotsugu grew sober. "I'm afraid we need more from you, young man."

"I know." He sighed. "Because of Inaba."

"Yes. He is a separate case in many ways. You know of the battle in which he was defeated in his earthly life, yes?" The one fought by Rialka, your ancestors and others?"

"Yes." Sho—and everyone in Ryu—knew that Inaba had kidnapped Rialka, the beautiful, beloved mistress of the Shogun along with his earth mage advisor. For days Inaba had experimented, using dark magic to try to make himself immortal and Rialka along with him. Only Rialka's sacrifice had stopped him—and begun a secret war that had lasted centuries. But Sho was distracted by something Kan'ami Kiotsugu had said. "Others? Others fought Inaba that day too?" He paused to think about it. "Oh. Yes. You mean the daimyo's men? The ones sent to track Inaba down for the Shogun."

"Yes." The elder frowned. "I hope you do not discount their part of the victory? They played their role then, as they do now and will in the future." He paused at Ken's frown and shook his head. "Never mind. That will become clear on its own and my time is limited. What is important that you remember now is that Inaba had those days to experiment, to manipulate natural laws and try one dark spell after another, warping both he and Rialka before he was stopped. When he died, he was no longer a normal man—and he is no normal spirit either."

"Is that a good thing or bad?" Sho asked with a shudder.

"Both, I must imagine. For Rialka banished him to the spirit world when she made her sacrifice. No matter how much energy and power he amasses there, Inaba cannot cross into this world, as I do now. Even if he wished to, which I could never imagine, I don't think he could abandon his personae and merge with the Ancestor. He is trapped—and it drives him mad."

"Good," Sho said with petty satisfaction.

"He could make himself comfortable in the spirit world, live there and be of use to himself and others, but because he stays true to his nature—he ceaselessly craves what he cannot have. He has never paused for a moment, he has done nothing but work tirelessly to find what he seeks. He has followed many dark and twisted paths, but it is only in the last hundred years or so that he has made significant progress."

"The Council at Ryu says that he has blended dark magic with science and technology." Sho watched the elder for confirmation.

"He has—with devastating results."

"It wasn't that long ago that we figured out that he was the one to cause all the destruction—the eruptions along the Ring of Fire and the Rift that destroyed Japan."

"Yes. His experiments. He has caused so much death and destruction," the spirit said, his head bowed in dejection. "The loss of cities, the pollution of so much of the planet and near extinction of entire cultures. It is beyond comprehension. The entire spirit world mourned, yet Inaba does not care. There is a vast emptiness inside of him. He won't stop until he conquers both this world and the next—and he doesn't care if he destroys them both in the process."

The elder sighed. "But the destruction cost him as well. *Yokai* and *kami* are spirits of nature at their core. The devastation, corruption and pollution—it does not sit well with them. Many of his allies have turned away from him. He is not as powerful as he once was—and yet there are whispers that he has found the secret he has been looking for at last."

"Who is whispering?" asked Sho.

"Many *yokai*, and even the mortals who labor for him. They share a sense of excitement, of long goals about to be achieved. But it is also being said that he needs a great amount of energy to accomplish his last, greatest experiment. And we . . ." He gestured toward the stage where the Noh play had disappeared, but a gathering of spirits stood instead. Sho looked and saw artists, playwrights, novelists, and musicians. "We think we know how he is going to gather what he needs."

They all stood there, watching him. From Vermeer to Hemingway and Jane Austen, from Johnny Cash to Michelangelo to Dickens and Homer, they waited.

"You saw the truth behind the movie posters," said Kan'ami Kiotsugu. "A sordid, almost ugly little story painted to look heroic and bold."

And Sho began to see the truth here too. An inkling of an idea that opened onto a flood. "Storytellers," he breathed. "Musicians. Artists."

"Yes. To capture interest, excitement, attention and admiration—it is a great source of power. It feeds all of us." He gestured at the diverse group again.

"And Inaba wants to tell a story—*his* story?"

"A fabricated version of his story. Because to invoke an emotional response—especially a *positive* response—is very powerful indeed. You've seen the power of attraction and affection, of true caring between two people? You've seen the effects of it with your *minding*, yes?"

Still staring at the crowded stage, Sho nodded. He saw Oscar Wilde, Janice Joplin, Bach. "Yes. It lights up the world."

"Imagine that sort of current between an artist and all of the many admirers of his work."

Sho pictured it and immediately understood. "What we feel for our favorite stories? Music? Poems. Art. All the affection, all the wonder and joy and satisfaction. It produces the same energy as the bond between family, between loved ones?"

The elder nodded. "It is what we have come here for, to make you understand."

"It must be enormous," Sho breathed. "So many sources. That's what produces enough to enable you to live on in the next world, your identity intact. Enough to allow you to travel between worlds."

"It is one of the sources of such energy. The strongest one."

Sho gaped. "You are saying that—literally—love is the greatest power in the universe?"

"I am. Essentially."

"And Inaba . . ." Sho's words trailed away.

"He intends to make the whole world love him—so that he can tear it apart."

26
___

Mei

"**H**ow's this one?" Ken hung off of an oak branch. "It's strong enough, and thick all the way through."

"Yeah, that's perfect." I was on the hunt for another staff. I'd been thinking more and more about the sword my father had made, the one that I had used to train with, but when I was in the woods, I wanted a bo staff—or a reasonable substitute. By now, Ken was used to this idiosyncrasy—and had seen the usefulness of it, too.

He started to chop at the branch. I noticed he used the *wakizashi* my father had given him—the partner to the *katana* that was on my mind—and wasn't surprised at how quickly it went through—my dad's work had been as much about function as it had been about beauty. All of his pieces blended both— just as he had done himself.

"Thanks!" I grabbed the branch out of the air as Ken tossed it to me and trimmed the ends with my own knife. "Let's go back to camp and I'll clean it up."

We hadn't gone far. I paused on the way back, peering in the dim light. Yep. There, in the shadow of a downed tree—a group of cream-colored morels. I managed to scoop a few up without Ken noticing.

It was darker beneath the trees and when we stepped out, back into camp, dim light still shone in the western sky. Hitomi was standing and staring toward the pond. "He still hasn't come back." She sounded worried.

"Give him a little time," Ken said. He'd taken his shoes off and went to stand in the water, ankle deep. "You said he felt something about this place. Maybe he needs quiet to meditate and use his *minding* to figure it out."

Sighing, Hitomi agreed. She moved the foil packets away from the direct heat of the fire and puttered about. I sat near the fire and examined my new staff, trying to decide if I would go to the trouble of skinning it. I twirled it idly, experimenting, but grabbed the branch in both hands as suddenly both Hitomi and Ken straightened into alertness, their heads tilted.

"Someone's calling," Hitomi said, low.

"It's not Boru," added Ken.

He came from the water as Hitomi grabbed her pack. Rooting around, she pulled out her mirror and beckoned me over. We crowded around as she settled herself. We waited. But it wasn't long before a fog crept over the reflective surface and a form began to materialize. Suddenly, I recognized the silhouette of the hair . . .

"Reik!" Hitomi cried in happy surprise.

He grinned at her. "Hitomi." Peering around, he nodded at me. "Mei. Ken." He craned his neck. "Is Sho—?"

"He's here." I waved my hand.

"Good."

An awkward silence stretched until Hitomi blurted, "Where are you, Reik? When are you coming back?"

"I'm . . . up North. It's cold up here, even for me." He made the same sort of nondescript motion I had. His gaze softened a moment as it settled on Hitomi. "But I'm not coming back."

"Then what do you want?" Ken asked harshly.

"Simmer down." Reik rolled his eyes. "I'm calling to warn you."

"Warn us?" Ken scoffed. "About friends who desert us?"

I nudged him. I knew he and Reik had a strained relationship, but I didn't want him to goad the other guy into running again.

"Well, yes." Reik appeared to be struggling with this answer. I stared at his handsome, almost-too-cool-to-be-real visage, with his spiked white hair and frame of blue rune tattoos while he searched for what he wanted to say. "Exactly that," he sighed.

"Just say what you want to say," Ken spat.

"I've got no time to soothe your wounded feelings, air-boy, so just listen. Inaba knows you are headed to JanFran. You have to be very careful who you trust."

"We think he's gotten to the gatekeeper here," Hitomi

agreed. "We've been tangling with some Jorogumo."

"Some? More than one?"

"At least two," she answered.

"Maybe more," I mused.

"That is odd." He hesitated. "But worse will be coming. You probably shouldn't go directly to JanFran."

"Where else would we go?" Now I was starting to get exasperated with him. "You don't have to be a rocket scientist to figure out that's where the fight is."

"Mei, if you have an idea to save Akemi . . ." He stopped, his head shaking.

"What of it?" I asked.

"Forget it," he answered flatly.

"Maybe *we* don't skip out on friends." Ken snapped.

"Enough, Ken." Reik just sounded sad. "Akemi is not coming back either. She's been in his clutches too long."

"Nobody knows if she's even there," I objected.

He sighed. "She's there. And you don't understand what he's like. She'll be his, now."

"No way!" Hitomi objected. "She's one of *us*. She's not stupid. She grew up in Ryu! She knows what he's done, what he's capable of."

"I'm telling you, it's too late. The list of people you can trust is small and she's not on it." He rubbed his brow, frowning. "Look, I called to tell you, now you do with it what you will. I have to go." He met my gaze directly. "Goodbye."

"Reik, wait!" Hitomi cried.

But his image was already fading and in an instant, he was gone.

"Jerk," Ken breathed.

"Ease off, Ken!" Hitomi stashed her mirror and stalked back to the fire. After a moment, Ken joined her. I stayed where I was. I knew Reik wasn't a jerk. He was trapped, caught between the people who had raised him and his love for his mother—a *yokai* who might not even be able to return his feelings, for all we knew.

Eventually I took my staff up again and joined them. We all sat in silence. Hitomi still looked upset, but there was no way I was going to defend Reik and set Ken off.

Suddenly, we all jumped. Hitomi gasped as the noise that had startled us faded across the water.

"What was that?"

We all faced the pond—and the long channels across the way. The scream had come from there.

"That wasn't Sho," I said, keeping my voice low.

"No. Not a cry for help, either." Ken motioned. "Everyone move away from the fire."

"It sounded like a war cry," Hitomi said, her tone uneven. She was already rummaging through her bag. "I'm going to look for him."

"We'll all go," I agreed.

"Bring enough flashlights for everyone." Ken was putting his shoes back on.

"Not for me," I countered. My hands would be full of my staff and my blade.

"Don't turn your light on yet," Ken told Hitomi. "But keep it at the ready."

We moved out, keeping watch in all directions, creeping along the edge of the pond. There was no further screaming, only the frogs and the crickets and their chorus. Past the swing we found a path heading off into the woods.

"He went this way," Hitomi whispered. "I saw him head in that direction."

We followed the curving path, our footsteps largely muffled by pine straw underfoot. I led the way, my staff pointing ahead and my blade in the other hand. We'd just rounded one long, sweeping turn and stepped out into a wider stretch of pathway when a noise sounded ahead.

We all stopped.

Footsteps were coming. Whoever it was moved quickly, not trying to hide. Ken whispered and we spread out across the trail, at the ready.

The steps stopped. "Guys?"

"Sho!" Hitomi stood straight, relief clear in her voice.

"Get down!" I ordered them both, spotting the glare of red eyes behind him. *Multiple* red eyes, behind and *above* him.

"What's that?" Sho said at the exact same time. "There's something behind you!"

Another nerve-shattering yell echoed through the forest just as I turned—and just as the giant spider above leaped for me. Instinct made me raise my staff. A flash of memory, an image from that other fight with one of these creatures reminded me of the vulnerability of the underbelly. I shoved the hickory branch into the hairy abdomen and swept the spider aside.

It scrambled up and disappeared back into the trees again, quick as a flash. I strained to see any movement, any sign of it in the dark.

"How many of these sharding things are there?" I heard Sho cry behind me.

The wind picked up. A light flared and flashed wildly while it swooped aloft, carried by a rush of air. It steadied as it lodged high in a tree, tucked into a space between trunk and branches. The beam aimed down and illuminated our spot on the path, where, behind us, Ken stood with Sho, facing another of the huge spiders.

"Hitomi's with you," Ken muttered and I nodded, sheathing my knife and grabbing my staff in both hands. I couldn't see her, but neither could the spiders.

I shook my head. Two of them? And in the trees? I wasn't sure we could get out of this one.

Suddenly the one I'd skirmished with dropped out of the canopy above. It hung above me, it's two front legs poised in front of it.

"Watch out!" Hitomi's voice came from the side. "It's got something."

The creature made a motion and tossed something at me. I swept my stick in the air above me again and caught a large net woven of spider silk. I let the end of my staff fall into the underbrush at the side of the path and entangled the silk there where it could do me no harm.

The spider made a chittering sound of frustration and when I crouched to face it again, it threw a line out to grab the end of the pole and jerked it. I stumbled a step before letting go and the monster pounced for me.

But I kept going, continuing my forward motion instead of jerking back, and I rolled back to my feet even as the spider landed where it had expected me to be. Backing up, I drew my knife and waited.

It turned toward me and I knelt, sweeping the ground around me with my free hand while keeping an eye on the monster. Finally, I encountered something, and came up with a long branch, the ends covered in fir needles.

"Use your Light!" a voice cried.

An unfamiliar voice. None of my friends had said that! I only had time to register that the tone was frustrated, as well as unknown, before the spider threw another line. It aimed for my knife hand, but I swept it out of the air with the fir needles. Trying again, it tossed a sticky loop into the fir and tried to yank this branch too, but I resisted, and using its own trick, pulled hard. Its spindly legs were an advantage in the trees, but they skated over the pine straw, unable to get a hold or brace it against my strong pull. This time I yanked the creature forward, making it lurch toward me and the knife I held waiting.

It let go before it stumbled into the blade and leaped upward again. Cursing, I watched it disappear overhead and hoped the boys were doing better than I was.

Only the slightest shimmy of leaves gave notice of where the spider was moving above me. It headed back, the way we'd come, and as I followed, leaving the circle of light, I wondered if it was doing it on purpose—if it meant to lead me into a trap.

But staring intently upward into the canopy reminded me of that first big battle back at Ryu, when I had closed my eyes and asked the vines in the earth to help—and they'd responded. I tried to find my way back to that place, where I could feel the connection and attention of the living things around me, but my nerves were taut. I couldn't focus on my link with the world around me when I was tensed and waiting for death to fall on me from above. It grew darker as I stepped further along the path and I decided to try something different.

The Light. Someone wanted me to use it. Who was it? And could I? I stopped and held still. And in the quiet, the connection started to come. Thinking back to that first surprising flash, I held that single note in my head, the one that had shaken me so. And it worked. Something rushed through the earth beneath me—*into* me in a blast of tingling energy. It roared through me and into my arm, thrusting my knife hand high and lighting it up with a sudden blaze of white.

I felt . . . calmer, suddenly. I could see now, but I could also *feel*. The light acted like a bridge, allowing me to sense the bond that existed between me and the trees, the shrubs, the bat winging in to catch insects attracted by the light—

I jerked back to attention as a great commotion started up in the branches above me. Leaves shook and branches bounced. Angry clacks and chitters sounded, followed by a deeper grunt. I cast about, looking for the source. It wasn't me. I hadn't gotten far enough to ask for help.

Behind me, the battle Ken and Sho fought raged suddenly loud, too. I felt a gust of air and heard Ken barking commands.

Then, from above, silence. The branches stilled. I ducked into a crouch, ready.

Suddenly a mass of silk shot down from the trees. It struck my knife hand with enough force to push it against my side— where it stuck. The light faded. My connection ebbed, leaving me alone once more.

Moving swiftly, I transferred the knife, but another blob hit me and my other hand quickly met the same fate. I was in trouble, with both hands trapped. The spider descended then, hanging above me and starting to loop strand after strand around my middle, pinning my hands irrevocably.

"Shards!" I shouted. "Hitomi!"

"Move left!" she answered, shouting back. Her voice carried from the side—and above me.

I didn't question it. My feet were still free. I shuffled to the side.

And suddenly the monster spider wasn't hanging several feet above me, but falling. Completely unprepared, it made a trill of surprise and hit the ground beside me. I flinched as Hitomi followed, dropping from above and landing on the spider with a thud. She didn't hesitate, but yelled the Japanese words and threw a seihoukei down into the creature, jumping aside as the familiar black outline raced around the struggling arachnid and slowly turned it to dust. She grinned, slapping her hands on her pants as the dust was swept away.

"Cut the dragline," she said with satisfaction. She waggled a finger at me and I saw the clawed dagger on the end.

"Good job," I told her. "Now, get me out of this!" I was struggling to turn as she began to saw through the thick silk. It had grown quiet behind us—and I had a bad feeling about it.

"What was that thing fighting up there?" she whispered as she sliced.

I stared at her. "It wasn't you?"

Our eyes met. She shook her head.

I glanced over my shoulder. We headed back to the circle of light.

The space was trampled, windblown—and empty.

"Come on," I whispered.

But there was no need. Another Jorogumo—slightly bigger?—stepped out onto the path. It held Sho grasped in several of its legs. He was trussed tightly in silk, his mouth covered and wrapped all the way down to his knees. The spider held him close, its gross fangs positioned above Sho's neck.

"No!" I yelled it and raised my blade, poised to throw it.

The creature inched its teeth closer.

Stalemate. We both stood, watching and waiting. Hitomi had vanished again. Though I faced the creature alone, I knew she was near. Where was Ken? The silence, the anticipation, our precarious position on the edge of loss made my hair stand on end.

Into the waiting stillness burst an explosion. A flash of movement like a blur. I gasped as it swung down from the branches above me—and stared as I realized what I was seeing—a man swinging from a nylon line. He swooped down, over my head, and crashed into Sho, knocking him from the spider's grasp.

The creature let out a string of outraged noises and reared back, reaching for the intruder. A bolt of light flashed and the creature recoiled a moment, keening. It came back, though, gathering itself and crouching into a massive leap.

I thought the man was done for, but he knelt where he'd landed and raised a round object toward his mouth. When the spider was just above him, he blew and a cloud of powder rose up and over the creature—and sent it flying backwards and into a tree.

The man followed, his movements a blur. He raised the

round object in his hand and I gasped as he said the familiar words of banishment—in English—and stabbed downward. He leaped back when the creature thrashed against the onslaught of the blackness. When it had gone the same way as its companion, the stranger turned to face me.

"Finally!" he said, his breathing only slightly heavy. His fingers were busy at his shoulder and I saw that the round piece was some sort of brooch as he fastened it to his clothes. "I was afraid I would never get you all alone!"

27

Mei

How long did I stand there, mouth agape?

No idea. Great Gods and Ancestors, though, he was gape-worthy.

The man—the young man—he looked to be only a couple of years older than me, on closer inspection—stood tall. Over six feet. Broad shoulders, heavily muscled . . . everything. His hair intrigued me. Shaved short on the sides, the top was long and gleamed with golden highlights in the flashlight's beam as it swept back from his face to end trimmed short in the back.

He stood, casual and confident, relaxed and at ease now—but ready. Everything about him breathed one word--*warrior*. That light—what had it been? The same sort of light I'd used against the Oni? I swallowed and sent up the fervent hope that this man would turn out to be on our side.

Ahead of me, Hitomi popped into view. I couldn't see her face, but I could read her eagerness in her erect stance and the quick rise and fall of her breathing. I hoped she wasn't wearing a dazzled grin, but I suspected she did.

The newcomer started when she appeared, but an answering smile spread across his handsome face—and that answered that question.

Off to the side, Sho struggled against his cocoon-like bonds. He wiggled his head side to side, moving his chin until he worked his mouth free. "A little help, here?" he croaked.

Wrenching my gaze away from the newcomer, I flew to him. "Are you okay?" I kept one eye peeled while I cut at his wrapping. "Where's Ken?" I demanded.

He pointed with his chin. "Look up."

I paused and searched beyond the still-frozen tableau of the Hitomi and the stranger. And then I saw him. Ken had been trussed up too—and hung halfway up a tree. His back to the trunk, his limbs were spread-eagled and locked down to branches. His mouth was covered, but his eyes glared, furious.

"Hitomi!" I kept sawing at the silk binding Sho. "Help him!"

"Huh?"

"Cut Ken loose? Up there!"

She was still staring, entranced, at the new guy. "Who *are* you?" she asked him.

"I'm Bard." He'd followed my gaze and spotted Ken. "Uh, oh! Let me help you."

He was halfway up the tree before anyone could respond. Hanging easily from a branch with one hand, he sliced at the thick web holding Ken with the other.

I cut the last of Sho's bonds and helped him brush the sticky silk off. He climbed to his feet and I gave in to a sudden impulse, reached out and gave him a hug.

He stiffened in surprise, then returned the hug, holding me tight for a second, before we both turned at a cry of warning and an ominous thud.

Ken had fallen from his silken cage and now lay at Hitomi's feet glaring up at the stranger who had set him free. "That." He raised a hand as the newcomer landed lightly beside him and pointed at the brooch on his rescuer's shoulder. "Is that a *seihoukei*?"

"Of a sort." The guy ran a finger over the handsome piece. I could see a raised figure on it—it might have been a dragon. "We modified the design a bit to make it more portable. What do you think?"

Ken stood slowly, an unfamiliar scowl on his face. "I think I'd like to know where you got it."

The stranger looked surprised. "In Ryu—where else? Your Toft is the only one I know capable of crafting such a marvel."

Some, but not all, of Ken's hostility faded. "You've been to Ryu?"

"*When* were you there?" Hitomi asked.

"How were they?" I blurted at the same time.

"Who *are* you?" Ken asked.

"I'm Bard," he repeated simply. At our continued blank looks, he frowned. "Has no one told you to expect me?"

"You were the one who threw the ninja stars, weren't you?"

I asked.

"Yes." He smiled. "I didn't want to show myself until I knew another one of those Jorogumo *yokai* wouldn't spot me, but it seemed as if you needed a bit of help in that alley."

"You know I did—and I appreciated it," I said fervently.

Ken frowned again. "*Should* we have been expecting you? Are you the help we were told to expect?" He glanced around at the rest of us. "We thought maybe they were sending the Eye."

"Yes. They did." Bard nodded. "I'm the Eye."

His face gone blank, Ken took a step back. "Obsidian's Eye?"

Bard nodded.

"Wait." Sho sounded skeptical. "I've met the Eye. He's an older guy, nearly fifty." He raised his head, casting back. "He has elaborate tattoos on his arms."

"My uncle." Bard sighed. "He's gone now." He met my gaze directly and stepped forward, speaking earnestly. "But I am fully trained. I can help you. I've been preparing for this my entire life." He raised a brow. "And from what I've seen, we've got some work to do."

I flushed, not used to being found wanting, frankly, but also more than a little excited at the thought of help—and of learning something—*anything*—that would help get the massive job before me done. So I swallowed my pride and looked around at my friends. "Who's going to tell me exactly what's going on?"

"Let's go back to camp," Hitomi said. "We can eat my salmon before it turns to jerky." She grinned at Bard. "And you can tell us everything."

* * *

"Wait." Ken stopped us as we emerged from the wood onto the mowed edge of the pond. "The campfire's blazing high."

"There's someone there," Hitomi strained to see and started to move closer.

Ken thrust out a hand to stop her. "More than one. Wait here. Everyone keep still and watch for a moment."

We all stared. Suddenly I spotted it, and my heart plummeted. "There," I whispered. "At the edge of the light."

It was another Jorogumo, and seated on the log right near

the flames . . . "Duri!"

"How many of these things *are* there?" moaned Hitomi.

Ken started forward and this time it was Bard who hauled him back. "Are you crazy? You can't go in there." He looked over at me. "You girls are going to have to handle this one."

Hitomi and I exchanged startled looks.

"Don't be insane," Ken began.

"You're the nutty one, if you think you can go in there after you've already been under her spell. She'll pit you against the rest of us."

"No, she won't. I'll . . ."

"Do what?" Bard demanded. He grabbed Ken's arm and headed closer, stopping when we could all see clearly into the ring of light. Duri sat quietly, and so did the giant spider, several feet away. "What do you see? How does she look?"

"Sad," Ken said quietly. "Maybe she wants to talk. Or maybe she needs help—"

"Uh, huh. No, no, lover-boy. You are not going anywhere near her until we get something to plug up your ears. You won't be able to follow her commands if you can't hear them." He started to retreat, catching up Sho along the way. "We'll be in presently," he said to me, over their heads. "But you won't need us. You can do this."

They faded back into the deeper shadows and I looked at Hitomi. "I hope he's right." I glanced back at Duri sitting so confidently at our campsite and hardened my heart. "Let's figure this out." I patted the cargo pockets on my pants. "What do you have on you?"

Several minutes later, I strode alone into the ring of light around the fire.

Duri looked up and smirked. Slowly, she rose. She was dressed in gorgeous robes of midnight blue, her tiny waist sashed with green. There was a shimmering light, and I had to squint as the brightness flared. Suddenly she was gone—and in her place stood an immense Jorogumo—easily twice the size of the others we'd fought—and of the one still perched on a log at the edge of the light. The colors of her fur echoed the robes she'd worn. She was beautiful in this form too, in a totally alien way.

She stood there a moment, just looking down at me, enjoying her dominance, no doubt—and then I flinched when something whizzed by my head, aiming straight for hers.

She didn't flinch. Almost casually, she lifted one of her many legs and deflected the *seihoukei*, knocking it out of the air and into the pond. Then the shimmer flared again and she was Duri once more.

She sat. "Please, can we just finish this? It's all starting to bore me."

"*Bore* you?" Anger blazed in my chest. "Bore you? You mean you are getting tired of losing, I'd say."

"Well, I wouldn't say that at all." She quirked the corner of her red-painted mouth.

I raised a brow. In my peripheral vision I caught a flash of movement behind her. Hitomi. I needed to keep Duri busy. Good thing she only had two eyes in this form. "No? Two of your minions banished to the spirit realm. Another weakened and wounded twice over—"

"Yes, yes." She waved a hand toward the other creature and I saw that it was the one I had battled in the alleyway. It held the leg with the missing foot aloft and the damaged great eye still oozed green ichor. "All true, of course. But that is not *losing*."

"Then what would you call it?"

"Efficiency," she laughed. "Minions? That is what you call them? Inaba would label them my progeny and act like I've been pining for them for millennia. Bah!" She sneered. "More his than mine, after all of his ridiculous experiments. And I name them nothing but burdens."

I stared.

"Well?" She shrugged. "They are useless to me. No ability to change forms. Barely the wit to understand human language. There is no art, lure or finesse to them. They do not seduce their prey or manipulate the situation to ensure the least risk of discovery. Instead they merely grab the first bumbling creature to stumble into their paths and so much for the consequences."

She heaved a sigh of exasperation. "No, you have done me a favor, ridding me of them. Now I will allow you to destroy the last of my ill-gotten children and in return I shall step back.

I'll leave here, taking but the one, and will share the location of the gate with you and your little band of child-warriors."

"We already know the location of the gate," I told her.

"Well, then you will make the bargain on peril of your lives." Rising up, she glared at me. "It is time. I shall be free. The blame for their defeat will fall on you—as will Inaba's wrath." She bared her teeth at me. "He's ready for you, you know, girl. We all heard the chime when you opened Rialka's gate. It echoed all through the spirit world."

My confusion must have shown on my face. Did she mean the tone in my head—the one that sounded when I took Ken's *wakizashi* and made it glow—the noise the Yamaworu had echoed?

She sneered. "You don't even know. *I* don't know why everyone is fussing over you. It's much ado about not much, as far as I can see."

I bristled—and hit her back where it would hurt the most— right in her vanity. "Well, my friends will speak of you, too. In Ryu they'll have theatricals depicting your defeat—if they can find a girl ugly and hairy enough to portray you."

She reddened, but brushed my remarks off. "Say what you will. I'll be long gone before Inaba thinks to question your victory. There are other ways to survive, far easier than keeping the gate."

I knew better than to think she would make any of this easy. And I caught another small flash of movement, much closer. Hitomi's camouflage was excellent but our timing had to be perfect. I couldn't let these creatures catch her slow shifting position. I stood, stepping back a little from the fire, drawing her attention and the smaller one's too. Mentally reviewing her words, I paused. "What do you mean, 'taking but the one?'"

She cocked her head.

"You said, 'I'll leave here, taking but the one.'"

She shot me a twist of a grin. "Don't be greedy, dear. You cannot save them all. You'll turn over the dew your group brought for me, of course. I must be able to shift. But that's not all I'll need." She raised her hand and made a quick clicking sound. The wounded Jorogumo instantly reached behind the log he'd been sitting on and hauled out Colin's bound form.

I gasped. Only the young man's hands were bound, but he looked pale, drained and exhausted. "No!"

"Well, I must eat," she said reasonably, then gave a bitter laugh. "Did you really believe that was pizza sauce on my face, back in that gym?"

I flinched. And tried not to gag.

"No," I repeated. Firmly, this time.

Her smile disappeared. "I don't care what your eyes look like, young one." She stood. "You may have defeated a couple of Inaba's minor lackeys, but do not grow cocky. I may look as young as you, but I have far more experience."

I sank into a ready stance. "That sounds like code for 'old and slow' to me."

"Insolent!" The shimmer started up. She began to transform—and a shower of liquid hit her from the side.

Hitomi popped into view, on her knees in the grass. "Ha!" She crowed.

I gasped. Effie Cout's potion worked just as the witch had intended. The light around Duri faded. The Jorogumo was frozen—and trapped mid-transformation. I was caught by the appalling sight of her face, stuck in between beauty and monster.

But the smaller Jorogumo had jumped to attention. It let go of Colin, who sagged against the log behind him. The wounded spider leaped for Hitomi and knocked her down just as she was climbing to her feet. It flipped her around and stuck its clicking mandibles close to her face.

"Hit it in the eye!" I called, leaping toward her. But Colin was up and moving too. He stumbled toward them, his bound hands digging frantically in his pocket. I reached the struggling pair first and swung my knife at the leg that pinned Hitomi's nearest arm.

The creature remembered the sharpness of my blade and pulled the leg away before I could slice through it. Hitomi shook her free hand and used it to punch the leaking eye. The spider recoiled, but didn't let go.

Colin stopped directly across from me. He'd found what he was looking for and held the small plastic spider he'd shown us in his bound hands. He met my eye, then took a step back, dropped it, and crushed it with his foot.

For a moment, nothing happened, then the creature convulsed. It made a strange, high sound, then exploded into black dust. We all stared as it hung in the air a moment, before starting to drift down. It wasn't swept away like the others. I couldn't take the time to think about what that meant as it started to land on and around Hitomi.

She sat up, choking and frantically wiping it away. I helped her up and we both went to support Colin. We cut him free and helped him stand—and then the three of us went to confront Duri's frozen form.

She looked grotesque. Legs were sprouting from her torso, half-formed. Colored hair had erupted on parts of her. Worst were her facial features, caught twisted and elongated in the journey between girl and spider.

Her malformed eyes shot fury at us.

"Maybe we should leave her this way," Hitomi said.

"She'll certainly never seduce another young man," I said thoughtfully.

"Yugh!" gagged Colin.

"Over her now, are you?" I asked.

He nodded frantically.

She made odd, formless sounds, all she could manage, but she imbued them with clear fury and promises of revenge.

"Maybe we'll free you," I told her.

She quieted.

"But we are keeping Colin. And you have to go away, remove yourself from this conflict between us and Inaba."

She held silent.

"How can we let her go?" Hitomi asked. "She'll just eat someone else!"

"She's a predator. It's her nature," I said sadly. "And isn't that what we are fighting for? To stop Inaba from manipulating others—and nature—for his own purpose? We cannot go and do the same."

"I guess you're right." Hitomi still didn't sound happy. But she beckoned me aside. I shot Duri a look and followed her. "Why don't we just use a *seihoukei* and send her back to the spirit world?"

"We could," I admitted. "But she's old and powerful. Ken said that those kind often don't take long to gather up enough energy to cross back over, right?"

She poked out her lip. "Yeah. I guess that's right."

"Better to leave her be and not push her into fighting against us, if she's going to withdraw, right?"

"Yes. It makes sense." She pouted. "But it sucks, too."

"No argument here," I sighed. "But let's do this. Do you have the antidote?" I asked.

"Yeah." She pulled it from her pocket.

I took it and sprinkled a couple of drops onto Duri's deformed face. It warped immediately into her regular human countenance, while the rest of her stayed locked in place. "I will make you suffer for this, human," she spat.

I sighed. "No, you won't. You said you were taking yourself away. Stick to that, and we'll free you. If you won't agree to take yourself completely out of this conflict, refuse to interfere or participate on either side, then I'll be forced to leave you like this."

"You cannot!" She glared. "You will not!"

"I can and I will. I'll refreeze you and donate you to some spook house or pop culture museum. You can helplessly watch people parade past you for a few millennia." I shrugged. "Unless you slowly starve, first."

"Colin, my dear," she looked to the boy, her face melting into a mask of sorrow. "Won't you—"

"No!" He nearly yelled it. He shuddered, and then looked to me. "I think we should just kill her and be done with it."

I shook my head. "You've heard the options, Duri. What will it be?"

Her lips pressed tightly together. I could see her weighing all of her options. Finally, she closed her eyes. "I'll go."

Colin grabbed his neck. "Do you know what she did? She told the police that Teague just left town. That I was mistaken about something happening to him." Hurt and pain colored his voice. "He didn't have family or a lot of friends. Now, those few won't even mourn him. Seriously. Let's destroy her."

"We can't. I'm sorry, Colin." I sighed. "Everyone step

back." I took out my own bottle of Effie's potion while Hitomi held up the antidote. "Go ahead," I told her. "I'll refreeze her if she tries anything."

Hitomi tossed the antidote.

Light flared and the humongous Jorogumo stood over us for a second, two legs waving in the air and her many eyes glaring hatred. But then she made a giant leap and landed in the tops of the hardwoods nearby. She turned and laughed. It sounded horrible coming from that monster throat.

"Run!" I said to the others, but it was too late. She'd shot a thick line of webbing at Colin and hit him square in the back. She braced four feet on two tree trunks and used the other four to start pulling him in. He kicked and fought, but was too weak to give her much resistance.

I pulled my knife. But it wasn't necessary. Ken stepped out of the trees beneath Duri. I could see his lips moving. He threw his *seihoukei* and in a moment, she was gone.

28
____

Mei

"*That* was truly impressive. Where did you get that potion? From the Granny Witch?" Bard sat down on one of the logs next to the fire, his expression gone unfocused. "Do you know how useful such a thing could be on a wider scale?"

"A wider scale?" Hitomi looked confused. "How many of these things are running around?"

"Oh. Jorogumo? No more than these. That I know of, anyway. But there are any manner of creatures that could be foiled in the same way." He began to tick them off on his fingers. "All the weres, Bakeneko, Skin-walkers—"

A wave of fatigue swept over me. I sat down heavily on another log. I had nothing left. No energy to contemplate other creatures, or new battles.

I stared at Bard as he continued to talk with enthusiasm. He was pretty; I'd give him that. Knowledgeable. A skilled fighter, from the little I'd seen and if the stories of his family were to be believed. He'd been sent to help. He would be an asset to our mission.

But how would he change the dynamics of our group?

Hitomi didn't seem to be worrying over it. She appeared more than a little enamored, listening to his stories of encounters with other shifters with fascination. Everyone else seemed to look as tired as I felt, as we gathered to share the foil dinner packets, making them stretch enough to feed our two new guests.

Colin, in particular, looked to be too exhausted and shell-shocked to eat. He would hold a bite and forget to eat it as he stared fixedly into the fire. I was all sympathy for him. I knew how it felt to have your life turned upside down by loss, trauma and the knowledge that the world was not as you'd always believed.

"You're going to need to eat, so you can get your strength

back," I told him.

He blinked, then focused on me, his expression suddenly alive and fierce. "I want to do what you do. These things . . ." He glanced at Bard. "There are more of them? Many? And different kinds?"

"Yes." I sighed. "But they are not all . . . predatory. Some are benign." I thought of Neil, of the friends I'd made of a pair of Kappa. "Some are even good."

"I want to learn," he said, insistent. "What they are, how to tell the good from the bad. My family—what if they ran up against one? They have no idea! I want to help—like you've helped me." I knew he was thinking of his friend Teague. "I want to *fight*."

He fell silent, his gaze drawn to the fire once more. I jumped, then, when he suddenly turned and grabbed my arm. "I never want to feel that helpless again."

I nodded. "You won't have to," I answered simply. "There is a place where you can learn and train. They will welcome you." I'd been where he was now. I knew it would be a while before he could go back to his normal life—if ever.

"Thank you," he breathed. He finished his portion and let Hitomi lead him straight to the pallet that she'd fixed for him. He was asleep even before she made her way back to the fire.

I stared at him, more than a little jealous.

"I'm about to fall asleep sitting up," I told everyone left. "But first, I need answers." I pointed at Bard. "You. Obsidian's Eye. Position on the Council of Ryu?"

"A sort of a link between our two families," Hitomi added.

Bard looked between us. "It's more than that. Much more."

"Tell us," Hitomi urged.

He swallowed the last of his meal and wiped his mouth. "It's true, our family was touched by Rialka's magic in the same way that yours was."

Just hearing her name made something inside of me catch— a yearning for the warmth and regard I always felt when I dreamed of Rialka—or when I stood in the presence of her tree at Ryu.

"Our family does not have *minding*, like yours. But we do have strength, agility, balance, all the skills needed to fight."

"We have those too," Ken said a little defiantly.

"Of course. I've seen it for myself." He continued. "We honor Rialka and our heritage. Every generation the greatest warriors in our clans strive for the honor to be named the Obsidian's Eye. Competition is fierce. And winning is only the beginning. The Eye's training is specialized. We receive in depth tutoring on Inaba and his history of subversions of magic and nature, we hear all of the stories of the incursions he's made in this world and the atrocities he's committed in his quest for a way back. We study *yokai* and train relentlessly so that we may be ready for when the day comes—when the Girl With the Stars in Her Eyes calls."

He drew himself up and nodded formally at me. "I am ready. I am here to assist and guide and teach you, in whatever capacity you require."

What do you say to a statement like that? I colored up and returned his regal nod with one of my own.

"Wait." Ken said, a little belligerently. "Only you? What of the rest of your warriors?"

Bard breathed deeply. "We have not followed the same path as the ninja of Ryu. You have stayed sheltered, isolated—"

"Dedicated to keeping Inaba where he belongs!" Ken corrected.

"Just so." Bard inclined his head. "But we have lived differently. We have sought out other warriors. We have traveled to every continent, met with, learned from, the fighters from every nation. There are other worlds connected to ours, other troublesome beings that seek to interfere here. We help to defend against them all."

"Other threats?" Sho sounded incredulous. "None can be so dangerous as Inaba!"

Bard inclined his head. "Which is why only the best of us may be named the Eye. And why I have the ability to call all of our clan to come in support of our efforts." He waved a hand to include us all. "But only the Eye carries the knowledge of the Light."

I sat a little straighter. "Yes. You kept telling me to use the Light."

He frowned, looking a little confused and some of his formality dropped away. "You've found it for yourself, right? The yamaworu told me that you used it to defeat the Oni."

"Just how long have you been following us?" Ken demanded.

"I arrived in Ryu right after you left. I didn't stay long, but set out after you within a day or so."

I disregarded all of that. "Bard, I need to know more about that Light. I used something against the Oni—and it nearly defeated me after it was through with him." I shivered, feeling once again those tiny dark wrigglers gnawing at me.

"Ah. Well, I'm here now." He grinned.

Ken snorted.

Bard shot him a look. "For thousands of years, we have passed the knowledge down, from one Eye to the next, keeping it safe and ready to be used when called upon by Rialka's daughters."

"What's your number?" I joked. "I'm calling."

He laughed. Ken scowled. "We will start training in the morning." He cocked his head. And I'm told we are supposed to try and find the Shihan? Good." He rubbed his hand together. "Think of what we can both learn, from someone as skilled as that."

With effort, I stood. Exhaustion felt like a load of rocks in my chest. I paused to look at Sho, though. "You didn't tell us. Did you find what you were looking for? What your *minding* was hinting at, about this place?"

His expression changed. He looked . . . excited . . . and sad. "I did. And it's big. You all need to hear it." He looked around. Everyone looked as tired as I felt. "How about at breakfast?"

I could only nod gratefully. "Goodnight, all."

The others stood too, and began to make preparations for bed. Except for Ken, who stayed and stared out into the night.

I watched him for a moment, then I searched in my back for a bit of string before slipping past the bunks and into the forest. It wasn't easy in the dark, but I found what I was looking for. Minutes later, I returned, and looked to find that Ken hadn't moved. I snuck over to his hammock, and then turned to find

Bard waiting for me.

"What are you doing?" he asked as I made my way to my own nylon hammock.

"Passing out. In three . . .two . ."

"No," he said firmly. Taking my arm, he led me to the makeshift bed of blankets Hitomi had cobbled together for him.

"Trust me, you'll rest better here." He tucked me in carefully. I didn't tell him that he'd left an arm uncovered and resting in the grass. I was too tired to care.

"I'll take your bunk?" he asked.

I nodded permission. He moved away and I saw Ken, still sitting alone at the fire.

He would find what I'd left him later. I hoped he'd take it as the sign I meant it to be.

I sighed deeply, asleep even before the deep breath had left me.

* * *

"Mei. Wake up."

I didn't want to. I was dreaming of Rialka's garden again. She sat before me, so lovely, and with the sweetest smile of encouragement on her face. She didn't speak. She never had. But she stroked my hand and I felt the silk of her robe and the warmth of her approval.

But the low voice would not leave me alone. The dream faded, but still I resisted. I felt like I'd just drifted off. But I also felt good. Refreshed. Warm and content. It reminded me of how I'd felt, lying on that rock in the river with Ken. Was he the one prodding me?

"Open your eyes. But don't move."

My eyes snapped open. Not Ken. Bard. He smiled and nodded. "Look. Don't move. I want you to see."

He gestured toward my arm.

The pallet I'd slept in had been set up under a low hanging maple. The grass was a little sparse here, except for a lush patch where my arm rested.

"Look."

I stared. Long, thick blades of grass stuck to the inside of my arm. I blinked, then raised my head. Outlining each blade was a thin band of light. Intermittent streaks of light moved away and further up my arm.

"What is that?" I jerked upright and the light faded as soon as I broke contact.

Bard stood, motioning for me to follow. He didn't speak, just put a finger to his lips then struck out along the edge of the pond. I cast an eye across the camp. It was early, the sun still hidden beyond the horizon, although the eastern sky was growing light. Everyone still slept. I considered a moment, then grabbed up a jacket, glad I'd changed out of my cargo pants before dinner last night.

We walked in silence around the pond, to the first toe-like extension. The water grew shallower as we followed it. After a few moments, we reached the end and a small, rounded clear space.

Bard walked to the center and began to stretch. Motioning, he made it clear that I should too.

"No. I need to talk about all of this first. What *was* that?"

"What do you think?"

"I think I feel amazing." I did. I felt exceptionally fit and ready. It wasn't the first time, either. I remembered the first morning after Ryu, fronds stuck to my forehead. Moving outside when I couldn't sleep at Effie's cabin. Willow branches. Rialka introducing me to a patch of clover. "It's happened before. A couple of times. Since we left Ryu."

"I thought it might have." He bent over and started wind milling his arms. His impressively long and muscled arms.

"I didn't realize it. Didn't connect it." My head was whirling. "It's like—"

He stopped and looked up, a brow raised.

"I feel like one of those old tabs, with a charging cord."

He laughed and stood up straight. "That sounds about right. But truthfully, haven't you always known that you had a special connection with nature?"

"Well, yeah. I always feel better, stronger, more at ease when outside, especially in fields or forests. But I thought it was because I grew up isolated in the mountains—it was what I was used to." I couldn't hold back a sudden frown.

"And because that's when you were happiest?"

It was my turn to raise my brows.

"They told me all about you," he admitted.

My frown turned into a scowl.

"Yeah. Hardly fair, is it?" He sighed. "Look—would it make you feel better if I told you something about me?"

I pursed my lips. "Something humiliating?"

"Really?" he asked, slightly disbelieving.

"Yep." I folded my arms, waiting.

"Humiliating. Huh. Let me think." He glanced about, then brightened. "Okay. When I was fourteen, I had an enormous crush on a girl. Berit," he sighed. "Berit of the flaming red hair."

I rolled my eyes.

"That's not the humiliating part. It took me forever to gather up enough courage to ask her on a date. She said she would go—if I could beat her to the top of a certain elm tree."

Now my hands were on my hips. "Are you going to tell me that the humiliating part is that you were beat by a girl?"

"No. The humiliating part is that I still, to this day, cannot beat her to the top of the tree. And that she still won't go out with me."

I laughed, but it faded quickly. I still had so many questions. "I saw you fight with the Light, as you call it. You blasted that Jorogumo away with it. Does that mean that you recharge with a roll in the grass too?"

Sobering, he shook his head. "Some people call it Star Light." He grinned. "It's a nice nod to you. Others call it Soul Light. I gather you understand why."

"Yeah." I remembered pouring myself into the battle with the Oni.

"Come, sit a minute. I'll tell you something else about myself."

We settled down at the edge of the water. Tiny fish moved there, and darted away from our shadows.

"So. I told you there are trials, fierce competitions amongst those who think they might be named the Obsidian's Eye."

"Uh, huh."

"Think for a minute. Try to imagine the fierce rivalry. Now, what would you imagine the final test to be like?"

I shrugged. "I don't know. I've never been involved in

anything like that. I've only ever been part of this group, ever, and that hasn't been for very long." I thought a moment. "Did they make you fight each other? Or against an entire regiment of your trained warriors?"

"No. They took us to a lovely, tall, glass-paned orangery. Like from the old Victorian times. It was full of trees, blooms, and exotic specimens from all over the world. They sent us each in alone. We were asked to select and bring out the most powerful plant in there."

"The most powerful *plant*?"

"Yes. Some thought it was a joke and refused to take it seriously. Others rigged ways to haul out the tallest tree. Some chose the specimen with the strongest scent. Others recalled their knowledge of plants and chose nightshade, because it can kill. Or foxglove—"

"Because it can both heal and kill," I recalled.

"Exactly. None of those were correct."

"What did you do?"

"I sat down and listened."

I nodded eagerly. "Oh, yes—I think I know what you mean. The first time I *really* knew I was a ninja of Ryu was when I did my first small, nature based magic. I asked a flower what color it wanted to be—and it answered."

"Exactly. I sat down and listened—and believe me, there was a cacophony of noise in there. But there was only one plant in there that . . . knew my name."

"What was it?" I was fascinated.

"A tiny sapling. Newly rooted and barely more than a twig, but it called to me and spoke with the greatest authority. When I picked it up, I heard a noise in my head, a strange, long note."

I sat up straighter.

"My hands flared with light. I felt it flowing out of me, encompassing the small pot."

"What happened?"

"The twig burst into leaves—and cherry blossoms."

"Oh! Was it—"

"Yes. It was a cutting from Rialka's tree."

I sighed a little—and then smiled. "Thanks for sharing that."

"Of course. But you must understand." He climbed to his feet suddenly, and reached down to help me up too. "Look," he said, pointing to his spot and then to where I'd sat. My spot looked different. The grass where I'd sat was longer and more luxuriant. "See the positive effect you have on the living things around you? You are the only one in which the connection goes both ways."

I stared. "Ken was the first to notice it. But I think it's happening faster now."

"Your powers are growing." Stepping away, he pulled out a small blade. He lifted it, holding it before me—and suddenly it lit up. The blade glowed with pulsing, white light. "I can hear nature's voices. I can generate the Earth Light—as still others call it. I harness the power of my chi, my spiritual self, to power it—but I cannot draw energy from the earth and her creatures in the way you can. It is a gift granted only to you— Rialka's daughter. The Girl With the Stars in Her Eyes."

I swallowed. "Oh."

He blinked and the light faded from the blade. He tucked it away, and then turned to me, grinning in a much more light-hearted manner. "Well, if you get the fate of the Earth dropped in your lap, you might as well get a kick-butt weapon to fight with, too."

I sighed.

"It's time you learned to use your gift to full advantage. Now, we train."

I stood up. "That, I can do. Let's get started."

29

Ken

"**Y**ou know they are just training out there, right?"

"Uh, huh." He didn't turn away from his steady contemplation of the pond. He'd been here since he awoke to find Mei and Bard gone. He hadn't helped Sho start to pack up camp and he hadn't offered to help Colin catch fish for breakfast. He'd just stood here, staring and telling himself to stop being an idiot—and fighting to keep a storm of angry, gusting winds inside.

A little brown wren fluttered near his ear, twittering in a soothing fashion. He waved it away.

"Listen, Ken, Mei is totally into you." Hitomi sounded exasperated. "You know it. I know it. And she hopes that you are into her, too. So if you are, you'd better be letting her know."

He didn't respond.

She huffed and started to turn away, but then whirled back. "And in case you hadn't noticed, *I'm* interested in Bard. And Mei can see it. She's not going to even think about him in that way, because it would totally violate the girl code.

"Okay." He still didn't move.

She left him then, and he took up berating himself in her place. He still practically burned with embarrassment about falling under Duri's spell. It happened, he knew. Scouts did fall prey to *yokai*—and he hadn't been the only one. But it still rankled. He hadn't suspected Duri at all. And he'd still felt her pull, even after seeing her change into a humongous spider. Even after seeing her horribly trapped in mid-shift. That was seriously messed up.

He cared for Mei. She was a jumble of sheer kick-assery and vulnerability and she called to him on every level. He didn't want to fail her. Ever.

And he didn't want her beautiful, unusual eyes following

some other guy, either. Even someone as annoyingly competent and unmistakably important as Bard.

Ken breathed deep. He had to get a grip. He had to be better than this. Bard was here to *help*. Ken had already reacted badly to Reik and his half-hearted interest in Mei. He wasn't going to do it again. He'd had her to himself for a while. He could still have that special part of her to himself if he stopped acting like an idiot. He hoped.

Things were changing. It was a good thing. He could do this.

He breathed deeply and the raging storm inside of him started to subside.

"Hey—why are you holding out on me, Ken?" Hitomi called. "I could use these for breakfast, you know. Or are you hoarding them for yourself?"

"What are you—" He turned to find Hitomi pointing accusingly at a large bouquet of mushrooms dangling from his hammock.

Just like that, the storm winds dissipated. His heart lifted as if he'd shot it skyward on a blast of wind.

"So, can I use them for breakfast?" she asked? "Roasted, they would go good with fish. Garlic or butter would be better, but we'll make do."

"Sure." His hair fluttered. He was leaking a breeze, but he couldn't help it, he felt suddenly so relieved and happy.

"Hitomi," he said suddenly. "Once we finally get through this gate and into JanFran, let's be sure to get some earplugs, okay? Good ones. For all of us."

"Sure." She stopped short. "Does that mean that there are *yokai* out there who charm the girls?" She sounded nervous, and just a little intrigued.

He laughed. "If there are, I'm sure we'll run into them." He struck out toward Colin. "Let's see if we can find some fish, shall we?"

30

Mei

"The fish were as surprised as I was," Colin said with a grin as we all finished breakfast.

I was happy to see him able to relax enough to entertain us with a story of learning how to fish via a waterspout instead of with a pole.

"Ken's handy to have around, even if he does use those spouts to cheat in a water battle," I teased.

Ken rolled his eyes, but Colin grew serious.

"I've seen what you all can do. I'm just . . . me. But I want to help. I want to fight. You've spoken of your village and Mei has mentioned that there might be a place for me." He leaned forward. "Will they take me there? Teach me? Even if I don't have . . . ninja magic?"

"My father didn't grow up in Ryu or have a *minding* talent," I told him. "And he fought with Ryu."

"They'll be glad to have you," Sho told him.

"How do I get there?"

We exchanged glances.

"Head to Asheville in North Carolina first," Hitomi said. "Find a general store called the Dragon's Eye. Talk to the owner Neil or his wife, Tomoe. Tell them what's happened here. They'll see that you are taken in."

Colin stood. "Thank you." Relief colored his tone. "You have your mission, I understand. I'm happy to have one of my own." He swallowed the last of his fish and went to roll up his bed. After a moment, Sho followed and spoke to him quietly.

We all moved to strike camp then, and eventually to bid Colin goodbye. He was eager to get on his way.

"I hope he'll be okay." Hitomi watched him disappear along the trail. "He's still weak."

"He'll be fine," Sho said.

Privately, I agreed with him. I stood, still looking, for

several long moments after he was gone, and then I heaved a sigh and went to organize my pack. I was just straightening when I felt a wind begin to rush around my ankles.

I knew what it was. Ken had snatched me up and into the air more than once when we were fighting battles. I looked around, but couldn't find him. And even though I knew, I still could not suppress a gasp when the eddy surged strongly up to my torso and I was lifted, carried aloft by a swirling column of air. Gently, I drifted over the trees until I reached a clearing—and I was set down slowly—right before a grinning Ken Sato.

"Show off," I said as my feet touched the ground.

"I figured it was my turn. Did it work?" he asked saucily. "Are you impressed?"

"Only in the usual way," I said lightly, and poked him in the shoulder. "But what is it? What's wrong? Is something going on that the others don't know about?"

"No. Nothing's wrong. But I wanted to thank you for the mushrooms."

"Oh." I shrugged, but he took both of my hands in his.

"No. Don't blow it off. I know it was a small gesture, but it meant something to me."

I met his gaze directly. "Good."

"I know I acted badly over Reik." He ducked his head. "But I gave myself a pass on that one. That guy has been jerking my chain since we were kids." He sighed. "But then I felt myself starting to slide down that slope, feeling ugly about Bard too—and I don't want to be that guy."

"Good," I repeated. "Because there's no need."

"I hoped you'd say that, Mei. I don't want to dance around this any more. I want to tell you how much I care for you. And how much I hope you feel the same."

"You know I do," I whispered. "I—"

His kiss cut me off. A little wind pushed my back and I was in his arms, our mouths entangled. His hands slid up to grip my shoulders, mine wrapped around his neck, and I was gone, lost in the play of lips and tongues, of hope and excitement and gladness flaring high. Minutes passed. I knew we should get back, but I couldn't let this go.

He stopped, finally, pulling back and resting his forehead

against mine. "I see that line between your brows, you know. It means you're worrying over something."

"I'm not . . . well, I am, I guess."

"What is it?" He sounded . . . tense, suddenly.

"Well. It's just that—when we first met—really met, you know?—you told me you'd been looking for me a long time. People in Ryu talked about it too, how you wanted to be the one to find me. To bring me back to the village. You said you'd imagined it—and I just . . . worry that I'm going to disappoint you."

He stared. "Never." It sounded serious. Like a vow.

"But the thing is . . . I'm not really all that heroic. Mostly, I'm just stubborn. And I'm slow to warm up to people. And I get cranky and suspicious." I sighed. "I was stupid, crazy jealous of Duri, you know. I wanted to rip her hair out even before we figured out she was Jorogumo. And I need to be alone sometimes—and I worry that I'm not going to live up to everything you imagined."

"Mei, stop." He ran an agitated hand through his hair and something inside of me jumped. "First—I realized my daydreams were blown the first time I saved you from that Tengu—and you drop kicked me."

I cringed, but he laughed. "Just like that, I knew I was an idiot." He rested both hands along my jaw, cupping my face. "Don't you know that I've been falling for you ever since that moment? You continually surprise me—and I fall harder every time you do something so unexpected, so adorable, so *you*. You put me to shame. You listen to people. You treat everyone with respect. You see the good in every person you meet— even Reik and *yokai* like those Kappa and, yes, even Akemi."

His mouth twisted. "Second—the irony is that I've been holding back because I totally felt like I could never live up to you."

"That's crazy," I said. "And we disagree over things, like my mask and Reik and—"

"Yes? That's allowed. That's *normal*." He laughed. "We've both been staggering around under the same worry— but I vowed this morning that I will do my best to be worthy of you. And I don't mean the *legend* of you." One of his hands drifted down to rest lightly over my heart. "I mean the stunning gorgeousness of the person you are inside."

I grabbed him then, holding him in the same way he had cherished me—but this time our kiss was harder, more demanding. He pressed close and explored my mouth and I reveled in it, desperately happy to let him and to follow his example and do some exploring of my own.

He wrapped me in his arms and I felt . . . treasured. My hands trailed over his muscled back and broad shoulders. It was bliss. It was—

"Mei!" Sho's voice rang out. "Ken! Where'd they get to?"

I realized he was close.

"We're ready to move out!"

We broke apart. It was over. But it was also just beginning. I smiled at Ken, dizzy with happiness.

He grinned back and took my hand.

We walked back, popping through the underbrush to surprise Sho. "We're ready," Ken told him.

"Good. Everything's broken down."

I let go when we hit camp and went to shoulder my pack. Struck by a thought, I looked over at Sho. "We still need to hear your story."

"Yes. Give me a bit to gather my thoughts? There's a lot to tell."

I knew just how he felt. Everyone agreed and we set out, moving easily in the cool morning air.

Bard didn't mention my disappearance, but he did say we could continue to work a little while we walked. So, periodically, I would stop and crouch, my knife at the ready.

"Open yourself up," Bard told me. "Feel your energy—and feel how it connects you with the world around us. Focus. Send it into the blade."

I did as he said, managing to set the blade aglow more often than not.

"I saw you . . . fling the light." I told him, eventually. "You sent it shooting out and into that spider, last night."

Bard nodded.

"How did you do that?"

"Practice." He shrugged. "We can see if you're ready—but

don't be discouraged if you are not," he said. "Now, summon the Light again . . ."

Demonstrating, he shot several blasts into the side of the paved road, but I couldn't quite get a handle on it. I could make the Light flare a little higher, but no more.

"It's your first morning," Bard said. "You just need more time and practice." He paused. "And I sense a hesitation. I think you need to understand a few basic truths."

I sucked in a breath. I felt a sense of urgency, a need to know. Who knew how much time we would have before we had to face Inaba? Everything was spiraling quickly, events coming faster. I wanted to be ready. "You said you were here to teach me. I'm listening."

"Why don't you try this?" Ken said, pulling the sword my father had given him from its place in his pack.

I was tempted. "Are you sure?"

"It worked that first time," he said with a shrug. "And with the Oni. Maybe the connection with your dad will make it easier."

I took it. Oh, and he was right. It felt good in my hand. Thoughts of my dad, our life in the mountains, his teachings—it all centered me. I felt calm, aware. Clear-minded, like I had when I sat in the meadow with my dad, meditating after a long day's training. Suddenly, it felt real, powerful, *alive*—that living connection between me and the world around me.

The blade flared to life quickly.

"Ready position," Bard ordered.

I obeyed. I felt ready. Open.

"Listen well, Mei. You are Rialka's daughter and Nature's champion," Bard said close to my ear.

The thought warmed me, but made me squirm a little too. "I want to earn their respect, to deserve it," I told him.

"Mei. Hear me. You already *have* it. You fight for her, for us—and we fight *with* you. The Light you summon holds Rialka's concern and regard, her hopes, the Mother's determination, all of Nature's blessing, the love of your friends and family."

Was he right? Shards, but I hoped so. Holding my breath, for the first time I opened myself to the currents, instead of just channeling them. And there it was. I could feel the truth of Bard's words. The caring, support and belief I received fed my soul—and the Light I wielded. I felt the warmth of it channeled right through the metal so carefully and lovingly shaped by my father. I wasn't alone in this, could never do it alone. It was a shift in thinking and some of my cares abruptly fell away. The Light flared suddenly brighter. For the first time, I knew I didn't have to be afraid of it, or of my responsibility.

"There are many evils in the world, countless selfish, greedy creatures who yearn only for their own desires, with no care for others, for balance. Inaba has become the biggest, most dangerous of these. Every blow you strike against his destructive hunger is a fight for us, for good, for caring, for respect and love for each other and the world around us."

I nodded. Niggles of fear still worried at me, but I ignored them, and latched on to feelings of purpose and determination.

"Now, strike a blow, Mei," Bard whispered. "We are all ready. Show us that you are too."

I imagined it. And then I felt it. Power gathered from my fingers and toes, it rushed through my chest and into my arm. It surged into the blade and I shot a bolt of energy that blew a pothole into the edge of the road.

Ken and Bard cheered. Ahead, Hitomi and Sho stopped and looked back.

I felt the triumph—and the drain of it. "Thanks," I said, panting a little as I handed the *wakizashi* back to Ken.

"Maybe you should keep it," he began, glancing at Bard.

"If Ken would be so generous," Bard started to agree.

"No." I sucked in a couple of deep breaths before heading to catch up with the others. "My father gave Ken that sword for a reason. We just don't know what it is." I still felt the truth of that, somewhere in my heart and brain.

Bard frowned as he caught up to me. "That was excellent. You're learning, but something isn't right. You got winded when you let loose that blast. You're using your own chi to power the Light."

"Isn't that what you do?"

"Yes, but it's not supposed to be what *you* do." He sounded frustrated. "You are nature's choice. Her champion. You can harness her vast resources. You won't tire. You shouldn't grow weary. Learn that and you will be unstoppable."

"I'm trying—" I stopped. This had been different from last night. I'd missed that connection, that rush of feeling from the earth and everything around me. "It's like I'm practicing the different moves to a form, or to a dance. I have to learn to put them all together."

"Yes—"

"Hey!" Hitomi waved, beckoning. "Someone's calling!"

We looked at each other and sped up.

"Hurry!" She jerked her mirror out of her pack as we jogged up. "It feels urgent."

There was no delay before Toft's strained face appeared in the small surface. "Are you at the gate?" she demanded without preamble.

"Almost," answered Ken. "Maybe an hour away?"

"Get there quick. We've got word from JanFran. Inaba's creatures have attacked the gate in the city. The keeper is fighting them off, but there's no telling how long he'll hold out."

"Why? What is Inaba going to do with the gate?" Hitomi asked.

"Destroy it before you can get through? Send something ugly your way? Who can know? You have to get through as quick as you can."

"We'll double time it," Bard stated.

"Bard? You're there? Good. Be ready for anything. We have no idea what you'll find. He's sent a second force to attack their stronghold there—and the kitsune are advancing on the wards here. I can't talk further. Boru needs us all."

"Go. We'll get there," Ken said.

We all looked at each other as she faded away, then we tightened up our packs and set out at a ground-eating jog.

"You've got to listen while we go," Sho said. "I've got a lot of story to tell and there are decisions to be made at the end of it."

He talked for a while and my heart plummeted the longer he continued. Why? Why did this already impossible situation have to get harder?

By unspoken consent, we bypassed the parkour site and proceeded straight on to the tiny cabin where Duri had lived while acting as keeper of the ley gate. Also by unspoken preference, none of us wished to go near her house. We kept to the edges of the small clearing, but as Sho finished, I came to a stop.

It was too much. I sank down to the ground, my back against a stump where someone had split logs for a fire. "Shards," I whispered.

"Mei?" They'd all stopped, staring at me.

"You heard Toft. We have to go," Bard said.

"I need a moment to freak out." I laughed, pretty sure I sounded unhinged. "Don't mind me."

Ken and Hitomi, thank goodness, looked as if they were still absorbing Sho's news, too.

"It's too much," I said.

"It's not," Bard countered. "Not more than you can handle."

I just stared at him, incredulous.

"I wasn't going to say anything. But Mei, what you learned this morning took me months." Bard shook his head. "I've heard you guys talk. I've seen you in action. Do what you have already been doing. Lay it out. Strategize. Follow up."

"Lay it out?" My voice rose and I fought to keep from sounding hysterical. "Okay. Let's do it."

I sat up straight. "Inaba is crazy determined to get back here and take over. So much so that he's destroyed significant portions of the planet." I held up a finger. "He's gathered or *created* a host of *yokai* to help." A second finger went up. "He's corrupted or attacked two ley gate keepers." Third finger. "He's got Ryu under seige." Four. "His underlings are right now assaulting our allies in JanFran." Five. "And now he's discovered that a vid franchise may just give him the obscene amount of power he needs to break Rialka's spell and push through the boundaries between worlds." I mimicked an explosion with both hands.

Everyone stared.

Sho blinked. "Well, yeah."

"*And* the Earth and her Elementals have decided that I must stop him, or we risk them deciding to wipe the human race from the planet—as just too danged much trouble."

"Hoo, boy." Hitomi dropped to the ground too. "It does sound bad when you put it all together."

Bard snorted. "Don't forget you've been gifted with the built-in, incredibly powerful weapon that can defeat him."

"*If* I can learn to use it in time."

"You will," Ken said soothingly. "You're not in this alone, you know."

I looked up at him, so grateful. He knew exactly what to say.

"We're all here. We have friends and allies. We have Rialka."

Reaching for calm, I breathed deep. "Yes. All right."

"We don't know what we are going to be jumping into, when we go through that gate. So we need to do what we always do. Assess our resources, marshal our strategies, evaluate our enemies, and plan."

"I'm not going with you," Sho said abruptly.

"What?" Hitomi and I chorused together.

"I'm not going with you through the gate. I can't," he repeated, determined. "I've been agOnizing over it all night and all morning, but I can't. I've been given my mission. I have to keep Inaba from telling his false story to a wider audience. We can't let him get that charge of power he's looking for."

"He's right," said Bard. "It's good tactics. Weaken the enemy while giving Mei time to grow stronger. And we should take it further, if we can. Move on to destroy the other sources that feed him."

"Other sources?" I knew my expression must have looked as bleak as my heart felt.

"Well, I don't know where they are, but I've heard the stories. Remote temples where he's worshiped like a god. Whole families living in servitude to his needs. Guilds of artisans and craftsmen laboring at his whims. Surely someone knows where these people can be found."

"I'll do it," Sho vowed. "Everything. All that I can."

"You can't do it alone," Hitomi said into the resulting

silence. "I'll go with you."

My head jerked up.

"Hitomi," Sho whispered.

"None of us should be fighting alone," she said fiercely.

I gasped and reached for her hand, fighting back the protests balancing on my tongue. Our little band—it meant everything to me. They were my first friends—my only friends. I couldn't bear to see us go our separate ways.

Except I knew I would have to. If we wanted to win.

Our hands gripped tightly.

"You go with the boys. Find the Shihan. Master your Star Light." She grinned at me. "And when this is over, and you've fought Inaba and reduced him to the tiny, squeaking little nuisance yokai he's meant to be, then you and I will get together and eat tacos and watch vids for *days*."

My breath caught. "Promise?" I whispered.

"Pinky swear."

I ground my teeth, refusing to cry. Even if we split up, they would be with me. I knew that.

Sho approached, reached out a hand to us both and hauled us to our feet. "Thank you," he whispered, pulling us in to a group hug.

I held out an arm to Ken and enveloped him in the embrace too. Hitomi arched a brow at Bard and said, "Oh, come on, already."

He laughed and stepped in—and we all squeezed each other tight for a long moment.

Sho was first to step out. "Let's see them through the gate," he said to Hitomi. "Then I was thinking we could head back to Hot Springs? Find out what we can about that film shoot—and what we can do to stop it."

She nodded. Then we all set out on the faint trail that would lead us to the gate.

31
____

Mei

"That's it?" Sho asked.

"*All* of it?" Hitomi echoed.

We stood in a small, shaded clearing, before a crumbling cement stairway. It had five steps that led up—and straight into a hillside. Bare dirt surrounded the stairs and scrubby brush started about six feet above the last step.

"Huh." Bard scratched the back of his head. "Maybe we should have thought twice before we sent the gatekeeper hurtling back to the spirit world. Or at least asked her some questions."

"Can we open it without her?" Sho asked.

"Yes." Ken dropped his pack and began fishing around inside a pocket. "Effie sent instructions with us, just in case of this kind of trouble." He pulled out a couple of sheets of paper. "Okay. Someone has to stand in front of the first step—"

"Me! I want to open it, at least, since I don't get to go through it." Hitomi stepped up.

"Go on then." Ken gestured. Hitomi took her spot and shook out her hands, bouncing in readiness. I couldn't help it— I stepped in and gave her a quick hug, then backed away.

"The command is simple enough, but it's in some ancient language. Listen—"

"Whoops! No need!" Bard pointed.

We all looked—and saw the space at the top of the stairs had begun to glow with white light. Everyone stepped back as it grew brighter, chasing the gloom from the glade.

And then something appeared in the midst of the white. A spiral. Blood red and black, it grew quickly until only the center shone white. I understood suddenly why Neelus had called it the spider's tunnel. It looked like a tunnel into the hillside.

A figure appeared, just a dark outline against the white. It grew larger, moving closer—until it stumbled onto the top step. With a whoosh, all the light disappeared and we stood, staring awestruck at the girl shakily descending the stairs.

Hitomi was the first to recover. "Akemi!" she cried. She rushed to steady the girl, relief and gladness alive in her tone. "You made it! We were so worried about you!"

Akemi still looked dazed from her trip through the gate. I watched Hitomi boost her up, while also eyeing the hillside. Would something else come chasing after her? But the gate stayed dark and quiet.

Akemi reached up and touched Hitomi's hair. "Is that really you, Hitomi? You left Ryu?"

"Of course! We're out here, fighting Inaba's creatures— and coming for you."

The sharp angles of Akemi's face softened. "That's so brave of you."

"Are you all right?" Hitomi asked. "Where have you been? How did you get away?"

Akemi shook her head. "I didn't think you would—" She sighed. "You are sweet, but I really wish you hadn't come." One hand stroked Hitomi's hair again, while the other, fist closed around something—struck a sudden blow to her temple.

"Hitomi!" I choked out her name and lurched forward, but she was slumping against Akemi, who let her roll to the ground. Sho grabbed her and pulled her away. Ken, all color drained from his face, stepped forward too, but before I could wrench my blade from my boot, Bard was between us, his now-familiar war cry echoing in the small space and his knife raised high and starting to shine.

I tried to step around him, but Akemi was on him in a flash. From her closed hand, she whipped a shining, thin chain. She grasped the other end with her opposite hand and stretched it wide.

I'd just registered what her weapon was—a *kusari-fundo*—a chain stretched between two weights—when, fast as lightning, she wrapped it around Bard's wrist, sidestepped so that they were back to back, continued on around to his front side, and pulled his knife hand up behind his back, with her chain stretching up and over his shoulder.

"Drop it!" she ordered, her color riding high.

Bard did it, still looking utterly calm as his blade fell at his feet.

With a snap of her wrist she recalled her weapon. The thing moved almost as if it were . . . *alive*. As it hit her palm, she kicked Bard's knee hard. He fell down on it heavily, but was up and moving back the next moment. This time Akemi whipped her chain out to tangle around his other foot. Eyes wide, he lost his balance, tumbled back—and I gasped out loud when his head hit the concrete stair with an audible thump.

He didn't move. Akemi straightened and turned to face the rest of us. She dismissed Sho, still bent over Hitomi, but she bared her teeth in a grim smile at me and at Ken. "Bet you didn't see that coming, did you?"

Fury rose, threatening to choke me. I looked over at Sho. He was staring at Akemi, his expression unfocused. After a moment, he blinked, glanced at me and shook his head.

I breathed deeply and tamped down on my anger. "Reik saw it coming," I told her.

She blanched and some terrible part of me cheered. I'd known that would hurt. Her feelings for Reik had been a bone of contention between us. "He called to warn us—told us not to trust you."

"And I didn't believe him," Ken said, suddenly stepping closer to her. "What are you doing, Akemi? You are one of us. You spent your life in Ryu. You know what Inaba is, what he's done. And now—what? Barely over a week and you can go to his side so easily?"

"You dare to ask me that?" she spat. "You don't even know what you are talking about. It's not—. He's not—." She shook her head. "Yes, I spent my life in Ryu—I wasted years trying to earn respect there," she spat. "And then *she* walks in and everyone is falling all over her in five minutes!" She flashed the chain at me, but I didn't flinch, not even when the weight at the end flicked to a halt in front of face—and hung there for a long moment.

"You had respect all along," Sho said from the side. "But did you ever really have it for yourself?"

"Shut up, Sho!" she raged, and the *kusari-fundo* snapped

back to her. "Quit staring at my insides! I don't know what you think *you* are going to do to Inaba? Chart his colors until he gives up in boredom?"

"Admit it, Akemi—what you've always wanted is fawning—and that's far from the same thing as respect." I raised a brow. "Is that what Inaba is giving you? Respect?" I eyed the weapon. "Or gifts?"

"Status!" she hissed. "And yes—respect! He believes in me. He listens to me!"

"For now." I struggled to remain calm—and not to look at Hitomi lying in Sho's arms or Bard's still form. I had to focus. And to gather myself and my power.

Help me? I asked it quietly, of just the surrounding trees and scrub, and the answering chime sounded soft and gentle—but I still felt the surge of strength anchoring me to the ground, tethering me to the life around me—and giving me the freedom to fight for us all. "What happens when you don't bring me back? That's why you're here, right? The Oni was supposed to bring me. He failed. And so Inaba sent you."

With a growing ease, I sent a channel of energy into the blade I still held at my side.

"Ah." Her shoulders dropped as she watched the Light flare and she heaved a big sigh. "I still wasn't really sure, you know? But you really are the one, aren't you?" Her mouth twisted. "Good."

With a quick, sideways lunge, she lashed her weapon at Ken. It curled around his neck eagerly—and she pulled it tight, choking him and dragging him close. "But you are wrong about one thing—I wasn't sent after *you*."

She began backing away, forcing Ken to follow. As she put a foot on the first step at the gate, white light began to swirl behind her.

"Akemi, no!" Terror raced down my spine. I could feel it clogging my channels, weakening my abilities. I couldn't stop staring at Ken. He'd shoved a finger under the chain, but his face was reddening and he sagged against Akemi as she half-dragged him along and up another step.

But a wind started up, trying to push them away from the gate.

"Stop!" I brandished my shining blade.

"Stay back, all of you!" She yanked viciously at the chain. Ken's body jerked and the wind died down. "I only have to get him back alive, not unbloodied."

"Let him go!" Fear and rage strangled me, obstructed the channels of flowing Light. I had to push to make the power flow past, but I managed. The wind was picking up again. Ken leaned low against her left side. I gave a hard mental shove and sent a blast of Light skimming over her right shoulder.

She flinched. A red strip of flesh appeared through her dark shirt.

"Let him go!" I roared again and flung another to open a thin line on her cheek.

"Come after him!" she shouted over the sound of the air now rushing down from above and behind her. She struggled against it like a weatherman covering a hurricane. "That's the message! Come and get him—and be prepared to pay."

"Let him go!" This time I hit the bicep of her right arm and she jumped, groaning and losing her grip on one weight. I saw Ken suck in a huge breath as the tension briefly loosened, but she gathered the weapon up in her other hand and kept climbing. The gate whirled faster behind her.

This was it. She was almost there. I was going to have to blast her directly. I raised my blade high—and the second stretched out into an eternity. I lifted my arm—and froze. With a smirk in my direction, she reached the top step and jumped back—her hair whipping wildly as they disappeared together into a swirl of red and black.

The roaring wind abruptly stopped.

"Ken!" His name ripped out of me with a force that tore my throat. I dropped my knife and sprinted for the gate. I'd just reached the bottom step when the hillside exploded. Heat and flame and scorched earth and molten metal hit me, carried me back on a wave of destruction. I hit the ground hard and the world went black.

32

Mei

I awoke, aching, to the sound of Sho calling my name.

"There you are," he said with relief.

"Ken?" I sat up.

Sho shook his head.

"Hitomi? Bard?" I struggled, trying to roll over so that I could get to my feet, but I felt sluggish and slow.

"They are fine. Both fine." Sho pushed me back. "Just rest a minute. Hitomi and I were far enough to the side, we barely felt it. The concrete steps actually protected Bard, but you took the brunt of it."

I felt like it. But worse than that, I felt the pain of that moment—

"Ken's gone!" I dropped my head in my hands. "And it's my fault."

"No." Hitomi dropped down beside me. "I saw it. Akemi—she took him. *Kidnapped* him!" She sounded harsher than I'd ever heard her. "How could she?"

I looked up—stared at Bard sitting and holding his head not far away. "That moment. I could have stopped her. But I would have had to seriously hurt her, probably kill her." I glared at him. "Is that what I'm supposed to do? Take this Light that comes from support and concern and caring and *life*—and use it to kill?" I couldn't hold back a sob.

"I'm sorry. You've just begun to learn—this came so fast . . ." Bard hung his head. "I thought we would have more time to train, to learn, to understand—"

"That I'm a hired killer?" I said, feeling sick.

He sighed. "It could come to that, Mei. I don't know."

I hung my head again. "With the *yokai*, we know they go on—just back in the spirit world—and some for only a short enough time. But . . . Akemi?" I shook my head.

"I think we need to see the Shihan, like Neelus said. Maybe

he can help us see everything clearly."

I sat up. "We're going to JanFran. We're going after Ken."

"You need more training, more practice. You can't go up against Inaba until you are ready."

I knew that. But I also knew I had to save Ken.

"We should wait—"

I shot him a look and he shut up. "The Shihan might be in JanFran anyway," he grumbled. "We were supposed to ask there."

I got to my feet and opened my eyes wide—not to see the destruction of the hillside, but to try and steady myself. Hitomi came over to prop me up and I clung to her. "How am I going to get him back?" I asked her in a whisper.

"We'll figure it out. Maybe there's another ley gate? We can ask. I tried to scry Effie but I couldn't reach her." She touched her temple. "Maybe it's the headache."

Sho gathered up Hitomi's pack along with his. He handed mine to Bard. "Let's head back to town. Eat. Rest. See if we can reach someone. Then we'll figure out what to do."

But I already knew what. Nothing was going to stop me from taking Ken back from Inaba.

It was only a matter of *how*.

Author's Note:

Thank you for reading ***Obsidians Eye!*** I sincerely hope you enjoyed it.

Would you like to know when my next book is released? Sign up for my newsletter at my website:

http://www.dmmarlowe.com

You can also connect with me on:

On Facebook

On Twitter

or at

http://www.RedDoorReads.com

And don't miss the first book in the Eye of the Ninja
Chronicles:

Eye of the Ninja

About the Author

D.M. Marlowe lives in North Carolina with her family and two cats. When she is not spoiling them all, she is probably writing. Failing that, she's likely lost in movie or a book, on a long walk, gardening, or hanging with her friends.

In her other life, she is a USA Today Bestselling Author of Regency Historical Romance for adults. You can find her other incarnation at www.DebMarlowe.com

www.ingramcontent.com/pod-product-compliance
Lightning Source LLC
Chambersburg PA
CBHW021649110726
47902CB00007B/1893